She'd been born into the most powerful crime family in the world, but all she wanted was to protect the innocent…

The water cascaded down her body, washing away the shampoo in her hair and the lovely smelling body wash across her skin. One thing the water couldn't wash away were her memories of the last twenty-four hours. Images of mangled and desecrated bodies filled her mind. The hard facts of her stay were burned into her memory.

Her DNA, the cells that made up her body, were infused with programming from Satan and his demons. All around her, thoughts invaded her senses—unconscious confessions of heinous acts casually tossed around, as if her relatives were planning their daily "to do" lists, like ordinary people.

Instead of picking up the kids from soccer or remembering to get milk from the store, these thoughts were hideous and grotesque. '*Manipulate John X into thinking his wife is having an affair. He's a prime candidate for murder-suicide. Work on another insider trading tip and pin it on poor Sally J. She doesn't have the temperament to survive public humiliation and ten years in jail. Once she's out of the way, her family land can be sold to a developer for a hundred times its worth.*'

Kate blinked back tears, trying to turn off the images in her head. On the one hand, she had an obligation to serve and protect but, on the other hand, the onslaught of thoughts was destroying her soul—one small piece at a time.

Unable to control the tears, she slid down the marble wall of the shower, knees drawn to her chest, her body racked with sobs from all of the pain, the anguish caused by her family. How could she fight that power? The family influence was everywhere. Was there anyone in the world with the ability to stop them?

New York Police Detective, Kate Morgan carries many secrets. The black sheep of America's most notorious crime family, she walks a fine line between her commitment to truth and justice and the obligations demanded from her family.

FBI agent Grant Anderson, embraces his role and place in the Anderson family, America's richest and most philanthropic example of good will and kindness. His loyalty ends, however, with his family's expectations of marrying the right girl.

For thousands of years, the Morgans and Andersons have been sworn enemies. Clans, steadfast in their loyalty and commitment as handpicked first families to the Devil and God. Both sides tread carefully, maintaining the balance between Virtue, Sin, and Immortality, enduring each other only twice a century, during the Summit of Good and Evil.

With the mysterious murder of Gus Morgan, the balance is threatened and the future of humanity in jeopardy. Treading through a minefield of treachery and deceit, Kate and Grant must solve this murder, face their attraction for each other, and stop a family feud before all hell comes crashing down.

KUDOS for *Surviving the Summit of Good & Evil*

In *Surviving the Summit of Good and Evil* by Christine Wall, Kate Morgan is a descendant of the devil, but she doesn't believe in following Satan. A detective for the NYPD, she believes in truth and justice and the protection of the innocent, much to the horror of the rest of her family who consider her a traitor to the cause. When she meets FBI Special Agent Grant Anderson, a descendant of God, they are immediately attracted to each other, much to the dismay of both of their families. But Grant and Kate are determined to control their own destinies. The two are thrown together when they attend the mandatory joint-family reunion at a luxury resort, where someone is killing family members. Now Grant and Kate have to investigate their own families to find the killer before he or she can destroy the balance between good and evil and threaten humanity. The story is well written, with a fresh and unique plot, plenty of surprises, and some hot sex scenes. What's not to love? *Taylor Jones, Reviewer*

Surviving the Summit of Good and Evil is the story of black sheep who don't conform to their families' expectations. Our heroine, NYPD Detective Kate Morgan, comes from the devil's bloodline. Her family is the first family of Satan on Earth, dedicated to causing mayhem and destroying innocence. Our hero, FBI Special Agent Grant Anderson, is a member of the first family of God on Earth, dedicated to protecting the innocent and overcoming evil. Needless to say, the Morgans and Andersons have been sworn enemies for thousands of years. But Kate and Grant march to a different drummer. They care for each other without regard to what their families think. When they both end up at the family reunion (the Summit)—that happens every fifty years and where attendance is mandatory—their families are appalled at their growing relationship. Both families try to interfere, but Gant and Kate happily defy family traditions.

Then when Kate's cousin Gus is murdered, Kate and Grant join ranks to find the killer before the balance between good and evil is destroyed, along with mankind. *Surviving the Summit of Good and Evil* is a far cry from Wall's first book, *Showdown at Evil High*, a young adult paranormal thriller. While both books deal with angels and demons, *Surviving the Summit of Good and Evil* is *not* a YA book. With a strong well-thought-out plot full of twists and turns, intriguing and realistic characters, spicy sex scenes, and slightly gruesome violence, this is *not* your grandmother's romance.

ACKNOWLEDGEMENTS

To my friends whose names end up in my books, know that my characters do not necessarily reflect my thoughts about you. I just like your names…

Nick S – especially you.

Laurelle and Annabelle – lovely women devoid of all evil.

JM – find your character (hint: not my JM) and know that you are still the most interesting person I have recently met…

Evroy – thanks for letting me borrow Nibs for the book!

SURVIVING THE SUMMIT OF GOOD AND EVIL

CHRISTINE WALL

A Black Opal Books Publication

GENRE: PARANORMAL ROMANCE/PARANORMAL THRILLER

This is a work of fiction. Names, places, characters and incidents are either the product of the author's imagination or are used fictitiously, and any resemblance to any actual persons, living or dead, businesses, organizations, events or locales is entirely coincidental. All trademarks, service marks, registered trademarks, and registered service marks are the property of their respective owners and are used herein for identification purposes only. The publisher does not have any control over or assume any responsibility for author or third-party websites or their contents.

DEDICATION

*To my Dad. A man of many hugs and few words, who read
all my books and supported my hopes and dreams.
Some of my best writing, including this book, was done
while happily indulging his love of playing slot machines.*

I love you, miss you and hope that I am making you proud.

Tony Fukumura (November 9, 1929 – December 9, 2015)

PROLOGUE

*A*nd I will give unto thee the keys of the kingdom of heaven. And whatsoever thou shalt bind on earth shall be bound in heaven and whatsoever thou shalt loose on earth, shall be loosed in heaven. ~ Matthew 16:19

CHAPTER 1

We are but fleeting moments. A fragile leaf blowing amid tumultuous winds, destined for the mysterious and desperate to know if an unknown God will steer us true."

She closed the journal and stared at the worn cover of dark brown leather. Sighing for a moment, she paused before looking up into the face of her therapist. Her sixth one in the last twelve months. Another recommendation from her best friend Melanie, who swore that this one would be the fit she needed.

"That's beautiful, Katherine. Thank you for sharing your most private thoughts. How does that make you feel?" The therapist stared at her thoughtfully, intent on keeping the momentum of sharing alive.

Kate opened her mouth, then closed it and frowned. How did she feel? Feelings were something of a treat she didn't often allow and certainly never shared. But lately—lately, with the reunion looming, she was forced to admit their existence and, no matter how hard she resisted, their rights as a part of her mind.

"I feel uncomfortable and anxious and I don't know why." Surprise, then annoyance, flashed through her mind. Kate Morgan telling the truth to a stranger. Well, that wasn't exactly the truth, but the less her therapist knew, the safer for her.

"Is it because of your work?"

"My work?"

"I would imagine working for the NYPD comes with a certain amount of anxiety and stress. Especially in the homicide department."

"Right, yes, of course, my work. Yes, the job can be downright gruesome sometimes."

Kate bit her tongue. *Shut up Kate. Shut up.* The woman had naively given her an out, yet all Kate wanted to do was to steer the conversation down a street not fit for travel.

The therapist seemed pleased for once and nodded, jotting something down on the Swarovski encrusted note pad that was a permanent fixture in her lap.

Any additional self-effacing remarks were interrupted by chimes from a stylish alarm clock on the doctor's desk. A wave of relief flooded Kate's mind, along with an ironic realization. She had been saved by an object whose days of usefulness were as numbered as hers. The woman glanced at the Rolex on her left wrist and put her pen down. "Well, Katherine, I do believe that our time is up. Shall we pencil you in for the same time next week?"

"Actually, Dr. Trask, I'm going on vacation, so it will have to be the week after."

Dr. Trask raised her eyebrows, a smile crossing her face. "Excellent to hear. I'm always glad when a patient takes some time for herself. I trust it will be fun and relaxing for you?"

Hardly, thought Kate, but she smiled and nodded. Family reunions were anything but fun or relaxing for her. Unfortunately, she didn't have a choice in the matter.

Kate thanked the psychiatrist and made a beeline for the elevator. The doctor seemed harmless enough. Vapid in thoughts yet genuinely interested in what Kate had to say. Perhaps there was someone who could help her after all. In the elevator, she felt the vibration of her smart phone and quickly reached into her bag, hoping to catch the caller before they hung up. She hated the days leading up to time off—there was so much to do at work, she barely had time to put her files in order, much less miss a call from her boss. Pulling her phone from the black hole slung over one shoulder, she felt her stomach drop when she read the number. It was her mother. Again.

Bursting out of the dark and onto the sidewalk of bustling Fifth Avenue helped to calm Kate's nerves. There was a certain comfort in being lost in a crowd of cynical New Yorkers. Everyone hustling to get on their way and no one caring about her problems. It was a welcome normality that she reveled in every day.

Kate took a moment, shoving her back against the cold granite of a nearby building. The heat was stifling and claustrophobic, another reminder of her Southern roots getting in the way. She took a series of deep breaths and unbuttoned the top button of her shirt, suddenly feeling like the garment was strangling her. Calling her mother back was out of the question. It wouldn't be long before ninety-eight pounds of criticism would be in her face. She didn't need another call ruining her day.

All she could think of was that damned reunion...summit...whatever you wanted to call it. She had missed the last one due to circumstances beyond her control, but nothing in hell or on earth would allow her to dodge this impending disaster.

"Pull it together, Morgan. They're just your goddamn relatives," she muttered, the pounding in her ears starting to subside. "So what if you despise them all?"

Pushing herself into a standing position, she sucked in some more air and continued her monologue. "It's just anxiety, you're okay, just breathe. What do you need? Coffee? Chocolate? Retail therapy?"

"Two shots to the head, one to the heart. No mistakes, no slip ups." The voice hit her full on, pushing away her anxiety. She snapped to attention, scanning the faces around her.

A burly figure passed by, so close she could smell the overpowering stench of his cologne. Glancing down, she spied the tattoos on his arm. Upside down cross with a severed head at the base. She identified with that tattoo better than the birthmarks on her own body. She knew the man and he was exactly what she needed. A collar that would make her day.

"Junior Malone, stop," she yelled, pulling out her nine millimeter, and aiming it in his direction. "You're under arrest for the murder of Stanley Bronson."

Junior stopped and looked at her. Smiling, he raised his hands and began cracking his knuckles. "Detective Kate, looking finger fuckin' good as usual." His eyes slowly swept her body, hungrily settling on the shirt that showed off the curve of her breasts.

"Get on your knees, Junior. You're under arrest for murder, kidnapping, extortion, and pissing me off."

"The only way I'm getting on my knees is if you're naked in front of me."

Kate rolled her eyes, half in disgust, half in annoyance that this idiot had managed to evade the NYPD at all. Before she could reply, she felt a surge of energy, a presence that threw her off focus and threatened her concentration.

"That's no way to speak to a lady, Malone."

The deep voice came from behind her. She could hear him but didn't dare take her eyes off her prisoner. "Whoever you are, move along," she called out to the man behind her. "This is police business and I don't need civilians interfering."

Junior started laughing. Wagging his finger between her and the mysterious stranger, he doubled over, letting out a loud snort, slapping his knee.

Kate didn't know what was so funny but every chuckle only made her angrier. "Hands where I can see them, Junior," she warned. "Now, shut up and let me read you your rights."

"That won't be necessary, Officer, I've got it from here."

Unable to avoid it any longer, she glanced back at the voice, ignoring the hysterical laughter from Junior. "It's Detective, you asshole."

He stood there, six feet tall, muscular and chiselled with a Glock in his hand. For a second, she was taken aback. Confidence radiated from him with a charismatic energy that took her breath away. Behind the Ray Bans and expensive dark blue suit, he could only be one thing.

With a smirk, he looked at her. "That's FBI asshole to you, and he's my problem, not yours."

Kate bristled in defiance. The entire department had been on the hunt for Junior and he was being dropped in her lap. There was no way anyone was going to get in her way.

"Back off," she warned. "He's my collar. I'm arresting him for suspected murder, ah—ass—Agent." She bit her tongue, choosing not to add "asshole" onto the end of her sentence.

"Well, he's mine now. FBI has jurisdiction over NYPD."

"The hell you do."

"At ease, Detective. Despite what you might think, I'm not the enemy here." He paused for a moment, struggling to keep his anger in check. "Look, this discussion is over. He's coming with me."

"Is he on your top ten most wanted?"

"No, but he's a piece of a larger problem that I need to solve."

"Well, he's at the top of my list. He killed a decorated war veteran in cold blood and I made a promise to his widow and two young kids that I would get justice for them."

Behind the sunglasses and stony expression, she could see that her words made an impact on him. The agent's jaw twitched slightly, his fingers shifted over the trigger as if he was silently daring Junior to give him a reason to shoot. After a moment he spoke, his tone softened just a little. "I admire what you're doing and I can promise justice will be served, but right now the Bureau's needs come first."

"Don't serve me bureaucratic bullshit. You want to flip him, and once he's in witness protection, any justice he deserves will be gone."

The agent's eyebrows rose as if she had read his mind.

"Trust me, lady, he'll get what he deserves."

"I'm not a lady," she spat. "I'm a goddamn detective and you're a bad liar."

Junior slowly backed away, shaking his head while the couple traded insults. "Wow, you're both fucking something."

"Shut up," they replied in unison.

Junior shrugged his shoulders then looked around. They were completely absorbed in angry negotiation and that was all the motivation he needed.

Kate whirled around in time to see Junior take off down the street. "Christ, I can't believe this," she swore. Holstering her gun, she whipped off her jacket and tossed it on the ground. Pointing her finger at him, she exclaimed, "This is your fault!"

The agent watched as she dashed after his suspect. "You've got to be kidding me," he muttered with the shake of his head.

Glancing down the street, he did a few mental calculations and looked into the sky. Pulling out his phone, he punched in a few numbers. "Yeah, Doug, it's Grant. Looks like we've got eyes on Junior Malone. Meet me near the corner of Broadway and West Twenty-Eighth." With a sigh, he took off after them.

Kate dashed after Junior, who was alternating between zigzagging and pushing pedestrians out of the way. He was just ahead of her, his lumbering body shoving people to the left and right of him.

Jumping over fallen shoppers and dodging little kids, she breathed a quick prayer of thanks to the universe for the skills she had picked up in her younger days. Running, swimming, and top of her class athlete. Being agile and fast had served her well and today was no exception. Kate had been chasing him for three blocks and, at the quarter mile mark, most of her perps started to slow down. True to form, he was starting to falter. Rounding the corner of Twenty-Seventh Street, he disappeared into an alley.

Kate stopped short, pulling the gun from her holster. "Junior," she warned. "Let's not do this the hard way. There's no escape. Give up and I'll go easy on you."

"Come and play, you crazy bitch. I can't wait for you to try."

She glanced through the dimness, cursing under her breath. The alley was a dead end, a passageway between two sets of apartment buildings. Looking up, she watched as lines of clothes strung across the structures fluttered back and forth blocking out the afternoon sun.

Kate stepped carefully, avoiding the holes in the cobblestone filled with water. At the end of the alley, the flare of a lit cigarette penetrated the darkness. She peered around stacks of garbage, following the scent of tobacco. She could see a figure and feel his eyes on her. As far as his thoughts went…well, she released the safety on her gun and moved farther into the darkness.

"Come. Come. I look forward to seeing you come."

His voice was almost hypnotic. His words rang with intelligent charm. On a good day, Junior's vocabulary barely ranked above third grade, his understanding of swear words even less so. This, she found this mildly amusing. "Why, Junior, I didn't think you had a double entendre in you."

The click of steel and the weight of an arm around her neck surprised her. She gasped as a low growl filled her left ear. Stumbling backward, she hit his broad chest, feeling his muscular arm shift downward to stabilize her. "He's not smart enough for puns," whispered Grant. "This is a trap. There's someone else here."

Kate drew in a sharp breath, overwhelmed by surprise, by his scent, and the electrical charge that ran through her. If he felt the same, he didn't show it, choosing instead to pull her backward to safety. She realized what he was thinking and broke her reverie, pushing him off and away.

"Junior, and whoever else is there, you're both under arrest. You have the right to remain silent. Anything you say or do can and will be used against you in a court of law."

"Your laws don't apply to me, Kate."

"The law applies to everyone."

"Not to us. You should know that by now."

Kate stepped farther into the darkness, creeping closer to the figure who looked like Junior. "I don't have time for riddles, jackass. Give yourself up and we can talk about this later."

"I think not, baby girl," purred the voice. "We have an appointment to keep."

Kate faltered for a moment, the term of endearment made her flash back to her past and her blood ran cold. Her mind raced, pushing away the alarm bells ringing in her head. Her past attacks hadn't happened with civilians around, but on the off chance this was really happening, she heightened her senses and prepared to fight for her life. "Who's 'we,' asshole?"

"Detective—" warned Grant.

"Shut up," she demanded, needing to hear the truth. "Who's 'we'?"

A wall of bone chilling cold hit her full on. She felt as if a million tiny needles were invading her body. Kate gasped in pain, temporarily paralyzed by the shock. She turned and felt herself plummeting, then the strong arms of Special Agent Grant catching her before she could hit the ground. A comforting warmth filled her body, her pain lessened, and the paralysis was suddenly gone. Again, she fought his help and forced her body to the spot where Junior last stood. Plunging through the darkness, she spotted a form on the ground, the showpiece of a singular shaft of light.

Kate gasped as she looked down at Junior. He was face up, eyes open, hair snow white, and his body contorting in pain. The strange energy shifted and she could feel Grant brush past her. He cursed then bent down, checking on Junior's convulsing form.

Standing up, he looked past her and yelled at his partner. "Doug, get an ambulance here. We have a suspect down."

Kate shook her head in disbelief. Something had aged

Malone. His expression was that of a corpse. The life was gone from his soul. She pushed away her shock, forcing her limbs to move and her eyes to scan the alley. Lifting her gun, she started a sweep of the area, looking for the second man. With no way out or up, her disbelief exploded in another bout of anger. "Where the hell did he go?"

Grant looked at her passively. "Who?"

His partner glanced from him to her, a confused look on his face. "Grant, what is she talking about?"

"You know who, the other man," Kate snapped, she felt her face warm with embarrassment. The smug look on his face made her feel like a fool. "The other one I was talking to."

Grant slowly shrugged his shoulders. "I didn't hear anything, and the man we were hunting is lying right there."

Kate let out a roar of frustration and shot out her leg, roundhouse kicking a set of garbage cans past the two men. The pompous ass was lying again and she didn't know why. "I'm calling this into my captain and he can deal with your director. The minute he recovers, he's ours. Don't think you can pull your jurisdiction crap with me."

Grant's mouth curled with amusement. "Fine."

His calm nature enraged her all the more. She had to get out of here. She had more important things to deal with than the infuriating man in front of her. Kate shot him a look of disgust. Without a word, she stormed toward the mouth of the alley.

"Detective."

Kate stopped and turned back to him. She knew that look, she had seen it before. It was a common reaction from the men, she encountered at her favorite bar. Some part of him wanted her and in that small moment, she held all the power. Glaring at him, she stood there for a second, allowing him to drink her in. Despite her anger, she begrudgingly admitted she had never seen a more handsome man. She felt the chemistry between them rise, but she'd be damned if she would do anything but stand there and stare back at him.

Grant took his time and slowly memorized her. The long legs, lean waist, the curve of her heaving breasts, and the stunning face of a 1940s movie star. After a moment, he smiled. "Have a good day."

Provoking her only fueled her anger, but he couldn't help himself. She was like a wild stallion. Defiant, beautiful, and hurting on the inside.

After a long moment of reflection, he turned to his partner. "All right, Doug, let's call in the team and shake the tree. Something bizarre just happened here."

CHAPTER 2

Kate stared at her computer, running through news reports, creeping around chat rooms and gossip sites, looking for any sign that *he* might be back in town. Yesterday's events replayed in her mind like an old record stuck on a scratch and replaying the same melody over and over until someone had the common sense to move the needle.

Common sense, that's what she needed. The only way to alleviate her fears was through logic and common sense. Lucas Morgan, her cousin, arch enemy, whatever name you called it, was back in New York. She had warned him in the past that he wasn't welcome in this town, not that her threats would stop him. She chewed on the end of her pen and muttered obscenities under her breath. What was he up to and was it connected with the family and their upcoming reunion?

"Morgan, wakey, wakey."

She glared at her partner, Detective Nick Salomons, as he flopped his lean body down on a chair beside her. "What do you want, Nick?"

He shrugged his shoulders, stretching his arms before looping them behind his head. "You tell me. Want to fill me in on what happened yesterday?"

"Nothing to tell. Had a day off and ended up collaring a perp."

"A perp who is now in FBI custody—that is if he ever

comes out of his coma. What the hell did you do to him, Kate? He looks like he was frightened to death."

Kate paused before she answered him. He was a nice enough guy, a new transfer from Los Angeles, which explained the blond hair and chiseled body of a surfer. It wasn't that she didn't trust him, she just didn't know where he stood. One minute, he was her got-your-back partner, and the next, he was kissing ass with the brass.

"Don't know what happened to Malone. By the time I reached him, he was flat on his back, pretty much the way you described."

"Uh, huh," he replied, looking anything but convinced. "And your G-Man friend? Can he shed any light on the subject?"

"Okay, not my friend and if you want his statement, just head on down to Washington, in fact, I'll point you in the right direction."

He shot her a grin and reached over her keyboard, grabbing the roast beef sandwich she had resting on her desk. Before she could snatch it back, he leapt to his feet and took a large bite.

"No need, Morgan. I'll just ask Special Agent Anderson, myself, since he's standing right over there."

Her eyes narrowed as she stretched over her desk, pushing his body out of the way. Special Agent Grant Anderson was leaning against a filing cabinet, staring at them intently. "Asshole," she hissed to Salomons.

"You're welcome, and thanks for lunch." He held up her sandwich and sauntered away with a cocky look on his face.

Kate rose to her feet and started toward Special Agent Anderson. As annoying as it was to see him again, she couldn't deny the strange effect he had on her.

Tall and handsome with piercing eyes that seemed to study her every move, today he was dressed in a black suit with pin striped shirt and a navy and purple tie, loosened at the neck.

Somehow he changed professional to sexual by shifting

his stance and easily commanding the attention of all the women in the office.

"God, he's beautiful."

"Please, let him be here to see me."

"Is he really here to see Morgan? Why on earth would he be interested in her?"

Kate glared at the women to her left, warning them away with a glance. It was bad enough she had to deal with the agent, but now the resident Barbie Dolls had their sights on him, and she would never hear the end of it.

"Special Agent Anderson, is it? What are you doing here? You commandeered my perp, are you here to take over my work place as well?"

He grinned and shook his head. "Had a hell of a time tracking you down, Detective. Are you aware there are fifty-five Morgans working in various precincts across the city?"

"One of the most common names in the good ol' US of A and fits with my lifestyle. I like to keep a low profile."

"Indeed."

The feeling of comfort and familiarity was the air, as if she lived in his universe all her life and frankly it annoyed her. Whispers filled her head, breaking through her thoughts. Kate cleared her throat, resisting the urge to turn around and yell at everyone to mind their own business.

"Look, can I buy you a coffee, Detective? There's something I would like to discuss."

"Are you returning Malone to the NYPD?"

"No."

"Then there's not much to discuss."

Grant rubbed the back of his neck wearily. "Fine, not a discussion then how about an apology?"

"For what, Agent?"

"For hanging you out to dry with my partner."

After his blatant arrogance yesterday, this was the last thing she expected. Somewhat taken aback, Kate nodded and followed him out to the street below. Once out of the building, she led the way, ducking into an old hole in the wall restaurant, as opposed to a brand new Starbucks across the street.

Heading to the back, she slid into a booth, barely noticing the shabby condition of the place, as if she had become so used to it, the cracked vinyl seats and scratched wooden tables were home to her.

Grant looked somewhat dubious as the waitress placed two glasses of water in front of them. "What'll it be, sugar?" she drawled. Giving Grant a quick once over, she gave Kate a knowing wink. "Want some ice cream to cool down your hot piece of pie?"

Kate shot her a disapprovingly look. "Just coffee, unless you want anything else?" she asked Grant.

"Coffee's fine with me."

The waitress sauntered away with a smug look on her face then returned moments later with two enormous coffee cups and two ceramic bowls, one with sugar packets and the other filled with tiny creamers.

Kate grabbed three packages of sugar and two creamers, adding them to the coffee before taking a sip. With the cup in her hand and her view of the almost empty diner unobstructed, she seemed to relax.

Grant looked down at the drink for a moment, his posture rigid, clearly uncomfortable with location she had chosen. She smirked at his response and, after a couple of sips, attempted to put him at ease.

"Relax, Agent. This place has the best coffee for ten blocks, despite the sketchy feel."

"You come here a lot?"

She shrugged her shoulders. "It's a good place to meet my CIs and not as high profile as the coffee shop across the street."

"You mean it's a convenient place to hide."

Her face dropped, unsure of how to answer such a direct and completely accurate observation. She chose annoyance as her response. "You said something about an apology?"

"Yeah, about that. I wanted to get your take on the situation."

"Hell of a way to apologize, Agent."

He drank the coffee, muttering something she couldn't hear. Drawing in a deep breath, he put the cup down and gave her his full attention. "I am sorry about the way I handled the situation yesterday. Something happened in that alley and I needed time to process it."

"And by processing it, you mean you were led back to me?"

He nodded, finishing his drink. "You're right, this is good coffee. So let's talk about the second voice. You know who it is."

His remark was a statement rather than a question. She scowled and glanced around the restaurant, wishing she was anywhere else. Of course, he was here about Lucas. He wasn't a stupid man, hell, he was FBI, for Christ's sake. In the past, when incidents like this happened, she had managed to keep it in house, disguised as any run of the mill crime. If this had attracted the attention of the FBI, there was no way she could explain it away.

Various ideas filled her mind, her analytical nature blowing reality out of proportion yet again. Maybe the FBI really had an X-Files division, a task force devoted to the strange and unusual. However, looking at this agent, with his no-nonsense approach to investigations, she somehow doubted it.

"I have an idea who it might be," she replied. "A perp with delusions of grandeur and psychopathic tendencies, although at this time, I can't prove it."

"What makes you think that?"

She sighed and picked up her teaspoon, tapping it absently on the table. Lunch time was approaching and the restaurant started to fill with people. Kate grasped for words, trying to come up with a tale of half-truths he wouldn't see through. She couldn't tell him about Lucas or the fact that he was her cousin. She had worked hard to disengage herself from her family name and she'd be damned if another psychotic relative was going to tear that all down.

"For the past six years, we've been trying to crack a string of unsolved homicides. Same MO—kidnapping then, after five days, death by strangulation. The victims are in their thirties, usually professional, good looking, with brown hair and an athletic build."

"Strangulation is personal. He wants a connection with his victims. Is that what yesterday was? Using Malone to lure you into the alley?"

"Possibly, but I don't know how they would know each other. The guy I'm thinking of comes with a more sophisticated palette."

"So this joker somehow knows you want Malone and uses the opportunity to reach out to you. Obviously, he's obsessed. What kind of information has he sent to you?"

Kate stared at him, wondering how he had made the leap so fast. She glanced around, hoping for a distraction to stop this interrogation. Almost every booth had filled, with the lunch counter on the opposite side of the restaurant quickly approaching capacity. She scanned the crowd of professionals and street eccentrics, hoping for some clash she could use as a diversion. Despite its ratty decor, this dive served good food and better stories. The locals hated the white-collar kids who took over their space, looking for an adventure to crow about at the office.

"He's never sent me anything," she replied, taking a deep breath. "What makes you think he's obsessed with me?"

"Well, for starters, you match the physical description of his victims."

She scoffed at his comment. "So do a lot of girls. I can throw a stone and hit ten brunettes."

"Maybe, but my instincts tell me there's more to this than you're letting on."

Through his words, a current of uneasiness settled over her. Something was happening around them that set her on edge and made her skin crawl. Kate studied the lunch counter, trying to convince herself that her instincts were wrong. Time seemed to slow down and, just for a moment, her thoughts went blank. She heard Grant's voice in the distance but she couldn't concentrate on what he was saying.

Putting her hand to her head, she closed her eyes for a moment and forced herself to focus on everything around her.

Office gossip two tables over, a homeless guy in the corner booth nursing an open-faced sandwich while quietly feeding the small dog in his jacket.

Not them, not them, she thought as she scrutinized her fellow patrons. Two hot girls at the end of the counter, wide-eyed and whispering, threw seductive glances in Grant's direction. A mysterious man, also at the counter, sat with his back to her. Collar up and hat brim pulled down low. His chatty demeanor didn't match his behavior and, more importantly, his thoughts.

"Are you listening to me?"

"No, but I get it. You don't believe a word out of my mouth." She barely registered what he was saying, her full attention now on the man at the lunch counter.

"Okay, what the hell is going on?"

She grabbed his arm, as he tried to glance back. "Guy at the counter has been doing his damnedest to distract the waitress. She's got the coffee pot on the counter. I think he's going to spike it."

As casually as possible, Grant turned around, just in time to see him dropping several capsules into the coffee. "Son of a bitch," he swore. "Why don't you get the coffee and I'll get the guy."

"Sounds like a plan."

Leaving the safety of their booth, they split up, Kate heading toward the waitress, who had just poured a Wall Street wannabe a fresh cup. She flashed her badge, grabbing the carafe from her while placing her other hand over the young guy's cup. Looking down at him, she gently tugged the mug from his hand. "You don't want this. You drink too much coffee as it is."

"What the hell, lady? Give it back."

"No."

A haughty look crossed his face and he grabbed her arm, trying to pry her hand from the mug. "Let go of my drink, you crazy bitch."

Kate sighed and gave him her best smile. "Fine, all yours." Shifting her wrist to the side, she let the cup tip and spill onto his pants.

The man jumped up, spewing profanities. "WTF? These pants cost two hundred bucks, bitch. Why the hell did you do that?"

"Why don't you cool off?"

"Cool off? My goddamn pants are ruined, thanks to you."

"Chalk it up to a life lesson, sport. Don't piss women off."

"How about I teach you a lesson?" Drawing back his arm, he balled his hand in a fist, ready to throw the first punch.

Kate rolled her eyes, secretly daring him to attack her. She was in the mood for a fight.

Before she could react, Grant was on him, shoving him away from her and into the waiting arms of two men in blue jackets. "Want to call the lady names one more time, asshole? Go ahead, I dare you," he hissed.

"Who the hell are you?"

"FBI, and you're under arrest for an attempted assault on a police officer." Turning around, Grant addressed the flabbergasted crowd. "Listen up, everyone. This place is closed. There has been a bomb threat and we would like everyone to vacate the premises."

No one moved. The crowd seemed unsure of what to do, until Grant glared at them. "Now!" he yelled. "Move!"

As the last of the patrons rushed the doors, Grant gave instructions to the waiting agents, detailing the protocol of locking down the building and starting a sweep for evidence. Taking the pot of coffee from Kate's hand, he handed it to one of his team.

Kate glanced around, at the team of people in blue jackets with FBI in yellow stamped across their backs. "Where did these guys come from?" she said to Grant.

He looked up from briefing his people and walked back toward her. "I called them. Meet the local branch of the FBI's emergency response team. They are some of the finest group of specialists brought together to contain a terrorist situation."

"You think one guy spiking a pot of coffee is a terrorist situation?"

"No, but when he disappears right in front of me, the situation warrants an investigation."

Kate felt her stomach drop as a wave of nausea washed over her. She suspected what he meant but didn't want to believe it. "What do you mean, disappear?"

"I mean, one minute, I had him pinned against this building, then I glance at my phone for a second and he's gone." He paused and frowned, looking her up and down. "You okay? You look like you've seen a ghost."

"Fine. I'm fine. It's just a lot to process."

He nodded and turned away, directing his team like this was an everyday occurrence. Disappeared in front of him? Only a certain type of person would attempt such a brazen act, and that person belonged to her family. Exposing family secrets in broad daylight? What the hell was going on?"

She sat down at the lunch counter, her mind reeling with questions. There was still five days to go until the reunion. No member of her family would be stupid enough to pull such a stunt in front of witnesses.

"Detective, you look like you have something on your mind. Care to share?"

She glanced up at him, dazed. Damn this man. He had the tenacity of a dog digging for a bone. There's no way he could be so dialed into her universe. Only people familiar with her world had senses that sharp. Her surprise turned to suspicion.

Quickly, she ran through a list of his qualities and silently swore for not doing her homework on the mysterious agent who had quickly inserted himself into her life.

"Detective?"

Her thoughts turned to confirming her suspicions. If he was who she suspected, there were a couple of subtle ways to find out, rather than going through official channels.

"Detective?"

"Sorry, yes, I mean no. No additional information about who the perp might be. Just hunches and suspicions."

His eyes narrowed, clearly unconvinced by her response. "Like what?"

"Like what was in those capsules."

"I can answer that for you."

They turned to see a member of Grant's team approach, a gorgeous blonde with bright blue eyes. She walked with an impatience that matched her response. Every part of her mannerisms screamed business, from the way she knocked her clipboard against her hand to the way she subtly eyed Grant, as if he was two hours late for a lunch date.

"Cassie, this is Detective Kate Morgan. Detective, this is Dr. Cassie Devereaux, chemist, microbiologist, and former teaching professor at Harvard."

"Nice to meet you." Devereaux nodded curtly, as if taking a second to exchange pleasantries was a waste of her time.

"You know what was in the coffee?"

"Unfortunately, yes. It is tetrodotoxin."

Kate blinked, stunned. "Oh my god. Are you kidding?"

"What's tetrodotoxin?" Grant replied.

"Poison from the Puffer fish. Extremely fatal."

"Wait, you mean the fish they serve at sushi restaurants?"

Devereaux, nodded again, lightly brushing a bit of dirt from Grant's jacket. "The detective is correct. It is extremely lethal and in a concentrated state, such as this, a sample the size of dot is enough to kill a man."

"He put several capsules in the coffee."

She shrugged her shoulders, clearly bored by his line of questioning. "Overkill, to say the least. There's enough poison in that coffee to kill the residents of a small town. Why waste it on a handful of people?"

"Cassie."

She shrugged her shoulders at his rebuke, a slight smile crossing her face. Kate looked away in disgust. She had seen that expression before. They were in the middle of a crisis and all the woman could think of was bedding her co-worker.

"Well, it looks like your team has the situation in hand. I have to get back to work."

"Detective, we haven't finished our conversation."

"I think we have, Agent. Tell you what, if I remember anything else, I'll give you a call."

"Detective, I—"

"Special Agent Anderson!"

They looked toward the agent calling them. He was on the phone and gesturing at the television on the wall above the lunch counter.

"Turn that up," Grant barked, to the manager as the conversation around them ground to a halt.

Kate turned to see a news report from Canada flash across the scene. Chaos filled the screen at what appeared to be a college campus. The pretty female broadcaster featured seemed overwhelmed as she struggled to get her words out in a composed manner.

"…we can now confirm that the mass killing of sixty-two university students this morning was linked to some type of terrorist attack. Minutes ago, the individuals responsible released a message to our station stating, and I quote, 'Other attacks will follow. One for every province and state around the forty ninth parallel.' To recap, about an hour ago, nine-one-one calls went out when students in this school suddenly became ill after visiting the school's main cafeteria. At this time, details are still coming in and the school remains in lockdown, pending the outcome of an investigation."

A roar of outrage overpowered the rest of the broadcast. Exclamations of horror, mixed with orders to obtain details on this latest crisis filled the room. What had been an exercise in averting a crime quickly turned into a mobile command center as people jumped on smart phones and lap tops, trying to draw similarities between the two incidents. Amidst the chaos, a young agent approached Kate with a pad of paper in his hand.

"Detective Morgan, I believe this is yours."

She gave him a quick glance then shook her head. "You're mistaken. I didn't drop anything."

"Oh, well, he said it was yours."

Kate took it and thanked the man, still entranced by the broadcast. Glancing down, she saw that she held an order pad, dropped by one of the waitresses, and did a double take. Scrawled across the paper was a note that made her stomach drop. Kate quickly ripped off the message then grabbed the man by the arm, spinning him around. "Hey, who did you say gave this to you?"

"Just some guy. Said to give it to the pretty brunette. I figured that was you."

"What did he look like?"

Grant answered her instead. "Who are you talking about?"

The young agent looked flustered at the amount of attention he was receiving. "This guy outside. I thought he was one of the diners who picked up a waitress's order pad."

Instantly, Grant was at his side. "What did he look like?"

"I—I dunno. Average build, average looks, I guess."

"Can you be more specific? Brown hair? Blond hair? Height? Weight?"

Sweat began to break out on his face. He started to shuffle around, unsure of what he should say. "Yeah, brown, no, blond. Um, I don't really know, it's a little hazy."

Devereaux rolled her eyes. "Idiot, how can you not know? You just saw him."

Grant held up his hand, stopping her. He motioned to another agent, then after a brief conversation the young man was led away.

"You want to tell me what's written on the book?"

"It's nothing. Not important. See it's blank." She held up the pad for them to see before tossing the book on a nearby table. Pushing past Grant, she forced her way through the mass of people and disappeared through a gathering crowd on the street.

"What the hell was that about?"

Devereaux looked down at the empty pad of paper in his hand and smirked. "Probably some poor sap giving her his number. Why do you care?"

Grant ignored the remark and walked over to the lunch counter. Grabbing a pencil from the register, he lightly shaded over the front of the paper. Sure enough the trick worked and words began to appear. Scowling, he read the message.

You can't save them all, baby girl, was scrawled in neat printing across the page.

"What the hell is going on?" he muttered, navigating his way past the rest of the team and onto the street. In the light of a warm September day, the situation seemed almost trivial with the good citizens of New York milling the streets, enjoying the sunshine, and oblivious to the local tragedy that had just been averted. Looking around, he swore under his breath. She was gone.

CHAPTER 3

Kate pushed her way through the crowd and on to the dance floor. After the events of today, she needed an outlet for pent up frustrations, and the atmosphere at Hellraiser fit her needs perfectly.

An hour before closing and the place was packed, just like any other club in Manhattan. The difference here was that all bets were off. Here, there were no rules. Here, she wasn't a detective and didn't care how many laws were broken around her.

Pushing past the packed bodies, she wiggled herself into the middle of the dance floor, pausing only once to turn around and punch a guy who had grabbed her ass. In the middle of the floor, surrounded by writhing people and the roar of music, she couldn't think, couldn't feel. All she could do was dance.

Kate raised her hands and jumped up and down to the beat of the music. Someone next to her thrust a half empty bottle of champagne into her hands. Closing her eyes, she took a long draw before passing the bottle onto another dancer.

This was exactly what she needed. All she felt was anger and this was the perfect outlet to work it off. Years of work to hide her past and now her future was in peril. Between Grant and Lucas, her family ties would probably be revealed, then it was goodbye to her career in law enforcement, the one thing in this world that kept her sane.

Somewhere, high above her, the crowd heard the boom of thunder. As if on cue, a loud metallic grinding sound filled the air and she looked up, watching the retractable roof slowly open.

The mob erupted in a melody of exclamations and yells. Soon, the rain would come down and cool an atmosphere several degrees above the current temperature of hell.

Kate closed her eyes again, striving hard to get caught up in the moment. She could rattle off a half dozen solutions that would drive her thoughts away and lose her in the sweet ecstasy of pleasure. Powdered, liquid, or breathing, she had tried them all, but nothing gave her the high of dancing her troubles away. She was far from naive, though. No solution lasted forever and she had long since given up believing that permanence in anything existed.

From behind her, she felt large hands grasp her waist. The fingers slowly explored the smoothness of her thighs and taut stomach. She sighed and opened her eyes, the moment lost forever.

Turning around, faced her molester, giving the beefy, drunk guy a sweet smile.

Raising her finger, she wagged her first and last warning at him. He smiled back and tightened his grip on her body. Kate sighed again and grabbed his hands with hers, wrenching them from her waist. A cruel smile crossed his lips and, before she realized it, he back handed her.

Kate staggered for a moment, tasting the salty tang of blood in her mouth. Quickly regaining her balance, she watched as the crowd parted slightly to give her room. With a sharp uppercut, she caught him across the chin, snapping his head back.

The blow should have fazed him, but it only seemed to motivate him more. He lunged at her, but she ducked, delivering two powerful blows and a momentary atmospheric high that dancing didn't deliver.

"I like it," he said with a nasty grin. "You want me to give it to you, don't you, bitch?"

"You know, I'm really getting tired of people calling me that."

With that, she round house kicked him into a few unfortunate bystanders and over a table covered with pitchers of beer. He leapt to his feet with a roar then signaled someone behind her. Before Kate could react, she felt herself pinned as powerful arms encircled her.

The man wiped blood off his face and charged forward. Before he could reach her, a figure from the crowd tackled him, throwing him to the ground.

Kate gasped as her rescuer turned to face her, giving her a quick once over. Grant Anderson stood before her with a look of anger that made her feel like a five year old, banished to her room. Seemingly satisfied that she was okay, he turned to the man.

"What kind of asshole are you, hitting a girl?"

The man slowly climbed to his feet and pointed his finger at the stranger. "One that's going to end you."

Grant rolled his eyes then glanced back at Kate and gave her a wink. She smiled, thinking similar thoughts, and nodded as he raised his fist again. His first blow coincided with a stiletto heel in the foot of her restrainer. Her attacker bellowed and loosened his grip long enough for her to spin around and knee him in the groin. Unlike his friend, the new guy collapsed to the floor and Kate spun around to watch as Grant knocked out his fighting partner with a strong one-two punch.

A roar of disappointment rose from the crowd when they realized the show had suddenly ended. Grant turned and charged at Kate. Before she could say anything, he grabbed her and tossed her over his shoulder, striding through the crowd that had parted for them in admiration.

"What are you doing? Let me down."

She writhed around, trying hard to pull herself off of his very broad shoulders.

"Stop it," he said, giving her bottom a hard smack.

"Ow, what the hell was that for?"

He barrelled through the back doors of the club and into the darkened alley, scattering a couple who were enjoying mutual pleasures. In between a dumpster and stacks of empty wine crates, he finally came to a halt.

"Last warning, Anderson. Get the hell away from me."

Grant ignored her threats and pulled off her heels before peeling her from his shoulder and planting her on the ground.

Overhead, the sky opened and rain came crashing down, but he didn't care. Kate barely had time to catch her breath before she found herself pinned against the wall, arms above her head and wrists caught in one of his hands.

His angry face was inches from hers, rain pouring down his chiselled features. Finding it suddenly hard to breathe, she gulped in air, staring into his angry eyes. "What are you doing?"

"Getting some answers."

"You're killing my buzz, agent."

"Then stop being a brat. What the hell were you doing in that club by yourself?"

Anger poured into her again. Not only was he stalking her, he was invading the one place where she could forget the world. She glanced down with the intent of kneeing him but he was one step ahead again. Through the haze of alcohol, she realized he was standing on her bare feet, pinning her in both directions.

"I was dancing and trying to forget about the world."

"While letting strangers molest you?" His eyes flashed with anger as he pointed to the back door with his free hand. "That place is a cesspool of degenerates, killers, and psychopaths."

"With great music and one-hundred-and-ten-proof drinks."

"Shut up. You could have gotten yourself killed."

"I work for the NYPD. I'm always in a situation where I can get myself killed."

"Not on my watch."

"I'm not your responsibility. I'm perfectly happy being left alone."

They glared at each other for a few moments more and she felt the mood shift. With quieting breaths, her rage subsided, and she sagged against the wall, unable and somewhat unwilling to escape his grasp. She cleared her throat, growing uncomfortable with just how comfortable she felt around him. "Why are you really here, Agent? Surely it's not to babysit me."

"You disappeared yesterday."

"Your team had the task well at hand."

"You ran away after you saw this." He held up the piece of the paper from the waitress pad.

She glanced at the paper, then averted her eyes as if the words gave her immense pain.

He felt her relax or, more appropriately, give up. Releasing her hands, he stepped back, watching her as she hugged the wall, shrinking in size against the building behind her. "Who is this guy, Kate?"

"A psychopath sending a message that he's the great and powerful Oz." She turned over one of the empty wine crates and sat on it. "You can't stop him, Grant. He's on an ego trip. Out to prove something and there's nothing that you can do."

"I can protect you and the people he's trying to harm."

She let out a bitter laugh, amazed at his naivety and shook her head. "No, you can't. More importantly, you won't be allowed to. It's the law of nature. People in this world die, and he's fulfilling a mandate."

"Killing innocent people isn't a mandate," he snapped, "it's the delusion of a sick and twisted mind. He isn't God. He doesn't have the right to decide who lives or dies. You decide your destiny. Stop acting like a victim. You don't have to be one of those people."

Kate leaned over and retrieved her heels, putting them on before standing up. She looked up at him, ringing water from the hem of her dress. "Yeah, sure. Victim, huh? That's a new one You don't have to worry about me. I can protect myself. It's the others like those poor students in Canada you should be concerned about."

"I will stop him."

"No, you won't." Shrugging her disbelief, Kate continued her walk to the corner and raised her hand to hail a cab.

"What's makes you so sure?"

Kate looked back at him thoughtfully. Maybe he was who she thought he was, and maybe he wasn't, but one phrase would tell her for sure. "The balance must be maintained, Anderson," she replied bitterly. "Isn't that what we're taught?"

Grant stared at her, stone faced, as she climbed into a cab. With her out of sight, he doubled over, putting his hands on his knees. Her words hit him dead on, and the realization hurt badly. She was one of those Morgans.

CHAPTER 4

Chateau L'Arc du Lumiere nestled itself between the base of the Adirondack Mountains and rolling countryside of upstate New York. More a castle than a Chateau, it had the distinction of being known as the twice-removed fortress. Once by a rich nobleman in the late fifteenth century, when it was uprooted from France to the Moors of Scotland, then once again a mere two hundred years later travelling stone by stone to the New World by some ousted arm of royalty who couldn't bear to leave his home behind.

Over the next four hundred years, it had flourished in its new home, first as a private residence, then, some said, as unofficial think tank of the Union Army, where Lincoln and his army of generals would retreat to plan their attack against the South.

Within the past century and the emergence of a more modern era, it held the distinction of spa and resort, offering world class fine dining and luxurious rooms to the New Yorker who fancied a more rural experience than the Hamptons without sacrificing the comforts of home.

For Kate, driving through the parking lot to the monstrosity of mortar was like entering a prison. A gilded cage of lies, deceit, and treachery. She sighed and gripped the steering wheel, forcing herself not to turn the car around. This was a trap, and she had no choice but to walk into it.

Pulling into valet parking, she greeted a cheerful man

who took her keys and carefully ignored her resistance to give up her only means of escape. "Miss Morgan, is this the only bag that you have?"

"Yes," she replied, handing him a generous tip in the hopes that he might remember her when she needed a quick getaway.

"Well, then. If I may direct you to check in, I believe the rest of your family will be arriving tomorrow."

Kate smiled weakly and headed through the main entrance, gasping just a bit at the incredible interior that awaited her. It was like stepping back in time. The soaring rooftop of stone and glass made her feel like she was in a cathedral. Instead of pews and alters, small areas of comfortable couches and antique tables filled the space. Everywhere she looked, flowers and greenery dotted the landscape and, though it was September, she could swear that the scent of hyacinths filled the air.

"Welcome to Chateau L'Arc du Lumiere. The Arc of Light for those who don't speak French," quipped a perky girl with a shiny brass name badge that read *Brandi* on it.

"Thanks. I'm Kate Morgan. Checking in for—"

"For the Summit and reunion, yes, Miss Morgan, I have a beautiful suite in the wing reserved for your family."

Kate smiled and shook her head. "No thanks. I'll take a room as far away from my family as possible."

The girl's eyes widened with surprise. She looked at her computer screen, then back at Kate with some confusion on her face. "I don't understand. I have explicit instructions to put you in the south wing with the rest of the Morgans."

Kate placed her Black Visa Card on the reception desk and smiled sweetly. "Brandi, this is a very large resort. Surely you have other rooms available."

"Of course, we have over seven hundred rooms and the only occupants are your family and the Andersons." She bit her lip and looked down, as if saying the name Anderson would bring down the wrath of God.

"Good, then there is plenty of room for little—"

A figure approached, and she paused her conversation. She couldn't see him but she could feel his animosity, his dislike toward the others here. He was a potential threat, and she needed to know why. With the sweep of her foot, she caught the man in a roundhouse kick, hitting him in the legs and flipping him onto the ground. With one foot on his chest, she pulled out her gun and aimed it at his head.

"State your intentions."

The burly man looked up at her, his hostility replaced by fear. "I was going to ask you if you needed help with your luggage. I'm a valet."

Kate glanced at his uniform and name tag as embarrassment set in. *What the hell are you thinking, attacking the people who work here?* Turning a dark shade of red, she lifted her foot off his chest. "No, thanks. I can handle it myself."

"No kidding, lady, I kind of figured that out."

She sighed and holstered her gun as he hurried off. Her skin crawled like it was on fire. She didn't want to be here—every little thing was setting her off.

Kate rubbed her neck in frustration then turned back to the front desk attendant. Her voice rose to a pitch that she only used with criminals. "Brandi, as you can see, I'm not in the mood to keep repeating myself, so why don't you give me a room as far away from my family as you can?"

Brandi turned pale and took a step back, unsure of what to say next. Instead of doing anything, she chose to look at her feet and hum a faint tune under her breath.

"Oh, for the love of Pete!" Kate said, throwing up her hands with frustration.

"Well, I would have chosen a different word, but that will do," replied a deep voice from behind her.

Turning around, she looked up into the smiling face of a tall man with dark wavy hair. As if on cue, the clouds shifted, filling the lobby with intense light. Kate blinked repeatedly, looking at the familiar chiseled features, kind eyes, and amused expression.

She stared at him, taken aback at the man who stood before her. Casual dress made him almost unrecognizable. A phrase from her Southern roots floated back from her memory. *A tall drink of water on a hot summer's day.* Athletic and lean in a well-tailored pair of khakis, his expansive chest hid under a button down shirt. He was wearing a black leather jacket and cradling a bag of groceries in the crook of his right arm.

She drew in a breath as an uncomfortable realization set in. "Oh, no."

"That's putting it mildly."

They stared at each other for several seconds with such an intimate exchange that it forced Brandi to cough loudly, trying to get their attention. "Uh, Miss Morgan, about your room?"

He nodded and, turning his attention to Brandi, gave her a warm and inviting smile. "Brandi, I sense a problem between you and Detective Morgan."

"Grant Anderson. Jeez, you're one of those Andersons," Kate said, interrupting his conversation with the clerk. "As in our families are mortal enemies, Anderson?"

"According to my overly dramatic mother, yes."

Despite her surprise, Kate couldn't resist showing a small smile. Unlike her last encounter, this version of the man was outgoing and charismatic. He complimented the sunny interior of the building, emitting a warm graciousness that seemed to affect everyone around him. She noted his talents were very appreciated, especially by the girl in front of her.

"Oh, Mr. Anderson. No problem," replied Brandi, her eyes wide as admiration flooded her face. "Just trying to get Miss Morgan checked in."

"And my room?" prodded Kate. "Far away from my family. Preferably in another wing or country?"

A pained look crossed the girl's face, Kate's humor lost on her. "You see? I'll have to check with my manager. I can't deviate from these instructions and well, you understand how these things go..." Her voice petered off into nothing, her look of pity only served to make Kate angry again.

"Look, Brandi," Grant whispered. "Why don't you put her right next to me? I'm in the farthest outreaches of the North wing."

"But you're an Anderson, sir. And the Morgans and Andersons aren't supposed to mix."

"Well, why don't we just create a new section? Call it the law enforcement wing of the property and Detective Morgan and I will promise to get along."

Kate looked at him with mild amusement. "Yes, the NYPD and FBI have always had a good relationship. We respect each other's jurisdiction."

Grant paused then turned his attention back to Brandi, choosing to ignore the dig about their previous encounters. "How about it? Let's make it our little secret."

Brandi grinned, her face alight with infatuation. "With pleasure, sir. There you go, Detective. Room 118, right across from Mr. Anderson. Can I get you a valet?" Her voice dissipated, lost in the wake of Grant's attention.

"No need, Brandi," Grant replied warmly. He scooped up Kate's Black Visa Card and handed it to her with her room keys. "I was heading there myself and will be happy to show her the way."

He gallantly gestured toward a long hallway that led from the lobby toward the north section of the property. Kate nodded in appreciation and followed him, pulling her overnight bag behind her.

"So a Morgan in the NYPD, with a Black Visa Card on a policeman's salary. That's interesting. I heard of the occasional beat cop coming from your family but never a wealthy detective."

"My family ties are as loose as possible, including their blood money. That doesn't mean I haven't learned a thing or two about investing over the years," replied Kate with a smile. Glancing sideways, she added, "You should talk. I haven't seen that much designer on one man in a long time."

He looked down at his clothes and mumbled something about personal shoppers before directing them around a series of left turns. They headed down a sequence of corridors that linked the stretch of buildings. It was obvious the previous owners had taken advantage of the rolling countryside to expand the resort. It was a maze of new and old architecture. "Interesting display of law enforcement training back there."

Kate blushed, looking away. "It's been a tough couple of days."

"Are we going to talk about the other night?"

"Nope."

"Detective."

"Okay, stop. From what I know of the rules, you can't do anything about problems out there mixing with, well, problems in here."

"You mean the Summit truce?"

"Yes."

"That doesn't mean I can't lay the ground work for when the truce is lifted."

"Spoken like a true law enforcer. Always on the job."

"So what's his name, Detective?"

"For crying out loud, call me Kate. I think we know each other well enough to be on a first name basis."

He smiled and nodded, temporarily suspending his interrogation, and, for the next few seconds, they walked in silence.

"Kate, you can't tell me you don't want to see him behind bars."

She threw up her hands in frustration. "Of course, I want to see justice done. Hell, I'd like to mow down half my family for the crimes they have committed. Why bother with jail? Why not just bypass the justice system and open fire on all of them. Believe me, that thought has crossed my mind a thousand times."

"Mass murder wasn't exactly what I had in mind."

Kate smiled. "Talk to me again after you've spent some time with my family." Hoping to put the topic behind them, she turned to him with a big smile, determined to take the heat off of her. "So, seeing as how we're stuck here for the next few days, why don't you tell me a bit about you? How did you end up in the FBI? I thought all Andersons were priests and nuns."

He raised his eyebrows in surprise. "Not really a fan of that lifestyle. I don't think we're much different than other families. We have our share of bankers, lawyers, and politicians. Of course, we prefer upholding the rules of society, unlike…well, with the possible exception of yourself, your family."

Kate laughed, matching him stride for stride, as they walked down the hallway. "You mean how does a member of America's most notorious crime family end up on the right side of the law?"

"Yeah, especially since…well, you know…"

"Since we are members of *that* family."

"Well, I wouldn't have put it so delicately, but now that you bring it up, yeah."

Kate shrugged and glanced up at the man with the talent to make her spill her life story. Judging by the clerk's response, she wasn't the only one easily influenced by his charms. Unlike her family, she didn't have an issue with the Andersons, never mind one who had just rallied to her defense. "I'm the family freak. The proverbial black sheep, the Marilyn to a family of Munsters."

"Well, you know what they say about sheep. Don't let yourself get led to slaughter."

An uneasy laugh filled her throat. "Been there and done that. Not a fan."

Grant paused and grabbed her by the arm, stopping her just short of room 118. "Wait. What? That's what you meant in the alley? Someone's tried to kill you?"

"Multiple Morgans and multiple times," she said nonchalantly, "Apparently there is no room for freaks in my family."

"But how did you escape?"

The stories of their victims were the stuff of legend. No one survived when they became the focus of a Morgan's sights. He stared at her, wondering if she was telling him the truth. After all, she was from the family committed to creating hell on earth.

"Yes, my family is evil, corrupt, and perfectly comfortable committing every heinous act known to man. How have I survived, you wonder? How did I know you wanted to flip Junior Malone, or that you have a penthouse overlooking Central Park with a beautiful husky named Nibs? It's my curse, Grant. I can read minds."

A moment of surprise quickly put the puzzle pieces into place. Every Morgan had some sort of talent, although reading minds was a new one for him. The girl had spunk, he had to admit that. He gestured to a door. "This is your room. I'm sure you'll want to get settled before the families arrive and sparks fly."

Kate reached out her hand, offering her gratitude. "Well, thank, you Special Agent Anderson. I appreciate your help."

He smiled and released her hand, shifting his groceries to his other arm while he fished for the room key in his pocket. Hearing the quiet beep of her door, he turned around. "Hey, Kate?"

"Yes?"

"I was wondering…"

Regardless of how she felt in New York, she was more than willing to put their differences aside for the sake of the Summit and possibly her survival. Begrudgingly, even she had to admit she was willing to hop on the Grant Anderson bandwagon for a short time. "Yes, Grant, I would like to have dinner with you. It would be nice to have an experienced guide show me the property."

His face flushed. "Right. Mind reader. Have to get used to that."

CHAPTER 5

S o you're an only child—"

"And I'm reminded of that on a monthly basis." Kate finished the last of an expensive burgundy and glanced around the half-empty dining room of Borealis, the chateau's three-star Michelin-rated restaurant. Random people in thousand dollar suits had been throwing them dirty looks all night.

Given the importance of this Summit, everyone without a name badge was an "associate," working for one family or the other, and it was obvious that none of them approved. She suspected her observations didn't go unnoticed by Grant but, out of respect for their dinner, he didn't acknowledge it.

"Why is that?" he said with a smile.

"Let's just say, if I had brothers and sisters, I wouldn't have been such a disappointment to my mother."

"Don't think you have a monopoly on unhappy mothers. I can introduce you to mine if you're interested in disappointment with a healthy dose of guilt on the side."

Kate let out a laugh of surprise. "Wait a second. Your family is the poster child for heavenly good. What about all that love, acceptance, and comfort?"

Grant let out a low chuckle then looked around and gestured to the waiter. "That's all there but so are the expectations. Perfection in all things, not to mention a constant reminder about following the 'family' plan. God forbid, I make the wrong career decision and bring about the next Apocalypse."

"And the right career decision was the FBI?"

"It feeds my need for truth and justice. I assume you have similar feelings about being a detective?"

Kate nodded, gazing into the trio of candles that gave their table a romantic feel. "It drives me, but of course my family detests it," she murmured. "I need to hold people accountable for their actions. I don't know, maybe because I saw in my family how easy it was to destroy the good in a person. As a kid, I kept looking for hope and all I found was evil."

"It must make your job easier, that combination of detective skills and mind reader."

She looked up at him with a half-smile. "Not really. You'd be surprised how many lies we tell ourselves. It's hard to distinguish a person's perception of reality from the truth. Besides, telling a judge that 'I know he did it because I saw into his mind' doesn't exactly hold up in court. I might know he's guilty but I still have to prove it."

He smiled in a way that made her catch her breath. Unable to look away, Kate held his gaze, the silence between them growing intoxicating as the moments ticked by. She glanced down, noticing his hand positioned dangerously close to hers. Looking up again, her smile faded as a tall man sauntered toward her.

"Speak of the devil," she muttered, sitting up straight, her body tensed and prepared.

Grant frowned as her hand slid away from his and toward the butter knife.

"Katherine, darling. So good to see you made it here safely, and you brought a friend."

He was tall and gorgeous with blond hair and the face of a god. By the furtive glances from the women around her, his impact had been widely felt. Carefully, he adjusted his cufflinks before extending his hand, flashing Grant, his signature million-dollar smile.

"Grant, this is my cousin. Lucas Morgan."

Grant started to rise, but Lucas waved him back, warmly shaking his hand. "Don't let me interrupt your dinner, just wanted to extend some Southern hospitality to an associate of our Katherine," he replied with an eloquent Southern drawl. "She tells us so little of her activities, it's nice to get a glimpse into her life."

"You got your intro, Lucas, so feel free to disappear."

"Now, Grant, you must excuse my cousin. No matter how hard we tried, manners just did not stick with her."

"Go to hell, Lucas."

Instead of shock, an icy look crossed his face. His perfect mouth contorted into a nasty grin. Lucas rounded the table, lightly touching the fine linen table cloth, then the curve of her shoulder, as if to massage her back, but at the last minute, thought better of it. He leaned over Kate, all the while scanning the room of admirers. With his lips grazing the outer edge of her ear, his whisper of words was anything but warm. "Play nice in front of the help, baby girl."

Grant tensed up and snapped to attention, looking closely at her cousin. Anger flashed in his eyes, but a subtle glance from Kate forced his feelings into check. Giving Lucas a tight smile, he replied, "Forgive me, I think there are some crossed wires here. I'm not an associate. My name is Grant Anderson."

This time it was Lucas who looked genuinely surprised. Kate felt the tension rise and, despite his control, heard a host of swear words pass through his mind. From her cousin's reaction, Grant Anderson and his name were well known. "Well, my apologies for the assumption. It's an honor. You have quite the reputation."

Grant nodded. "As do you. I hope the Summit is fruitful for you."

With a polite acknowledgement, Lucas glided away, as Kate exhaled the breath she didn't know she had been holding. After a moment to compose herself, she shot Grant a weak smile. "Family is complicated."

"That's him, isn't it?" he hissed. "He murdered sixty-six people."

"I thought there were sixty-two victims from the Vancouver massacre."

"Four of the students were pregnant."

Agony flooded her face. She didn't need to say a word, her look confirmed it all. Before he could do anything, she took a deep breath and put her hand on his arm. "You can't touch him here and we have no proof. He probably is responsible, but for now, we're stuck, so cool off."

For a minute, she thought he was going to bolt, her words not making a difference at all. After a few minutes of silence, he relaxed slightly, sitting back in his chair. "You're right. It can wait for now."

"Patience is a virtue, right?"

"Huh, never thought I'd hear those words from you."

Kate blushed, throwing up her hands in defeat. "Touché, Agent. My preference is to leap over this table and attack but, when it comes to him, specifically, biding one's time is not such a bad thing."

Intimacy became an uncomfortable silence between them. Thankfully, for Kate, the moment was interrupted by their waiter, pushing a trolley of enticing desserts, spirits, and coffees.

She looked up at him and, grateful for the intrusion, smiled. "No sweets for us. We're not dessert people." She frowned for a minute, then blushed again. "I'm sorry, I don't know why I said that. I don't know if you like that sort of thing or not."

"No, you're right. Was never big on sweets, but I am a fan of something else."

Grant perused the cart for a minute before pulling a bottle of Talisker from the bottom tier. Grabbing two glasses, he stood up and gave the man a quick nod. "Charge this and the dinner to my room and add a thirty percent tip for yourself."

"Of course, Mr. Anderson. My name is Walter if you need anything else during your stay."

"Thank you Walter, I think this will be a nice start."

Kate eyed the bottle of eight hundred dollar single malt with amusement. "Scotch?"

"Drink of the trade. Besides, we're going to need a healthy dose of this to get through the next few days. Follow me."

"Where are we going?"

He smiled and gave her a wink. "My family loves this property and I promised you a tour, so we're going to go to the parts that I like."

She followed him out, completely aware that all eyes watched them leave the dining room. The disparaging thoughts were almost overwhelming. Sanctimonious hypocrites who would do better to keep their mouths shut. She didn't doubt that once the enormous doors closed, the conversation would raise a decibel or two.

Once away from prying eyes, he walked them out a side door, around the main courtyard, to a satellite building around back. Going through a double set of doors, Kate found herself on the threshold of a medium sized chapel complete with altar and wooden pews. "A church? Really?"

"Come on," he said, pointing to a narrow stone staircase. "You can enter a house of worship, right? You're not going to burst into flames on me?"

Kate rolled her eyes and pushed him up the stairs. "Very funny, altar boy. I never attended church, but I'm pretty sure you're not supposed to drink in one."

"No, but all those years of sitting through three-hour Easter masses made me want to."

The choir loft had been updated and converted into a seating area. It soon became clear to Kate that the chapel was more for the occasional wedding than weekly service.

Grant sat himself down on a large plush sofa in an alcove at the back of the balcony, pulling an army knife from his pocket. With more than a measure of expertise, he fished out the cork and poured them both a healthy dose.

Kate joined him and took her glass. Looking out into the room, she felt a sense of calm overtake her. "Nice. It's very peaceful here. Like a sanctuary from the world."

"That's why I like it. When I come here, no one bothers me and I can think."

He took a swig and let out a sigh, propping his feet up on the wooden coffee table in front of them. "Tastes as good as first time I shared a glass with ol' Hugh MacAskill, the founder of Talisker, himself. Cheers."

"Cheers," she echoed. "When was that?"

"Hmm, just after they started production so I'm guessing 1835? Yeah, that sounds about right."

"Wow, you're that old and not looking like a day over forty?"

His eyes twinkled. "Hey! People used to say not a day over thirty."

Kate took another sip and sat back on the couch, slipping off her heels and curling her feet underneath her. "So what goes on at these conferences, anyway?"

His eyes shot up in surprise, the question catching him off guard. "Wait a second. This can't be your first one?"

"Let's see, they are held every fifty years, so technically this would be my third one."

"These events are mandatory, so how did you get out of the first two?"

"Well, the first one I attended was when I was five and don't remember it, and the second one, I was dead."

Grant furrowed his brow, his drink forgotten in a sea of thoughts. "So if I remember how the life code works for your family, then this is your second life."

Kate tossed back her drink and reached for the bottle. "Third. And final I might add."

He shook his head in disbelief.

"No, really," she added with a smile. "I might look like I'm in my thirties but I can show you the gray hair. I've started to age like a normal person."

Accepting her offer of more scotch, he watched as the liquid filled his glass. After a long moment, he cleared his throat. "How? If you don't mind me asking? Your family?"

She let out a musical laugh, the alcohol proving to be a better catalyst than any therapy technique she had encountered of late. "No, no—at least I don't think so. The first time was in 1968, just two days before the last 'reunion' as I call it. I was practicing medicine in New York and a patient with a death wish decided to take me with him while I was trying to talk him off a ledge. The second time was about fifteen years ago. Some kind of car accident, I think. I don't actually remember the details of that one."

"And the attempts?"

"Ah, yeah, those. So a couple of highlights. At age six, it became clear that I didn't tow the family line, and every year, my resistance strengthened. By the time I hit fifteen, my mother reasoned that killing me was for the best, hoping that awaking to my second life might reset me, so to speak. So that summer, Lucas tried to drown me in Jackson Lake on a family vacation.

"The Lucas I just met?"

Just for a moment, she saw his eyes blaze with anger. She nodded and watched his grip on the glass tighten, then the calm exterior returned.

"Another time, there was an associate bent on proving her love to my cousin Aaron. She attempted to poison me and...well, I could go on and on. Let's just say they get more creative all the time."

"I can see why you aren't so excited to be here."

"If there was a way, short of death, I would have fought it, but as you know it's preprogrammed into us." She caressed her glass. "Besides, you can only run so far from family responsibilities."

He paused for a moment and she didn't have to read his mind to see the conflict on his face. "You haven't completed The Joining, have you?"

"You know about that?"

Grant nodded and took another swig of his drink. "When you have enemies trying to burn down your family tree, you get to know as much about them as you can."

Kate looked away, the intimacy of his pain resounded in his words. It was a realization she found hard to bear. He wasn't the coward that she was. While she ran, he clearly chose to fight.

"Sorry about that," she murmured. "Most of them pride themselves on the code of responsibility. It's a sick tribute to Satan, himself."

After a moment, Grant stood up and wandered over to one of the windows. Glancing up at the moon, he stared at it for a long time. "So what are your responsibilities, Kate? Are you going to complete The Joining?"

She wandered over and stood beside him, leaning against a shallow divot in the wall. "Not if I can help it."

"They'll force you."

She shrugged her shoulders. "I'm on my third life with a career that doesn't have great retirement odds. I won't see another reunion, so why should they care? I just have to survive the next four days and, hopefully, they'll leave me alone."

"Hope alone is not a good plan for survival. Believe me, I found that out the hard way."

She pondered his words, silently agreeing. "I'm sorry, I didn't mean to kill the mood. Forget about me. I'm a survivor. Hell, if I can thrive on my idea of home cooking, no one can kill me. Besides, the politics are vicious between my cousins and there are bigger Morgan fish than me to fry."

Grant looked down at her and smiled. "You're a brave woman, Detective Morgan," he whispered, caressing the side of her face. "Naive, but brave."

She fought the urge to lean into him, the pull to be in his arms almost impossible to resist. Tearing her eyes from the compassion in his face felt like ripping out a part of her soul. Kate cleared her throat and pulled away, returning to her place on the couch. "So, yeah, what can I expect at this Summit of Heaven and Hell?"

Grant rubbed his eyes and tossed his hands in the air. "Not sure what your side has planned but it's pretty dry unless you're on the High Council or part of the first families. The sides meet to plan out what the next fifty years will look like for humanity and how to maintain the balance. They discuss past and future events, making sure the checks and balances are in place. There are discussions on equalizing world events, managing catastrophes—you know, that kind of thing."

"What, no discussions about demons and angels? How about a hundred and one ways to corrupt mortals?" she said with a laugh.

"Just say no to evil?" he added, taking another drink.

"Temptation from the beyond. How to resist the pleasures of Hell," she replied, laughing hysterically.

Grant wiped back the tears from his eyes. "Don't joke," he exclaimed. "I remember lectures from several priests that might have been called that."

"Ahh, I can't wait. Four days of seminars on how to be bad and a decade's worth of lectures from my Mother. You're going to be one hundred and fifteen, when will you do something with your life? Why can't you work for the family and settle down? What's wrong with being a woman of leisure?"

"A woman of leisure?"

"Yeah, my mother is a combination of a martyr from a Tennessee Williams play and refugee from *Gone with the Wind* with the Scarlet O'Hara accent and evil cunning to boot. She has been clinging onto her last life forever. At this rate, she'll be a thousand years old and still ranting about my lack of Southern values."

Grant let out a hearty laugh and looked at the beautiful girl curled up beside him. He couldn't remember the last time someone had reignited his sense of humor. He liked her combination of truth and sarcasm. She was the real deal.

Kind heart, good soul, and beautiful face all rolled into one.

Kate looked at him sideways, a puzzled look on her face. "What?"

"What do you mean what? You can't read my mind?"

She blushed and lowered her eyes, feeling self-conscious for the first time in a while. "I can turn it off and sometimes I do. Besides, it might be a reflex for me, but deep down I think it's kind of rude."

"One of the few perks of being an emissary is the special powers we each receive. You can't be ashamed of it, any more than the family that you're from."

"Easy for you to say," replied Kate, lifting the glass to her lips. "You don't have to navigate a group of psychos."

Grant laughed again and finished the last of his drink. He offered the bottle but she shook her head, trying unsuccessfully to stifle a yawn.

"And on that note, I think it's time for bed."

"Absolutely," Kate added as she rose to her feet. "You can't walk into a den of tigers without your wits about you."

She looked around for a minute, finally seeing the heel of her shoes peeking out from under the couch. She quickly maneuvered her feet into them. Perhaps too quickly, for when she turned toward the stairs, she fell forward, right into his arms.

He caught her easily, one hand supporting the small of her back, while the other grazed the top of her arm. A smile of amusement crossed his face as he watched her flush with embarrassment. "Okay to walk?"

"Yeah, just not sure if I want to." She looked up into his eyes, wondering if this complex man was real. She wasn't used to this type of openness, especially with someone she barely knew.

"Hello, anybody there?"

"Did you hear something? There's someone here! We should go. I told you this was a bad idea."

"Shut up. I'm trying to hear."

The mysterious male voices from below quickly killed

the mood. With lightning-fast reflexes, Grant pulled her behind a heavy curtain, concealing them in a shallow alcove against one of the walls. It wasn't the best hiding spot but enough to cover them if the mysterious figures attached to the words chose to investigate further.

Flabbergasted, Kate looked at him, "What are you doing? We're not kids. We have a right to be here."

"Sticking to the shadows," he murmured. "I've learned from experience; covert actions are never a bad thing at these Summits."

She searched his face, unsure if he was kidding or not. Behind the curtain, she was trapped between his body and the plaster wall behind her. The alcohol made her feel lightheaded and carefree. His scent, the heat that radiated from his body next to hers was intoxicating. One of his fingers gently stroked her hair before finding its way down the curve of her neck. She closed her eyes and steadied herself. It took everything in her power not to place her hands on his chest and her mouth on his.

Standing on tip toe, she whispered into his ear, "Sure you're not over reacting, Agent?"

"Probably, but that's never a bad thing either."

They stood in silence for the next few seconds as footsteps echoed off the roof of the building. Grant leaned in, placing his hands on either side of the wall behind her. For a long moment, all she could hear was their combined breaths in unison, their eyes locked and ears open as they strained to hear creaks from ancient floor boards that would signal the approach of the mysterious male voices from below.

The echo of footsteps ceased, only to be replaced with the sound of groaning then the creak of a wooden pew. "You're being paranoid as usual," chided the first voice with distain. "It's a goddamn church. There's no one around."

"Out of all the places," whined the second. "Why do we have to meet here?"

"Call it poetic justice."

The first voice let out a sound that mixed annoyance and acceptance. Kate froze again, amazed at the acoustics of the chapel. It felt as if the men were having the conversation right next to them.

"So what's the plan?"

"The plan is none of your concern. Only the outcome."

"So, two shall die. Correct?"

This time Grant stilled. His mouth closed and formed a hard line. Kate blinked in disbelief, her alcohol-infused euphoria long forgotten.

A grunt of response from the first voice and the man reluctantly finished his thoughts, "Fine. Fine. If that's what it takes to put things right."

"Of course that's what it takes," blustered the first man. "Don't be such a moron. Meddling fools, blustering around in the dark. They will surely disrupt the plan."

"And you're sure it has to be them?" A slight pause, then the first man continued his query. "Okay, okay. I'm not doubting your power, just that this will make things more complicated. Draw attention from the Council that we don't need."

"You let me worry about the Council. Just stick to the plan. I want this done before the end of the Summit."

Echoes of exiting footsteps had Grant pushing back the curtain and sidling over the edge of the balcony to ensure the way was clear. He walked around in circles for a moment, running his hands through his hair.

"Did you recognize either of the voices?"

Kate shook her head. "I avoid my family like the plague. A couple of run-ins by accident, the occasional outing with some of the cousins that I actually like, but that's about it."

"There must have been fifty people at dinner who I didn't recognize. Those voices could have belonged to any of them."

She retrieved her shoes and started for the exit. "It's not that dark out, I'm sure if I run, I can catch up to them."

He was at her side in seconds, grabbing her around her waist, pulling her back from the stairs. "What the hell do you think you're doing?"

"Hopefully, preventing a murder or two. Why are you stopping me?"

Before she knew what had happened, Grant lifted her and pushed her squirming body against one of the walls. He pinned her between the cold stone and his warm hands. "Listen to me," he growled. "You need to check that ego and know when not to interfere. It's not safe."

Her blood was ablaze with anger. "You keep forgetting that I'm good at protecting myself and great at surviving. I can handle a couple of men."

"Those aren't men, they're probably part of our families."

"So what? No one is above the law."

"And that would be true if you were dealing with normal people. You need to get it through your head, Kate. Everyone one here has powers. Powers they have been perfecting for years. Ignorance may have been bliss for you, but at this Summit, it will get you killed."

His grip changed to a light caress. "You said it yourself, you're on your last life and are clueless about your powers so until you find out, you choose your battles, okay? For once, please listen to me and stop being so hot headed."

She relaxed and admitted defeat, knowing in her heart that he was right. "What if the target is an Anderson? What if the balance is jeopardised? Is it even possible to kill one of your side?"

Grant nodded and released her. "While our life code works a little differently, in the end both families are still mortal. As much as they would like to deny it, they can be killed if you know the proper way."

"And if their plan is successful and the balance destroyed?"

He looked out at the chapel below, its serenity broken by the weight of this revelation. He turned to her and, for a moment, envied her innocence. Looking away, he pondered her words before replying, "Hell on Earth."

CHAPTER 6

Kate stumbled into one of the main banquet rooms, blinded by a combination of morning and hangover. The streams of light blazing down from multiple skylights gave her new understanding to the name Chateau L'Arc Du Lumiere. It was indeed a place of light.

"Well, this should be fun," she remarked, looking around the half empty tables.

It only took seconds for Kate to find her mother in the middle of the room, dictating orders from the end of a long table, her gestures and facial expressions visible even from where Kate stood. The woman was the oldest of four siblings—Kate's mother Elizabeth, sisters Annabelle and Alice, and brother Leland. Her mother's mother was from a brood of five but not as evenly matched. She was the only girl in that bunch, and that gang made up the Morgan side of the Council.

Come to think of it, Kate reflected as she wound her way past tables of relatives and their associates, she was the sole party of one. The lone Morgan with a conscience. The only freak in generations if you didn't count her cousin Julian, and he was only shunned because of his lifestyle. He had proven his worth to the family at age nine when he lashed out and killed a classmate in anger.

Her mother had a way of ruling their arm of the family, despite her offspring's deficiencies. She sat with her sisters on either side of her and, for the moment, some of their children. Together, they took up the entire table, and that suited Kate just fine.

"And there I was at the crack of dawn in the lobby with a trunk of the finest clothes for my only daughter and I went up to the clerk expecting to be directed to a suite next to her and, to my surprise, when I settled into my room and knocked on the door next to me, my niece Lesley opens the door."

"Good morning, Mother,"

"Yes, yes my family," she continued with a dramatic sweep of her hand. "This daughter. This daughter of mine, whom I discovered after knocking on every door in the wing, was nowhere to be found."

Kate shoved her hands in her pockets and let out a loud sigh. All eyes around the table glanced up at her expectantly. She stared back, stone faced. To her mother's right sat her sister Annabelle, to her left, her twin sister Alice. Around the rest of the table sat an assortment of Kate's least favorite cousins, all pretending to hang on her mother's words.

"Aunt Annabelle, Aunt Alice," Kate murmured.

Her mother made a disapproving sound with her mouth. "Speak up, child, and greet your cousins."

Kate rolled her eyes and, with most of her sarcasm in check, began her salutations. "Hello, Gus and Sophia, Jim and Jim's wife Rebecca, Ivan, Veronica, Bess." She paused to take a breath.

Jim interrupted her. "It's Rochelle."

"Excuse me?"

"My wife's name is Rochelle."

Kate snapped her fingers, then smacked herself in the head. "My bad. Rebecca was your first wife who died under mysterious circumstances and whom I actually liked."

Rochelle's expression was unreadable while Jim muttered something that Kate didn't catch. Not that she needed to, given the images of Rebecca's body flashing through her mind.

"Mmmm, well, Rochelle, welcome to the family. Tip for a long and happy life. Stay away from trips to Mexico or any offers to sail on Jim's yacht."

Jim let out a roar and leapt to his feet.

"Don't even think of it, Jimmy," Kate taunted. "Remember, I'm a police detective and very well connected."

"Jim, sit down. Katherine, enough. I will not let you antagonize your family because it amuses you. Now I grow weary of your impertinence. Where are you staying?"

"I'm here in this lovely building, Mother. That's all you need to know."

"Probably camped out on the grounds somewhere or hiding with the servants," replied Gus with a sniff. "Low brow always was her style."

"Servants?" Kate replied irritably. "What freaking century are you living in?"

"Well, that does it. I will speak to the manager and have you moved to our wing."

"No you won't, Mother."

Elizabeth Morgan let out a dramatic sigh and picked up a cloth napkin, wringing it with her fingers. "Why do you vex me, child? Why won't you spend time with your family?"

Kate gave a long glance to the group of people whom she barely knew. Their expressions ranged from smug condescension to bored indifference. "Because I hate you all," she replied, emphasizing each word loudly and slowly, so there would be no mistaking her message.

Her mother gaped at her, then burst out in tears, turning to the comfort of her sisters. Kate rolled her eyes and turned on her heel, heading for an almost empty table on the far side of the dining room. Plopping herself down, she flipped open the menu and graciously smiled when the waiter promptly arrived with a large craft of coffee.

Five minutes with her mother and she had almost lost her appetite. Talk about a new record. "Just a bowl of strawberries," she said to the waiter, before diving into her morning indulgence.

"Well, well, well, little Katie Morgan, stirring the pot again," said a voice from across the table.

Kate glanced up, looking at the old man across from her. He was somewhere between asleep and awake, his head, bobbing dangerously toward the bowl of oatmeal in front of him. She frowned and looked around, knowing the comment couldn't have come from him.

"Jules?"

From next to her there was a flash of light and suddenly he appeared. Julian Morgan, brother to Jim, Bess, the twins Wade and Will, grandson of Damian, and one of the few cousins that she liked. He was flamboyant, artistic, and a fellow black sheep to the family.

"Katie! Darling! So glad you could make it. I was beginning to think you would fake your death again to skip this event!"

"Funny, you're reading my mind. If there was a way, I would have. Unfortunately, we're like salmon going to spawn. Can't avoid the pull of reunions."

"Too true, but at least we avoid their fate. Death, darling, does not become you."

She couldn't disagree with that comment. "Your brother Jim is being an asshole again."

"Again?" he scoffed, "Katie, you should know better by now. When is he not?"

Kate sipped her coffee and smiled. Julian Morgan was the most colorful person in the room and not just in personality. Gold lame pants with a dark silk shirt that sparkled. His hair was short in the front, spiked in the back, and every inch of skin was covered in some kind of sparkly bauble. He looked like a combination of side show clown and Liza Minnelli impersonator.

"Jules, what are you up to these days? Last time I saw you, you were working in Vegas."

"Darling Katie, while the lure of show biz will always be in my blood, I have made an actual name for myself as an artist. I am more famously known now as JM."

"JM? Why do I know that name?"

"Sweetie, I have been featured on the covers of the finest magazines in the art world. My work sells for hundreds of thousands of dollars."

He snapped his fingers and a copy of *American Canvas* appeared on the white tablecloth in front of her. Kate looked down at the somber man, dressed all in black, staring back at her. It was a direct contrast to the larger than life Hermes scarf who sat beside her.

"Oh my god, Jules! That's you?"

Julian clapped his hands in delight, grabbing her by the shoulders. "I know. I look so grown up! I decided to go for the brooding genius with a slightly constipated look. The critics just eat me up!"

"I've seen your work before. There's a gallery in Soho that I walk by on a regular basis."

"The Silver Swan, yes that's my home base."

Kate glanced up as the waiter returned, a large plate of Western Omelette, overflowing with green peppers and a small mound of strawberry garnish, in his hands. He placed it in front of her, wincing slightly as she shook her head. "I didn't order this. I hate green peppers."

The waiter gave her a side glance. "Sorry, ma'am, but your mother insisted. She said that you are not to receive anything else."

Kate looked at Julian with exasperation. "She knows I hate all peppers and this is her exerting her dominance. What am I five?"

He shrugged. "Better do what she says, honey. You know how she gets."

Kate glared at him, then turned around to see her mother looking at her, smugly. Kate silently shook her head, but before she could get up from the table, her mother's voice popped into her head.

Katherine, I know you can hear me. You need to eat a proper breakfast and if you refuse what I have sent you, the waiter will suffer the consequences of your actions.

Kate paled slightly. After a moment, she regained her composure. "Proper breakfast, my ass." She turned to the waiter and looked at him sweetly. "You can leave this one and bring me fifteen more, exactly the same."

"Excuse me?"

"You heard me. Fifteen more."

Julian smirked as she waved the waiter away. "What did Aunt Lizzie say to you?"

"That she would kill the waiter if I didn't comply."

He rolled his eyes. "That's an empty threat. She knows the rules. If anyone dies during this Summit of the two Hs, there will literally be hell to pay."

"Yeah, but does that include the employees?"

Julian helped himself to her craft of coffee and sat back in the chair, searching his memory. "Let's see, there are usually rumors about staff gone missing after these things. At the last one, a go-go girl disappeared. Before that it was a scullery maid or two. Ah, who can remember? That was a hundred years ago."

"And what should I expect at this conference? Aside from my mother and her antics."

Julian grabbed the magazine and started flipping through it. "There's not much required from us, Sansei. The elders attend joint meetings about stuff to do with the balance. Oh, sure, they'll try and get us to attend seminars on how to strengthen our powers but all we really have to go to are the opening and closing ceremonies plus the ball on the second night."

"Sansei?"

"It's Japanese. Mean's third generation. Most of this revolves around the first generation elders. Then there are the second generations like your mom and her brothers and sisters. From our level there are a few chosen emissaries like Lucas, Ivan, and Gus who are expected to learn the ropes. You know, how to deal with *them*."

"By them, you mean the Andersons."

He rolled his eyes and scoffed. "Of course, them. Who

else am I referring to? The people who have chosen to make hospitality a career?"

His eyebrows raised as the waiter returned with friends, each balancing four plates on their arms. "Darling, protein is good, but in this quantity, you're just going to get fat."

"So are we allowed to fraternize with the enemy?"

"Well, it's not forbidden. After all, we're supposed to use this time to build relations. But realistically, the two sides usually avoid each other."

She nodded as she stood up and leaned over the table. "Good to know."

He watched as she dumped a bowl of sugar cubes onto the tablecloth. Using the bowl, she collected the garnishes from each of the plates until it was overflowing with strawberries. Turning to the waiter, she pointed to the plates. "See about arranging for this to go to a homeless shelter in the area."

Julian howled in delight, realizing that once again, Kate Morgan had beaten her mother at her own game. She glanced over at the table and raised her bowl in salute, choosing to ignore the withering glances from her family.

"Jules, did you bring any samples of your work? I'd love to see some of it in person."

He stood up and bowed to her. "Come on, Katie, you naughty girl, reading my mind. Of course I brought several masterpieces and we have just enough time before the opening ceremonies begin."

CHAPTER 7

They wandered down the corridor of banquet halls, eating strawberries and chatting about old times. Both had met as children, Kate on her first life and Julian on his second, reincarnated after an unfortunate accident had ended his nearly-thousand-year-old first life. Strolling past the room reserved for the Anderson family, Kate fought the urge to stick her head through the door and see if Grant was there. It was no secret that any relations between the families were at best tolerated and at worst…well, she didn't doubt there had been heavy casualties from both sides.

Still, she couldn't shake the events of last night. Not just about Grant, which for his safety, she had to hide, but, more importantly, the message they had heard. *Two will die,* the voice had said. Her detective instincts were ringing off the hook. What two and, more importantly, from which family? There had been an uneasy peace for generations. One side killing another would have repercussions that might not only affect the world but the future of millions.

Passing the restaurant where she and Grant had eaten last night gave her an idea. Kate stopped Julian at the doors, grabbing his arm. "Do you remember the game we used to play as kids?"

He crinkled his nose for a moment, then broke out into a huge grin. "Of course. What's going on, Katie? What have you got up your sleeve?"

She pulled open the doors to the closed restaurant. "Call it an itch I need to scratch. Something's rotten here."

"Darling, you're with our family. Everyone's rotten here."

Kate looked around the empty dining room, searching for something that resembled a hostess stand. Tucked around the corner, she spied it parked next to a large ficus plant. With a quick glance, she dashed over to the podium, pulling open drawers and flipping through papers.

"What are you looking for?"

"Fancy place like this would require a reservation to get in, right?"

"Of course."

"Good, then I need to see their list from last night."

Kate scoured the station, finding nothing but an elaborate computer tablet attached to the base of a table beside it. Hearing the sound of footsteps, she stepped away in time to see the restaurant manager approach.

"Good morning. Can I help you with something?"

"Yes, I was wondering what time you opened for dinner? I had such a lovely time here last night, I would like to book a future reservation."

Kate glanced past the man to Julian, who was standing behind him. She subtly scratched her left eyebrow, while glaring at Julian to create a diversion.

"Well, of course. Let me just check my list."

The man strolled to the computer screen and with the swipe of a finger pulled up the reservation screen. "Let's see, we have an opening for tonight at eight o'clock."

"Tonight's not good. The start of the conference and all."

"Oh, yes of course. Would you be a Morgan or an Anderson?"

"Neither, darling. We are the entertainment," replied Julian. He stepped in behind them and guided the man away. "Great, that I caught you, are you also in charge of sound for the banquet today?"

"Why yes of course, although I didn't realize there was entertainment."

"Last minute decision by the Morgan's, darling. And we can't disappoint them, now can we? Why, one wrong step and half your staff could disappear."

The man's eyes widened, a light sheen of sweat breaking out on his forehead. "Yes, I have heard rumors—"

"Excellent, well, why don't we discuss karaoke and disco balls?"

Kate shook her head with amazement as Julian lead the poor man away. Stepping quickly to the computer, she swiped through the reservation list. Pulling out her camera phone, she snapped the names of last night's diners and their hotel room numbers. Hearing the pair returning, she quickly swiped the screen then, glancing down, realized two things.

"Son of a bitch," she murmured to herself.

Reading the manager's thoughts, she quickly darted from the room and back into the hallway.

A few minutes later, Julian joined her in the corridor. "Find what you were looking for?" He asked with a yawn.

"Thanks to you," she said, opening her bag to reveal the computer screen. "It's a tablet," she added.

Julian looked at her like she was crazy. "Darling, you're rich. Why do you need to steal a second hand tablet?"

"I'm not stealing it, just borrowing it."

"What on earth for?"

"Come on. Remember when I said rotten? Let me tell you about something I heard."

They reached the main hall of the chateau, a long room that in the past had housed royal thrones and many of the celebrations that gave it a reputation for opulence and excellence. Today it was more of a large connecting corridor, adorned with thick stone columns, Persian rugs, and comfortable sitting areas. At the back of the room, the former wall turned into a series of exits connecting additional buildings. Julian stretched out his arms and gestured to the walls. "Voila," he cried. "What do you think?"

Kate gasped at the multiple canvases. "Oh Jules, they're magnificent."

"Just something I threw together. Had a hunch it might fit the setting."

She turned to him, shaking her head. "I'm serious. You have a true gift. These are spectacular."

The paintings were an exhibition of eight large canvases, each about twenty feet long by fifteen feet high. No two were alike and, from what she could tell, no particular theme or painting style was present. Kate wandered up to the first one, a hypnotic vortex of colors, swirling together in modernistic style. It was a harmonic clash of colors that changed from disturbing violence to calm synchronicity, depending on where the observer stood.

The second canvas was the complete opposite. An ode to the old masters, it was a pastoral setting, imagined in England's history. A small cottage sat surrounded by countryside and, in the distance, an artist's idea of Stonehenge before it became a pile of stones.

"Jules, what were you thinking when you painted this one? It's so peaceful."

"I was thinking how to get out of marriage to a druid girl."

Surprised, Kate turned to him. He rolled his eyes then slung his arm around her shoulders. "Ah, Katie, I forget how young you are. It's from a part of my first life. But forget about the painting, tell me more about the murder plot. We have ourselves a regular whodunit to solve."

"Jules, be quiet. Absolutely no one can know about this. I can't find the perp if you go around blabbing that I heard something."

"Perp," exclaimed Julian. "Such macho talk. I love it." His eyes widened. "So is that why you stole the tablet?"

"Borrowed," she scowled. "So help me, Jules, if you don't shut up—"

A squeal erupted from the other side of the room. Both

of them turned to see a very attractive, petite blond running toward them. "Oh my God! Oh my God, you're JM, aren't you?"

She barrelled toward Julian, almost knocking him over with her bear hug. Following on her rear was a less-impressed older woman with an even lesser-than-impressed look on her face. Looking past her, Kate's eyebrows rose, for the third person in the party was none other than Grant Anderson.

"Mother, Grant, you have to meet JM!" the young woman squealed, pulling him toward the group. "He's only the world's most finest artist and this is new work. OMG, fabulous! Look at his new work!"

Kate wasn't sure what was less forgivable—the use of bad grammar, the perky way she bounced around the room, or the fact that she knew Grant. Julian stuck out his hand and greeted the party like the New York socialite that he was.

"Julian Morgan. JM to the art world. This is my cousin, Katie Morgan."

"Chrissy Wentworth, your number one fan, and these people are my mother Georgina Wentworth and my fiancé, Grant Anderson."

"Christina," replied her mother sharply. "He is not your fiancé, yet. Not until the courting is complete."

"Oh, Mother, such a stickler for details. Of course, we're going to get married."

Chrissy grabbed Julian by the arm and dragged him over to a painting that looked mildly like a retelling of *St. George and the Dragon*. Her mother pursed her lips and chased after her, as if just breathing the same air as a Morgan might turn her evil.

Kate stared after them then up at Grant. "Well, if you will excuse me," she said coldly.

As she brushed past him, he grabbed her by the arm, pulling her behind one of the many columns that littered the room. "Hold up, you're not excused. Let me explain."

"No need. You like teenagers. That makes things very clear."

"She's twenty-two."

"Oh, that's much better. Twenty two and what are you, three hundred? Yeah, that's a perfect match."

He sighed and ran his fingers through his hair in frustration. "Look, this is another ambush by my mother. She's been trying to marry me off for...well, generations. I had no idea who that girl was until this morning."

"And the whole 'courting' thing?"

"Something that has involved everyone in my family, except me." Grant reached out his hand and gently caressed her arm. "Look, they've tried this before and I've made it clear that I decide how my life is run."

She nodded, pushing him away. He raised his eyebrows, stepping back with surprise.

"No touching in public. You don't know me around *them*. The walls have ears," she whispered.

"I don't care."

"Well, I do. Certain members of my family would kill you just to spite me."

He let out a quiet laugh. "Thanks for the concern, but I can take care of myself. Besides, you really think it's that easy to kill me?"

"You forget who we represent. Everything comes easy for us."

"Noted, Detective. Now, want to tell me what's in your bag?"

Kate gave him a puzzled look, then remembered the tablet. *Impressive powers of deduction*, she thought with a smile.

With a subtle nod, she walked over to Julian's fourth painting, a series of crystal cubes suspended over a winter scene of snow and ice.

Staring at the picture, she murmured, "I borrowed the reservation computer from the restaurant. Thought whoever might be behind the threat may have eaten there last night."

Grant joined her, looking at the artwork with interest. "Good thinking, Detective. Any leads?"

"Haven't had a chance to look it over. Here's the best part, though. The tablet is hooked into the main reservation system for the hotel. I can get a list of each room and who occupies it."

"How do you plan on getting past the passwords? Things like that aren't just left in the open."

She rolled her eyes and strolled ahead to the next painting. He casually caught up, waving to Chrissy and her mother in the process. "Right," he said, after putting two and two together. "Mind reader."

"Bingo. A couple of minutes lazing about the lobby and I can have a half dozen passwords. Once I get access, I can copy down all the details."

"I think I can do one better. Give me the tablet."

Kate opened her bag and handed Grant the computer. Glancing over at Julian, she scratched her eyebrow with her finger. His eyes widened and he grinned, making the "okay" symbol with his fingers. Turning to Christina and her mother, he opened his arms. "Chrissy, darling. What would you think about sitting for me? I would love to do your portrait."

Chrissy's screams of joy rebounded off the cathedral ceiling, attracting the attention of others who had been enjoying the exhibit. Within seconds, they were lost in a sea of curious well-wishers and autograph seekers.

Grant ducked behind another pillar and turned on the tablet. Fishing a small device from his pocket, he plugged it into an open port.

Flipping through the first screen, he gave her a lopsided smile. "Got one of those passwords handy?"

She peered at the screen. "The restaurant manager's code should work. Try alpha, three, echo, echo, nine, nine, two."

An administrative screen popped into view. Grant nodded and flipped through multiple menus. Everything from room assignments to designs for the conference ball.

She watched in fascination as the box he attached downloaded a copy of everything on the tablet. "Is that a...you know...God thing?"

He chuckled. "It's an FBI thing. Clones hard drives in nothing flat. You don't think I would pass up the opportunity to spy on America's greatest crime family, do you?"

"I wouldn't expect anything less. What else can I do?"

He unplugged his device and handed the tablet back to her. "Get this back to the restaurant before they suspect anything, go to the opening speeches, and be good."

"I want to help with a list of suspects. And what do you mean, be good?"

"There'll be plenty of time for that after the opening conference. You make nice with your family."

"But—I—" she sputtered. "Why on earth—"

"Because if we need to butter people up for information, it will be a lot easier if they like you. Right?"

Kate scowled, crossed her arms, and started walking away from him. He grabbed her by the elbow and pulled her back behind the pillar again. "Come on, Kate. Don't be angry. Talk to me." She looked up at him, the hint of a smile breaking across her lips as he ran his finger across her bottom lip. "No pouting."

"All right. I'll play nice." She sighed. "But not too nice or they'll get suspicious."

"Deal. And speaking of..." he said as Julian approached them.

"Well, well, well, Katie," declared Julian smugly, looking Grant up and down. "When you said itch...well, I can see who you'd like to scratch."

Grant's face reddened slightly and he nodded politely to Julian, walking quickly away. Julian turned to watch him leave, then grabbed Kate by the arm. "Yum, yum, yum, girl! Katie, you have outdone yourself. Stealing some other girl's fiancé, not to mention canoodling with a sworn enemy will put your mother over the edge."

Kate watched them leave, Georgina Wentworth shooting dirty looks over her right shoulder. Kate sighed and shoved her hands in her pockets. "No, Jules. It's not...well, let's just leave it at, it's complicated."

"Complicated, my ass, that's one fine-looking man and there is nothing complicated about that. Come on, girl, you can spill all the details on the way to the opening ceremonies." He paused then slapped his hand across her bottom. "Let the games begin!"

CHAPTER 8

The largest ballroom at the Chateau L'Arc Du Lumiere, while meant to impress, had the opposite effect on Kate. Grandiose and aged, its fresco embossed walls and ornate ceiling reminded her of a cheesy banquet hall in New Jersey. Over-the-top chandeliers glittered and reflected off the polished Italian marble floor, while strategically placed mirrors made the room feel like it went on forever. Unlike the rest of the chateau this room felt out of place—cold and impersonal. The perfect place, she rationalized, for a clash of the titans.

Contrasting to the setup from their breakfast room, round tables covered with white tablecloths dotted the landscape. Red table numbers for the Morgans and white ones for the Andersons were interspersed around the floor. At least here, Kate reflected, was some effort to bring the sides together.

Standing in the doorway, she marvelled at how ordinary the room looked. People in business suits milling about, introductions that were made, and hands that were shook. To any outsider, it looked like an average business conference, joining the thousands of other business conferences held across America every day.

What differed from those thousands of other meetings was the uneasy tension. The feeling of dread that filled her soul. This felt wrong. The kind of wrong after a mistake is made that can never be undone. That feeling that if you could just rewind time and take a different path, make a dif-

ferent choice, or stop to acknowledge the instincts screaming in your head, kind of wrong.

But what could she do? She had already stepped aboard
the Titanic and the iceberg was heading her way. She just
had to figure out how to find a lifeboat in time.

"Are you ready?" asked Julian, nudging her past the
doorway.

Kate took a deep breath and pushed the darkness away.
Reflection was a dangerous thing. Nothing mattered, not her
curious new attraction to Grant Anderson, not her Mother
and her devious motives, nothing mattered except survival.
She grabbed onto the one thing she could rely on—her belief in herself. Kate Morgan excelled in no-win situations.
After all, she had endured enough of them. "Not really."

"Too late now." Julian dragged her to the registration table and smiled at one of the event coordinators.

A kindred spirit perhaps? Something in her memory said
he looked familiar. He was an older gentleman with specta-
cles and an expression that said he wished he was anywhere
else but here.

"Julian and Kate Morgan, reporting for duty," Julian said
with a salute.

The old man tapped his pen on the table, looking at the
pair over his glasses. He sat back in his chair with folded
arms and smiled at them. "Well, I'll be. So this is the infa-
mous Kate Morgan."

Kate looked at his name tag and frowned, trying to place
the name, A. Anderson, with anyone in her past.

"I'm sorry, do I know you?"

"Nope, but I know you. Ambrose Anderson. Retired cor-
oner and former state forensic examiner for New York. You
have quite a reputation with the boys in blue at the Fifty
Sixth Division. Nice to see a Morgan on the right side of the
law for once."

She extended her hand and shook his warmly. The name
Ambrose Anderson was legendary in New York. He was
known for helping to close ninety percent of the homicide

cases that came across his desk. Now that she knew he was one of *those* Andersons, she wasn't surprised why his track record was so stellar. He looked so ordinary, she couldn't help wondering what his powers might be. "I'm pleased to meet you, sir. Was sorry to hear that you had retired."

He smiled and handed her a large manila envelope. "Well, would have looked too suspicious if I had stayed around. At my age, the faculties are supposed to go, not improve. Anywhoo, it's nice to meet you. Now on with the formalities." He pushed a bin toward her. "Any weapons to surrender?"

"I have my gun, but I left it locked in the room."

He nodded and jotted a notation on his paper. "Additional guns? Knives? Poison? Explosives or any device that could render harm to an Anderson or a Morgan?"

"God, no." She paused and did a quick sweep of the room. "Although judging by the crowd, maybe I should have."

"And how about you?" he said, gesturing to Julian.

"Just my wicked charm and devilish good looks. They've been known to kill a man in his tracks."

"Right. Smart ass, huh?"

"At your service."

Looking satisfied, Ambrose ticked off the remaining boxes and turned the page over. Clearing his throat, he took a deep breath. "Now on with the legal stuff. This is a reminder that for two thousand years the Morgan's and Anderson's have held these peace talks without incident. No harm has come to either family in accordance with the agreement between God and Satan dated 102 B.C. As a good-will gesture, it is expected that you, as emissaries will uphold this agreement and refrain from the use of your gifts for the purpose of intentional harm, coercion, or treachery, so help you God." He paused and looked at the both of them. "Or in your case, Satan. Do you agree?"

"I do," they both replied.

"Excellent. Sign here, please. Know that this agreement

is binding with both councils and violation of it, without plausible justification, may result in death."

"Jeez, they've really stepped up the legal. Used to be just a handshake and a promise to be good," replied Julian, signing the paper with a flourish.

"Well, you know, now a days, everyone is a damn lawyer. They'll dispute anything not on paper."

Ambrose collected their documents and gave Kate a mock salute. "I look forward to trading war stories with you, young lady. For now, I'm going to hand you off to my niece, Ellie Anderson, our event planner."

Kate greeted the wide-eyed redhead and watched as Julian worked his magic on her. "JM, I had no idea you were coming," she gushed. "What do you think of the decorations? This is my first event for the family so I decided to go sophisticated and elegant."

"Nice touch with the colors," commented Kate. She picked up one of the red place cards. All that was missing was a pitchfork beside her name. "Glad to see you veered away from stereotypes."

"Well, like I said. Elegance is my middle name," Ellie replied, missing the sarcasm in Kate's voice. "So you are sitting here, and JM, why don't you come over to the VIP table?"

Julian looked at Kate as she shrugged her shoulders and sat down at the empty table. "Oh, darling, I don't think I should," he said, looking at her like she was a puppy that had been left out in the rain.

"It's right beside the bar and I stocked it with only the best…"

Julian looked at Kate again. She waved her hand, giving him her blessing. He turned back to Ellie, throwing his hands in the air. "Oh, all right, you darling angel. Any champagne around?"

"Dom Perignon okay?"

"Perfection my dear. Now about these decorations…"

Kate watched them leave then glanced around as the

room began to fill up. Seizing the opportunity, she quickly switched seats, preferring to sit against the wall. Better to keep track of friends and foes, if she didn't have to watch her back. She glanced at the other place cards—names of people still to arrive. Three were family she hated, two were people she didn't recognize, and, thankfully, none were her mother.

Arriving early gave Kate time to survey the room. At the front, on a double-raised stage, sat a long table, she presumed, for the first generation of both families. The ancient ones who influenced winners and losers in history. Under their guidance, the world had seen unbelievable horrors and inspiring triumphs. They were the whispers in the halls of justice and those responsible for destroying millions of lives. Who knew what horrors had been committed, what sacrifices had been made in the name of maintaining the balance? She shuttered at the idea that she could ever play a part.

Lower down were several large tables meant for the second generation of both families. Close to the sides of the front, on the floor, was the VIP area, complete with gold colored tablecloths and kiddie tables nearby for the assistants of the rich and famous.

Opening her package, Kate pulled out a program outlining the opening and closing ceremonies and her invitation to the ball. Attached to the documents was a red piece of paper with a list of dates and times, but nothing else. Kate frowned and opened the envelope again, this time dumping out a notepad and a red Swarovski crystal pen. The final item was a scrap of paper and on it a series of digits that looked suspiciously like a phone number.

"Hmm, curious, but I'll bite." Pulling out her phone, she punched in the numbers and held her breath.

Three rings in and she was beginning to think this was a bad idea. On the fourth ring, a familiar voice answered the phone. "Well, it's about time. I was beginning to think you'd never open that envelope."

"Grant," she answered with a smile. Hearing his voice gave her the confidence she so badly needed. "Where are you? I don't see you."

"Just walking in now. Somehow, I got elected to double check security on this dog and pony show."

"Hmm, I'm disappointed Special Agent Anderson. No metal detectors or pat downs? You know you're not dealing with the most honest bunch of people."

From across the room, he locked eyes with her, a playful smile crossing his lips. "Already factored in, but if you really insist on a pat down, I'm sure I can arrange something later."

She laughed then covered her mouth with her hand. Three of her cousins were headed her way. "I'll hold you to that. 'Someone wicked this way comes.' Gotta go."

Kate dropped her phone into her bag and tipped back her chair, balancing it against the stone wall behind her. "Hello, Laurelle. Larry. Lee. How's it going?"

They sat themselves opposite her, all in a row like a firing squad. Three of the six siblings who belonged to Leland Morgan. Lucas, the oldest of six, was noticeably absent, then came Larry. Lee, Lesley, and Lila who had chosen to sit elsewhere, and the baby of their family, Laurelle. Age wise, they were no more than seven to ten years older than her, though with a variety of first and second lives between them. Larry, with his pot belly and receding hairline, easily looked close to sixty in human years.

"Kate the Fake, it's good to see you. It's been too long." Laurelle's voice dripped with condescension. "Whatever have you been up to?"

Kate gritted her teeth. "Homicide detective in New York City. How about you?" The nickname from her childhood set her on edge. Giving a helping hand to a friend in distress had not gone unnoticed among her cousins. They'd called her a fake Morgan and taunted her for showing compassion ever since.

"Senior partner with Morgan, Morgan, and Power. Engaged to a Demplemeier and I just received notice that I'm going to be featured as one of Atlanta's top Thirty under Thirty movers and shakers."

Kate opened her mouth then closed it. She bit her tongue, knowing she should let it go but this was too good an opportunity to pass up. "Congratulations, even though you're closer to a hundred and thirty."

"I'm a hundred and ten," she barked.

"Laurelle, come on. Fooling yourself is beneath you. I'm a hundred and fifteen, and I know for a fact, I'm the youngest of our generation."

Lee stopped checking his smart phone to let out a bellow. "She's got you there, Sis. Always admired that mouth on you, Kate," he said, wiping the tears from his eyes. "Goddamn gift of yours. You should have been a comedian." He let out a final guffaw and went back to his phone while Laurelle flipped open a laptop and chose to sulk in silence.

"So you're all lawyers?" asked Kate after a few minutes of uncomfortable silence.

"Lee and I are criminal and Laurelle is civil," replied Larry, not bothering to look up from his phone.

"Makes sense. Family business. And how's Uncle Leland?"

"Well, you can see for yourself. He's about to give the opening address."

"Attention, everyone, we are finally ready to get underway," said Leland Morgan. With his booming Scottish accent and distinguished manner, the room quickly quieted down.

"Thank you. Clan Morgan, Clan Anderson, and distinguished guests. Welcome to the Summit of First Families to God and Lucifer. This is the fortieth peace talks between the pure bloodlines directly chosen to represent Heaven and Hell on earth. As key players in history, we have directed nations to war and peace, decided the fates of billions, and orchestrated the rise and fall of every civilization known to man. Though we work in the shadows, as emissaries for good and evil, we exist to serve mankind and influence the future of generations to come."

He paused as a rousing round of applause circled the room. "It gives me great pleasure to once again act as a catalyst for the balance. The keeper of all that is sacred, a shining example of tradition, and purveyor of understanding and mutual respect between the two families."

He paused again to another rousing round of applause, this time as Kate noted, more from her family than the Andersons.

"Before I hand over the microphone to our gracious host, Jonathan Anderson, I would like to introduce or perhaps reintroduce our esteemed Council."

Kate looked at the ancient faces that filled the panel, then back across the table. For the first time, she noticed her cousins had abandoned their technology, focusing intently on the words their father was saying.

"From my right, head of the Anderson clan and elder, Jonathan Anderson. Second son, David Anderson. Third son, Paul Anderson, and first daughter Marion Anderson Lowell."

A spirited round of applause filled the room and Leland joined in, egging the crowd on in a fashion that Kate remembered vividly from her childhood.

"On my left, esteemed elder of the Morgans, Damian Morgan. Second brother Ronan Morgan, First sister, Lilith Morgan and third brother, Nero Morgan."

Kate joined in the applause more out of show than interest. Somehow with wading through the dread of seeing her mother, she had forgotten that Grandma Lily was going to be there as well.

With the introductions over and her cousin's attention back on their phones, she picked up her pen and pad and perused the crowd for possible murder suspects.

Table by table of Morgans, she jotted down the most obvious contenders, based on a combination of family rumors and rap sheets she could recall from memory.

"And finally, before I hand over the microphone..."

Kate glanced at her watch, not surprised that Leland had used that phrase again in his endless recap of previous conference highlights. He had been droning on for twenty minutes and, from what she could tell, even her mother who was sitting at one of the VIP tables was getting antsy.

"I would like to announce that after two thousand years, Lilith Morgan has decided to retire and offer her place on the Council to a new member." Leland paused for a moment, looking a bit surprised. It was obvious that this announcement had also caught him off guard. Holding up a sealed envelope, he continued his announcement, this time unable to hold back his surprise or excitement. "After fervent discussion by both sides, a short list of names has been decided and will be announced on the second night at the end of the Grand Ball."

The room erupted into a fervor of comments and whispers. Kate looked around, more out of curiosity than genuine interest. Catching Grant's eye again, she could see the announcement was just as much a mystery to his side. He gave her a puzzled shrug of his shoulders before an older gentleman diverted his attention by whispering something in his ear. Her cousins reacted quite a bit differently.

"Oh my, what is Granny doing?" asked Laurelle.

"Did she tell you this was going to happen? She didn't say anything and we had lunch last month," said Lee.

"Laurelle, text Lucas, Lila, and Lesley, see if they know anything," added Larry.

Kate rolled her eyes, tossing her pen down. Their grandmother had a heart of stone and a mind filled with intent just as dangerous.

She doubted Grandma Lily would spill secrets to any of Leland's six children. Kate's own search for a possible killer was equally as mysterious. The list of suspects had grown so large, she finally gave up and wrote *entire family* across the bottom of the page.

"Big deal," Kate said with a yawn. "So Grandma Lily is retiring. Who cares?"

"Who cares?" asked Larry. "Are you kidding? Do you know what an honor it would be to sit on the Council? To be able to actually dictate the decisions that will end up in the history books. To decide which terrorist group to fund or who will be the next dictator? Can you imagine the power?"

"No, because no one should have it."

"The world is filling with maggots. Insignificant people, who in the past would have been weeded out by war, pestilence, and poverty. Now they suck up resources, interfere with our plans, and muddle up the blood lines. They have to be eradicated so room can be made for the chosen ones. The true children of Lucifer."

"Wow, you're goddamn insane," Kate replied angrily. "It's bad enough you're a psychopath, now you want to be a dictator too?"

Larry turned two shades of red and puffed up like a blow fish. He shoved his finger in her face. "That's why you're the family freak. How best to pay homage to Lucifer if not to turn as many as these mortals to his ways? We pride ourselves on service every day. We use the law to his advantage. Do you know how rewarding it is to watch children of violence grow and accept his ways into their hearts? To watch hope die, only to be replaced with a twisting desire to inflict pain and suffering. It's glorious and it makes me high."

Kate glared at him then kicked her foot at his chair, pushing it off balance and him to the floor. She leaned over him and whispered. "You listen to me, Larry. What you do is sick. Your firm is sick, and this whole family is sick, you hear me?"

"Remind me to take a piece out of Lucas when I see him," Larry hissed back. "He should have killed you when he had the chance."

"Yeah, Larry, that sounds like you. Too chicken to do your own dirty work."

Larry heaved himself off the floor, lunging toward her. Grabbing her hair, he wrenched her head back and pulled her toward him, one arm locking around her neck. Kate winced as she felt the strands of hair ripped from her head, but that was minor to the pressure of his arm around her windpipe.

She pulled at his fingers, intending on breaking his wrist before he could complete his choke hold. Before she could act, she felt his body pulled away, followed by a loud crashing sound. With the pressure gone, she fell against the table, gasping for some much needed air. Staggering to her feet, she saw Larry pinned against the wall with Grant's arm against his back.

"Assaulting an officer of the law is a felony, Morgan."

"This is a family matter, Anderson. Besides, I'm a lawyer and I know my rights. I was defending myself. I have witnesses."

"You bet you do. I witnessed the whole thing myself and I didn't see her lay a hand on you."

Grant whipped out a pair of handcuffs and handed them to a pair of security officers that had appeared to assist him. "Put Mr. Morgan in a holding cell until he decides to cool down."

Grabbing him by the lapels of his three thousand dollar suit, Grant pulled him close. "Family matter or not, no one is going to disrupt the integrity of these talks, Morgan. Got it? As part of the hosting family, it is my duty to inform you that any additional behavior of this type will not be tolerated for anyone and, especially, not you."

The officers hustled him off down a side passage before he could disrupt the conference further. Grant glared at the remaining siblings, before turning his attention to Kate. "Detective, I'm going to have to ask you to come with me."

Kate nodded, flushing from a combination of embarrassment and anger as triumphant looks erupted from Laurelle and Lee. Shoving everything back into the envelope, Kate grabbed her bag and followed Grant through the door.

CHAPTER 9

With the door closed, he stormed off down the corridor at such a pace, she had to run to keep up. "Hey, wait up, where are you going?"

Grant turned down a narrow passageway and through a double set of doors to an old stone staircase. With the doors shut firmly behind them, he stopped suddenly at the top of an old winding staircase. For a moment, he stared out into space then turned and looked at her.

"What the hell were you thinking?"

"I was thinking how I wanted to kill that bastard."

"Wrong answer!"

In the short amount of time, she had known him, she had never seen him this angry. He stalked around the landing, a variety of unpleasant words filling his mind.

Turning, he pointed his finger at her. "What the hell am I going to do with you?"

"Nothing. Okay? How many times do I have to tell you that I can take care of myself?" Now, it was her time to be angry. She wasn't chattel and resented being treated like his property.

Her words only fed his fire. "How many times do I have to tell you? You don't have the skills to deal with these people. God, why won't you listen?"

"Because you don't own me!"

She'd had enough of his lectures. Striding past him, she headed for the door. Before she could reach it, a large oak barrel rose from the floor below and crashed into the wall above the door. Before her eyes the pieces of wood rear-ranged themselves into a barricade, blocking her from leaving.

From below them a wiry man dressed in a sharply pressed suit and bow tie emerged from one of the climate controlled rooms. Grant turned for a second and pointed back to the open door.

"Leave us," he bellowed.

Kate took the distraction as opportunity and tackled him from behind, sending both of them tumbling down the winding staircase and into a nearby sitting area. Kate was faster and on her feet first. Grabbing an ornamental sword from a wall display, she leveled it at Grant's throat.

"I might not have your tricks but I'm a quick study. Do not under estimate me again."

With the wave of his hand, the sword flew across the room and he was on her, pinning her to the wall.

"Still think you can handle yourself?" he growled, pushing her flat against his body.

She scowled at him. This wasn't a battle of wills any-more, they were both fighting to feed their egos and if he was going to play dirty, then so could she. Kate turned her head, the one part of her body with movement, and pressed her lips to his throat. With her teeth and tongue she ran the length of his neck, ending with a gentle tug on his earlobe.

Her plan worked. Much to her chagrin, it worked too well. She felt him shudder then weaken his grasp on her. His hands moved to her hair, pulling her mouth to his. Kate let out a small gasp, as his soft yet demanding lips captured hers in a sensual kiss. She struggled to remember the plan—weaken him, then get the upper hand and show him who the real boss was—but all thought flew from her mind. All she felt was the pleasure of his lips exploring hers, his hands, trailing up her spine with such soft pressure, she felt her knees buckling and her soft curves firm and harden against his body.

All desire to fight drained from her body. The only thing she wanted, the only thing she needed at this moment, was him. Long moments passed before he broke the kiss and, for a moment, there was silence as they both struggled to catch their breath. With the sweep of his thumb, he lightly touched her hair, carefully brushing it away from her face. A string of curses murmured from Grant as he stared at the imprint of fingers around the base of her throat.

"Does it hurt? Are you okay?"

"Yeah, I'm fine," she replied meekly, as she fidgeted then shoved her hands in her pockets. "Look, I'm sorry. I let him get to me and that wasn't professional."

"If I have my way about it, he's the one who's going to be sorry." Releasing her, he stepped back, leaning against the back of a leather couch with concern in his eyes. "Kate, you have to learn to control yourself. If you can't contain your temper every time one of your relatives opens their mouth, I'm going to be breaking up fights all over the place."

Kate stared up the stairs, unable to look him in the eye. He was right again. They were using every trick they could to bait her and she was falling for it. "I'm sorry, I'm sorry, you're right."

"What were you two fighting about?"

Kate threw up her hands. "Politics and propaganda, I guess. He's a high level attorney in Atlanta. He was crowing about how he gets off on seeing children of crime turn into the very thing they despise. That it's our duty to corrupt as many innocents as we can to glorify Satan, and I just lost it."

Grant nodded and sat down. Looking up at her, he blew out a long breath. "Yeah, I can see why that might be upsetting."

"Actually, I just wanted to rip his face off. If I had had my gun—"

"I'd be arresting you for murder right now, and that's not something I want to do."

"I know, I know. You're right. I just need some kind of a filter to stop me from going too far."

Grant looked up at her, an idea forming in his head. "Hmmm, that's not a bad idea."

Puzzled, Kate stepped over to him. "I don't understand what you mean."

Before she could react, he pulled her down and on top of him. Lacing his fingers through her hair, he crushed her mouth to his, kissing her soundly, taking his time and thoroughly exploring her mouth with his own.

Kate sighed and collapsed onto him, her body eagerly molding and bending to his demands. His kisses set her on fire. When he touched her, she couldn't think, couldn't breathe. All she could do was feel. Desire, passion, want, need.

Running her fingers up and down his chest, she felt the hard expanse of his abs as she straddled him, pulling him closer. He groaned and, grasping her waist, flipped her, pinning her against the cold rock of the cellar floor.

Her skin ignited in a blaze of sensitivity, the desire to have him so strong, she thought she'd scream. Unable to stop himself, Grant tugged at the buttons of her shirt, peeling back the starched cotton to reveal her silky skin. Hands encircling her rib cage, he traced a line with his mouth, down the curve of her neck to the delicious indentation between her breasts.

Her fingers combed through his thick dark hair, eager for his touch, for the caress of his lips on hers. Then suddenly he stilled, and came to rest on her chest.

With every ounce of strength he had, he pulled his mouth from her and rolled away, staring up at the ceiling and breathing heavily.

For a moment, the only sound was the rapid beating of hearts. He turned on his side, fingertips making small circles on her stomach, unable to resist the feel of her smooth skin. After a moment, he cleared his throat. "If I don't stop, I'm going to take you right here and right now."

Kate drew in a deep breath, the wave of desire between them making it hard for her to speak. "I'm really okay with that," she gulped after a moment.

"I'm not. You deserve better than a cold stone floor. Besides, I don't have any…you know…protection on me."

Kate smiled. It was charming to see that he was so easily embarrassed about a little thing like birth control. "Well, you don't have to worry because I have that more than covered. I have no intention of ever reproducing."

He frowned and pushed himself into a seated position. "Really?"

"If the odds were good of producing offspring that had no empathy and no soul, would you be running out to buy baby clothes?"

"Good point."

"Besides, there are plenty of kids in this world that need a good home. Adoption is always a possibility."

"So you don't have a problem with children?"

She shook her head. "Babies and dogs love me and I feel the same way. Some day with the right guy…well, who knows what the future holds. If I make it through the Summit, then I'll happily give it more thought."

He let out a quiet laugh. "Good to know. So how about we trade cold stone for my warm bed?"

Her eyes lit up with excitement. "In the middle of the day, and while you're working? Special Agent Anderson, how wicked of you."

He grinned and leaned over, caressing her lacy bra before fastening the button in the middle of her blouse. "Okay, let's get something straight. I'm not running security here. I am a guest, just like you. Let Ambrose and the one hundred officers assigned here do that work."

Kate propped herself up on her elbows, letting her blouse fall open around her stomach. "So that speech about guarding the integrity of the talks?"

He leaned over and feathered a line of kisses up her midriff. "More like guarding you from your relatives."

Kate's breath caught as another wave of desire hit her. She stared up at the ceiling, trying to resist the effect he was having on her. "Okay—uh—if we don't leave this…this…" She paused, looking around. "What is this place?"

"Wine cellar," he mumbled, giving her a hickey just above her navel.

"Right," she said breathlessly. "Well, if we're going to go, it had better be now because in about ten seconds I won't be held responsible for my actions."

Grant nodded, pushing himself up and off her. Grasping her hands, he pulled her effortlessly to her feet. Watching her button her blouse a smile crossed his lips.

"What?"

"What kind of power are you holding over me? I've never felt this way before."

Kate let out a short laugh. "No powers, just good old fashioned chemistry. My only gift is reading other people's minds. Something I'm trying really hard not to do with you."

He frowned, crossing his arms. "Wait, you said you're on your third life. What about your other two powers?"

She shook her head as she finished up with her blouse. "I don't know what you're talking about. I only have one trick up my sleeve."

"Really? You might want to check with one of your relatives. The norm is one power per life and sometimes the powers are compounded. There should be a way to activate the other two if you haven't figured them out yet. There'll probably be a seminar on honing gifts in your package."

Kate picked up her envelope and tapped it against her hand. "Another thing I didn't get. The page that listed seminars was blank."

Grant laughed and shook his head. "Check the paper again, the list should have appeared by now."

She opened her packet and pulled out the paper with times and dates on it. Beside each was the title of a seminar. "Son of a gun," she muttered.

Opening the door to the hallway for her, Grant nodded. "It's a precaution to stop the other side from knowing what trade secrets might be discussed. Because we are hosting this conference, the paper stays blank until the beginning of the speeches."

"Yeah, because everyone wants to learn 'Creative concealment and advanced lipid reduction,'" she said sarcastically, looking the sheet up and down. After a moment, she hit his arm, flabbergasted. "Hey, that's code for disposing a body. Damn it, I'm going to have to go to that just to see who shows up."

"Interesting," he said, taking a look over her shoulder. "What else does it say?"

"Take a look for yourself," she replied, handing the paper to him. Taking the page, they watched as the sheet turned blank.

"DNA detection built in," he said, handing the page back to her. "No Anderson can touch it."

"Trade secrets?"

"Yup. Stuff, I wouldn't mind knowing if you can take notes."

She followed him down the hallway past the now-empty ballroom. Glancing into the open doorway to the tables inside, she pondered, "Do you think we missed anything important?"

"Nah, I think that announcement was the highlight. If you think your Uncle Leland is long winded, you should hear my Granddad. Besides, I think we made much more productive use of our time."

Kate looked up at him, somewhat troubled. "No argument there."

"But…"

"But I can't help thinking about what's coming. How are we going to stop someone from being killed when the list of suspects is practically endless?"

"We approach it like any other threat. Come up with motive then see who has the most to gain."

Kate sighed and gave a reluctant nod of approval. "Lies, deception, and manipulation. Yup, this is a Morgan event for sure."

Grant shot her a disapproving look, then before she could react, swung her off her feet and into his arms.

"Hey, what are you doing? Put me down," she protested.

He strutted down the deserted hallway, carrying her as if she was his conquest. "Not until you learn to trust me and believe that someone in this world has your best interest in mind."

Kate alternated between threats and demands but it did no good. She was helpless in his arms and begrudgingly admitted that it pleased her this way. "Okay, okay, I give up. Put me down and I will never question your decisions again."

Grant slowed his pace, finally putting her down a few doors from the entrance to their hallway. He grasped her shoulders and looked her squarely in the eyes. "I don't think you're getting what I mean. I want you to question what I do and what I don't do, but I also want you to trust that not everything is about seeing through the lies."

Kate nodded. "I know, it's just hard for me. Questioning everyone's motive is what keeps me alive."

"Well, Detective, perhaps I can teach you some new ways to see the world."

Before she could reply, the door to room 105 opened and Ambrose Anderson appeared in the doorway. Looking at the pair, he rolled his eyes, then opened the door wider, inviting them inside. "I wouldn't teach her anything just yet, Grant. We're going to need some healthy suspicion to get through this conference. Your lead is starting to pan out."

CHAPTER 10

What looked like an empty hotel room transformed as Kate stepped through the doorway. Overcome by a slight feeling of vertigo, she watched in amazement as the setting changed around her. Gone was the bed and dresser, replaced by glass walls of conference rooms and rows of desks with busy people manning computer stations.

"Wow, what just happened here?"

"We call it a Rainbow Bridge," Grant replied. With his hand steadying her, he guided her to a place around a large glass table. "Ambrose hates that term."

"I hate that term," echoed Ambrose. "It's not a bridge, it's a link between two destinations created through the bending of space and time."

"And in this case, I am assuming, this is the FBI?"

"Sort of. There is no official connection between religion and government, so this is an offshoot division called Zion. Self-sufficient in funding and one of the most profitable areas of government out there."

Grant leaned over to Kate, whispering, "Ambrose is very proud that his division stands as one of the few revenue positive areas of the US Government."

"*Only* one," corrected Ambrose briskly, "and I might be old, Grant, but I'm not deaf."

"Ahoy, Captain, my Captain," replied Grant with a grin. "What have you got for us?

SURVIVING THE SUMMIT OF GOOD & EVIL 91

A good-looking man in a suit and tie handed Kate a holster and gun, then slid them a file, waving his hand across the table. A series of pictures scattered themselves across the desktop. "Based on your intel from the restaurant tablet and cross-referenced with security videos, the voices you heard belong to the following people."

"Kate, this is my cousin, Mark. He's Uncle Ambrose's son."

Mark looked strangely at Kate and Grant then, nodding his head slightly, he reached out and shook her hand. Focusing back on the table, they watched as his fingers flew across a virtual keyboard, and its surface changed again. Police records, IRS files, and crime scene photos splashed across the top before dividing themselves into piles.

"Mark's a Texas Ranger. The Morgans keep him very busy down there."

"Drug running and human trafficking across the Mexican border. I'm not surprised. I hope you're tossing them in jail, Mark."

"Yes, ma'am, I am. So, in the absence of security cameras within the chapel, we pulled surveillance feed from the courtyard and discovered that only two people entered after you."

They watched as the feed showed them entering the chapel, followed by two additional people about half an hour later.

"Drinking in a church, Grant?" Ambrose remarked sternly.

"That was fifty year old scotch and it's not a functioning church. It deserved to be enjoyed in an appropriate setting."

Kate smiled at the banter between the two men. Lightheartedness was not a common characteristic among the Morgan clan.

"So here are the two suspects," Mark continued.

Two pictures floated across the desk. The first was a business profile of a younger man, taken from a major business magazine.

The second picture, Kate recognized as her cousin Gus. "Son of a bitch," she muttered. "Why am I not surprised?"

Mark pointed to the first man. "Andrew Parsons. Entrepreneur and business man. It is believed that he is here on invitation of Laurence Morgan. The second is your cousin, Gus Morgan. Son of Alice Morgan, Grandson of Ash Morgan."

"Larry, I totally get," Kate said, "but Gus? That's surprising. I didn't think he had the intelligence or bravado to try something like this. They used to call him gutless Gus when he was a kid."

Grant quickly flipped through the files. "Any idea who the targets might be?"

"Does it matter?" Kate asked. "If this is typical Morgan feuding, then one less one is not a big deal."

Mark smiled, shaking his head with disbelief. Kate stared at him, not understanding what was in his mind. "What do you mean, 'just like fifteen years ago'?"

"What?" Mark replied, his smile fading fast.

"Your thoughts just now. You were remembering a case that we worked on fifteen years ago. How is that possible? I've never met you before."

Grant stared at him, his eyes narrowed with suspicion. "She's right. Isn't she, Mark?"

Mark looked down at the table, an uncomfortable silence filling the air until Grant added, "And if you *have* worked with her before, you know that she reads minds so you might as well spill, cuz."

"'We,' not 'me.' We worked together," he drawled, "all y'all."

"Stop speaking Texan, Mark," Grant growled. "What are you talking about?"

Ambrose pulled up a chair and sat down, his full attention on his son. Mark looked irritated and took to tapping his cell phone on the table in conjunction with his story. "In a nut shell, fifteen years ago, Grant and I were working a serial killer case in the panhandle." He pointed at Kate.

"She showed up because two of the victims had been traced back to missing people in New York City. Together, we were able to find the killer and solve twenty-two murders."

"Why don't I remember this?" Grant and Kate asked in unison.

"Probably because of that," said Mark, pointing his phone at the both of them.

"What?" they replied.

"That. That weird chemistry between the both of you. At first, you two were like oil and water, then…then…"

"Fire and ice, and you kept wondering when we would get a room," murmured Kate, flushing with embarrassment.

"Then what happened?" Grant asked angrily. He looked at Ambrose for some kind of explanation but the man seemed as mystified as they were.

"I don't know if you two had sex—" Mark exclaimed

"Not that, Mark. The memory thing."

"How should I know? All I know is the day the case closed, Uncle Matt showed up and both of you were suddenly gone. I figured you had run away and eloped or something. You certainly seemed headed that way," he replied awkwardly. Glancing down at the table, Mark excused himself, grateful his ringing cell phone interrupted their conversation.

Grant tossed the files on the table and turned on his heel, heading for the door.

"Grant," Ambrose yelled. "Wait. Don't do something rash. You know your father's not well."

"He's well enough to interfere in my life."

"That was fifteen years ago."

"Ambrose, he erased our memories. What other violations did he commit? First, Mom, with her arranged marriages, and now this? I am done with the meddling."

"You made a promise, Grant."

"That was three hundred years ago." He paused and looked in Kate's direction, "And I intend to keep my end of the bargain."

"We hold these things as sacred, Grant. No offence to Kate, but getting involved with a Morgan was not part of the deal."

Kate looked away, stung by his words. "No problem," she mumbled.

"Kate."

"No, no, don't worry about it. It's fine, and he's right. I'm sure there was a good reason fifteen years ago and it's probably a good thing now."

"Kate, come on."

She pushed away the rejection, the affirmation that she would never be good enough—as a Morgan or anyone else—then put on a brave face. "Like you said, we all have responsibilities. Finding out who's trying to derail the Summit should be our first one."

Mark waved his cell phone around. "She's right. Keep your saddle oiled and your gun greased, y'all. Gus Morgan's just been found, dead."

CHAPTER 11

Kate raced down the hallway, more because she was running away from Grant, than the need to investigate the death of her cousin. As much as the murder was a problem, she was grateful for the distraction. She could feel herself falling for Grant and knowing now that her family ties would destroy her happiness again made the idea more than she could handle.

The path to Gus's body was illuminated through whispers, thoughts, and feelings. She lived among personalities that celebrated their psychopathic nature. None of the Morgans felt remorse for Gus's death. Their feelings revolved more around curiosity and fascination than grief.

Through the gallery to the rear courtyard, she ran, unsure of what she would find. As she and the rest of Ambrose's team burst through the sets of French doors, she looked around at the group of people milling about. "Where's the body?"

The courtyard was spotless. Gray pavestones mixed with the tidy landscaping of boxwood hedges and fragrant flowers. A large stone fountain in the middle of the space lent the soothing sound of water to a harmonious picture.

Grant touched her elbow, his eyes looking toward the heavens. Kate glanced up and gasped. From the top of a large flag pole hung the body of Gus Morgan. He was a grotesque sight of bone and flesh. Strung up by the neck, his extensive girth aided in pulling the flesh away from his body at its weakest point, exposing the bone and cartilage of his spine as if someone had started to fillet sections of him, then thought better of it.

Below his body, a series of flags, one American, one Scottish, one French, now muddled together and wrapped around the pole, weighed down by the collection of his blood.

Kate watched as Ambrose and his team sprang into action, closing off the scene and shooing onlookers away. She stood quietly, pushing away her issues in favor of reading others for guilt. At least twenty-five Morgans; a collection of Andersons, from the number of people making the sign of the cross; and the riffraff, as Julian liked to call them. They were the assistants and associates who had figured out the true nature of both families and hitched themselves to an ill-conceived idea of fortune and glory.

Kate stiffened, feeling the subtle touch of Grant's hand on her back. "Before everyone disperses, any guilty thoughts?"

"Nothing stands out among my family. Just the usual indifference."

She scanned the crowd again, her eyes stopping on a pair of fashion-forward women who appeared to be in their twenties. They were looking up at the body and whispering something mildly amusing.

"Grab Barbie One and Two on your left, the chain smoking man leaning on the wall behind the last set of French doors and the priest making the sign of the cross."

Grant gestured to a nearby officer, his mouth set in a firm line. "Sure, no one from your side?"

Kate shoved her hands in her pocket, her eyes scouring the crowd of Morgans. "I'm sure there are plenty of people from my side. I can give you a top fifty list of suspects but no one who is going to stand out in this crowd. One thing my family excels at is not reacting to a crisis."

Spying her mother through one of the French doors, Kate's eyes narrowed. "That's the problem when you deal with psychopaths. They're very good at hiding their true nature." Making a start toward her mother, she added, "It's time for me to do some family detective work."

"Why don't you let me interrogate that bastard?"

"No way. You said it yourself, keeping the peace is more important than vendettas. Let me handle this."

Kate wandered through the French doors to the place her mother was standing. As she approached, Lucas appeared, offering his arm to her mother, his linen handkerchief ready in case she needed it.

"Mother. Lucas. Any insight you'd like to share about this crime?"

Lucas scowled at her, "Any insight you'd like to share about partnering with the enemy?"

Kate glared back at him. "This is what I do. I investigate crimes. I would think that you would care more about who killed Gus, than keeping tabs on the people I interact with."

She accepted the handkerchief, holding it close to her face. "So you think Gus was murdered?" asked her mother.

"Well, he didn't string that fat body of his up there himself."

"Katherine. Show some respect."

Lucas walked over to the windows and glanced up at the corpse hanging limply above him. "Such a shame. He'll be missed."

Kate bit her tongue, trying to be civil. It was a challenging task when all she could see were thoughts of lost revenue floating through Lucas's mind. Gus was a lawyer at a subsidiary of Morgan, Morgan, and Power in Greensboro.

"So I assume he was on his third life?"

"Katherine," chided her mother, "We do not discuss such things. You have no concept of manners or boundaries. That is a private matter."

"Well, if he's going to come back from the dead, I would like to know. It would certainly narrow down a list of suspects if he could tell me who did this to him."

"You don't have to worry, baby girl. He's gone to embrace our father, to the place where we all belong. There won't be any resurrection coming from him."

Kate bit her tongue again, Grant's request to play nice cutting through the sarcastic thoughts that saturated her mind. "Stop calling me that. Now what about his powers?"

"Katherine! The impertinence of such a question. How could you bring that up so casually? Stop acting this way."

"Mother, I'm not asking about his sex life or if he cheated on his taxes, I just need context for this killing. Did he have any enemies? Were there secrets that put him in this situation? Is there anyone else who might be a target?"

"Of course, poor Gus had enemies. We all do. We're living under the same roof as a hundred of them, just look around you."

"Aunt Elizabeth is right, baby girl. Why are you interrogating your own when you should be looking at your law enforcement friends?"

"Because they are here to maintain the peace and uphold the law. They haven't been preprogrammed to cause chaos in the name of an asshole."

"Katherine! You do not disrespect your deity."

"He's not my deity, Mother. I worship no one."

Lucas turned from the window, a flash of distain filling his eyes. "Best be careful about who you piss off, baby girl. Gus isn't the only one on his third life."

Kate's eyes flashed with anger. Clenching her teeth, trying to hold back the rage she felt inside, she uttered, "You want another go at me, Lucas? Give it your best shot. I beat you once and I can do it again."

Lucas smiled and walked back to her mother, extending his arm. "Aunt Elizabeth, I think I should get you away from this unpleasantness. It is far too taxing for a dignified lady like you."

Elizabeth Morgan raised her hand to her forehead, nodding in agreement as she took his arm. "You darling boy, you are so considerate. Why did our maker forsake me and not give me a son like you? Leland must be so proud."

Lucas bent down and gave her a kiss on the cheek. "Now, Aunt Elizabeth, Father is equally proud of all six of us. He doesn't play favorites."

"Well, darling, I will be sure to tell him how you helped me in my time of need." Turning her attention to Kate, she scowled, tapping her lightly on the arm. "I will forgive your transgression toward our maker because you are young and foolish and have always been mentally deficient in some way. You can play the rebellious card and hide from the family but, let me be very clear about this. You fail to make the proper choice at The Joining and I will kill you myself. Is that clear?"

Kate bristled slightly, the shock of her words, quickly replaced by anger. "Crystal clear, Mother."

"Good, my dear. I expect to see you at breakfast tomorrow."

Kate watched them walk away and annoyance filled her mind. A few days ago her mother's words would have instilled dread, but now they were empty and meaningless—a shining example of their relationship from days past. She would threaten and Kate would run, but no more. She was tired of running and, if she was going to take a stand, once and for all, it would have to be here.

"What's The Joining?" asked a tiny, high-pitched voice behind her.

Kate turned around and saw a slender, teenage girl standing there. She was pale with big eyes, long blonde hair, and dressed in a long skirt, billowing blouse, and hand crafted jewelry. Kate was reminded of a flower child from the sixties. She didn't stand, so much as swayed back and forth, like the branches of a Willow tree on a gusty day.

The girl was a mixture of timid and curious, as if she didn't want to ask the question but couldn't help herself. Kate smiled, glancing down before looking around.

"Um, it's a ceremony in the Morgan family. A marriage of sorts. We take a blood allegiance to the head of our family who, if you didn't know, is Satan."

The girls eyes grew twice as large and she clasped her hands together nervously. "Oh, wow. You can't do that, no, it wouldn't be good for you at all."

"That's what I keep telling myself," Kate replied grimly. She glanced down the hall where her mother and Lucas had previously walked. "That's why I keep running away."

The girl bit her lip nervously then looked around. "You can't do the ceremony. It will change you. It will make you like them."

Kate smiled at the girl. "Believe me, I'm doing my best not to become like them." She stretched out her hand. "I don't think I've had the pleasure. My name is Kate Morgan."

The girl smiled shyly and placed her hand in Kate's. Her touch was cool and limp, like it was the first time anyone had shaken her hand. "I'm Sapphire Anderson."

"Sapphire. What a beautiful name."

Sapphire blushed and glanced down, quickly pulling her hand away. "Everyone calls me Saffi. You can call me that too."

"Well, Saffi, call me Kate."

The girl smiled and looked down at her fingers again. For a moment, her eyes scanned the assortment of wristlets on her arm, her fingers lightly touching them before settling on a shimmering blue and gold bit of string. Taking Kate's hand, she tied the bracelet around her wrist. "Here, this is for you. I make them. It's a protection bracelet so don't ever take it off. It will heighten your instincts and make you wary of evil's eye."

Kate glanced down at her wrist, overcome by the generosity of the girl. "Saffi, it's beautiful but I can't accept such a gift. You should be wearing this, not me."

"No, it was made for you. Just like you were made for him."

"Who?"

"My Uncle Grant."

"You're Grant's niece?"

Saffi nodded shyly. From across the room, a voice called her name. Saffi looked around then back at Kate, her eyes large and mischievous. "I have to go now, Kate. Dad is coming and he doesn't like Morgans very much."

"Sounds like a smart guy. You should listen to him."

Saffi twirled around then stopped and gave her a wink. "I know, but your family is so interesting and I can protect myself. You should talk to your cousin Lucy. She can help."

Kate frowned trying to understand what she was saying. "Help? You mean with this investigation?"

Saffi laughed and shook her head. "No, silly, with your powers. You're going to need them all very soon."

With a wave and a flounce, she was off. Kate glanced down at the bracelet. It was a finely woven mix of gold and shades of blue. So light and airy she barely felt it on her wrist. It was impeccable workmanship, indeed. She couldn't tell where the fine strands of thread began and ended.

Wearing a haggard look and moving like a man who hadn't slept in days, Grant caught her eye.

She looked at him, then down at the bracelet from the girl who believed in her more than she did. Perhaps she was giving in too quickly. *Obligations and responsibilities*, she heard in the back of her mind. What about joy and love? In the midst of turmoil, she'd experienced a taste of happiness and, for once, she was going to hold on to it.

She watched Grant stride across the space, only to be stopped by a tall, distinguished gentleman. They traded a few heated words, ending with the man grabbing Grant's arm and forcing him to look at a paper the man was holding. Grant skimmed the sheet before shoving it back at him and storming over to Kate.

"Grant, who was that?" she demanded. "What's wrong?"

He dismissed the man with the wave of his hand. "Don't concern yourself with my brother, Chase. It's nothing, and we have bigger problems." He paused and shifted his stance, uncomfortably.

She had never seen him so upset. "What's going on?"

After a moment, he let out a weary sigh. "More bodies have been found."

CHAPTER 12

Grant led the way through the gallery to the front of the building. At the lobby, he took a left and slipped down a service corridor. Kate followed in silence, unsure of what to say. He was acting differently from before.

As much as she wanted to read his mind, out of respect she chose to rely on her skills as a detective and old fashioned observation. They walked the service corridor to a heavy steel door on the left.

Pulling open the door, she took the opportunity to stop him, grabbing his arm. "Grant, what's down there?"

"You don't know?"

"Of course not," she replied with a frown. "I won't read your mind again. Not unless you tell me to."

The conflicted look on his features lightened a little. "I'll explain everything in a minute, but not here."

Silently, she followed him down the steel staircase to a cavernous room below the chateau. Kate looked around at the enormous boilers that filled the room. Despite the vastness of the space, she felt claustrophobic, as if they were entering a tomb, and not a common work space.

Around them was a flurry of activity—men and women wearing blue jackets with FBI stamped in capital letters on the back. Some were familiar from the attempted mass poisoning in New York, others were new faces, who she suspected came through the Rainbow Bridge.

"Kate, what do you know about the history of our two families?"

The question caught her by surprise. For the last few minutes, he hadn't said a word. Aside from the occasional nod to people who passed them, his expression was a study of silent fury and worry.

"I—not much beyond the more recent history of our families," she confessed. "Yours represent God's will on earth and we're emissaries of the Devil."

"What about your family history?"

Kate exhaled a long burst of air. "Umm, there are a number stories ranging from we're the descendants of the Morgan Le Fey from the King Arthur fables to the one we all learn as kids, the one from the Bible."

"And what would that be?"

"An addendum to the Genesis story of Sodom and Go-morrah. It was said that one of the elders of Sodom arrived home from trading abroad to find the entire town destroyed by God. His name was Moriah and, in his rage over finding his children dead, swore an eternal oath to Satan. In return for the resurrection of his family, he and his descendants would carry out the Devil's work and destroy God's people in every way they knew how until the end of time."

"And what do you know of my family?"

"Not that much. Just that a lot of famous popes and saints have come from your ancestors."

Grant stopped outside a large metal sliding door, corroded with age and rust. He turned his back, leaning against a painted metal pipe that extended from the wall. "True, but our history goes back farther than that. Anderson means 'Son of Andrew.' We're descended from the Apostle Andrew and, while our family is committed to God, they are also committed to keeping mankind safe."

"You mean safe from my family."

"I mean safe to progress at its own pace. To maintain the balance and find its own way to peace and goodwill."

"Balance," she scoffed. "What kind of balance is there

when everyone lies, steals, and cheats their way through life? You think my family are the only ones responsible for hell on Earth? You're giving them way too much credit."

"What I am saying is when stuff like this happens, it disrupts the balance and if that isn't maintained, the end result is bad for everyone involved."

"Bad things like what? Gus's murder?"

Grant shook his head and walked over to the metal door. Giving it a tug, he pulled it open and unveiled the contents of the passage way in front of them. Kate gasped as she surveyed the scene in front of her. Miles of cable stretched down the service corridor. Every ten feet or so, the mass of wires was attached to a detonator so complex, she couldn't begin to understand how to disarm it.

"My God. Where does this corridor lead?"

"Under the north wing of the chateau," Grant replied with a sigh.

Kate stared at him, stunned. "That's under our wing and under the Anderson wing."

"Uh huh, with enough explosives to level the entire building and blow a crater miles wide."

"Who would do this and why?"

Grant rubbed his neck wearily. "Someone very stupid or very smart. This is a message and not just a threat."

"What do you mean?"

"Look closer at one of the detonator boxes. Someone's trying to make a point."

Kate glanced at him then carefully stepped closer to the wall. Her focus on the image was so strong that she ignored the pool of liquid soaking through her shoe. Amongst the sea of cable and wire was wrapped a strange concoction of white and red fabric. she blinked and stared harder at the wall. Hollow yellow tubes wrapped in red and beige stared back. Feeling liquid seep through her shoe to her toes, she looked down and moved her foot, realizing it was resting in a pool of blood. Her eyes were playing tricks on her. There was no way such a feat could have been performed.

"No, it's not possible," she said quietly.

"It is. I wish it wasn't, but it is."

She stepped back, chills wracking her body. "Grant, that's the skin and sinew of a person in there. Someone wove a person into the bomb!" Kate's mind reeled at the savage possibility. She had spent most of her first life as a doctor. She knew the look and feel of the human body. How pliable the tissue was if treated in the right way. "How many feet does it go?"

Grant shifted uncomfortably. "At least a couple of thousand."

"And each box is dressed the same way?"

He didn't reply. She didn't need him to. His expression said it all. "There could be a dozen people or more down here," she choked.

A dozen lives that could have been saved if her family didn't exist.

She turned away, the taste of bile filling her mouth. She had been a doctor. The sight of human remains was not new to her. As a detective she had seen mankind at its worst, but this was revolting, nauseating. The idea that she could be related to someone who would do this made her sick to her stomach.

She stumbled down the corridor, blind to the people around her and Grant's voice, calling for her to stop. It wasn't until she had reached the bottom of the steel staircase that he caught up to her, grabbing her by the arm.

"What?" she gasped, her voice hoarse with restrained fury.

"You don't know," he replied, guessing her thoughts. "You don't know it's one of them. One of your family."

"Really? Who else would do such a thing? That's the work of a sick, sick person. Oh, hell, maybe a group of people. I'm not the only doctor in the family, you know."

"Kate—"

"No, Grant. This is what I grew up with. Psychopaths all around me who would laugh and joke at that abomination like it was modern art. It's a goddamn nightmare. My life is one long nightmare and I can't wake up."

He pulled her to him as the tears started to flow, wrapping her in his arms. She crumbled against his chest, her sobs muffled by his embrace. Tightening his grip, he kissed her hair, letting her grief wash over them both. As she cried, he felt a wave of warmth sweep over them, the flurry of activity around them seemed to subside. A series of popping noises made him look up. They were alone, the agents that surrounded them, suddenly gone.

"Kate. What just happened?"

She raised her head from his chest, wiping the tears away. "What do you mean?"

"The agents that were just here. They're all gone."

Kate looked around, disorientated by the scene around her. Gone was the command post wedged between two of the boilers. The room was quiet except for the hum of machinery. Disengaging herself from his arms, she moved to the bottom of the stairs then turned back toward him at the sound of the heavy fire door opening above her. "Someone's coming. Should we hide?"

"From what? If this is what I think it is, you can't interact with the people. You can only observe."

She looked up then drew her gun, just in case. From above her she could hear the baritone voice of a man. He was humming the Battle Hymn of the Republic.

Kate turned and headed back toward Grant.

Down the stairs the man came, dressed in a black overcoat and matching fedora, carrying a valise that reminded her of an old fashioned doctor's bag. She stumbled to avoid his path, tripping over a section of pipe that some worker had left strewn across the floor.

Before she could hit the ground, Grant caught her, but the force from her foot sent the cylinder shooting across the floor.

The man paused, stopping to look at the pipe. Kate held her breath as he slowly shifted around, hoping for a glimpse of his face. Although he turned a full three sixty, staring right through them, all she could see was a flash of one striking gray eye.

Satisfied that he was alone, the man resumed his whistling and continued through the room and out of sight.

"That was strange," murmured Grant.

"We should go after him," declared Kate. "He's the one who's responsible."

"No, wait, you can't."

"Sure we can. We have to stop him."

"Kate—" Grant said quietly.

She turned and headed after the man, taking about five steps before the noise stopped her. She turned to look at Grant. He was yelling something but she couldn't hear what he was saying. All around her the clamor increased and shadows started to appear near them.

"Grant!"

A loud rushing sound filled her ears and a wave of vertigo hit her full on. The room around her started to spin and, just when she felt like she was going to hit the ground for the second time today, she felt an arm around her shoulder, steadying her.

The room was back to normal, a flurry of agents comparing notes, taking samples and snapping pictures. Morbid chaos surrounded her, yet everyone acted as if this was mundane and routine. Kate gasped, looking around in confusion. She felt Grant's hand gently take her gun from her fingers and holster it back on her hip.

Panic filled her mind as she struggled to process what had just happened. Paralyzed with fear, she forced her legs to move as he guided her from the crime scene, up the stairs, and back down the deserted service corridor. Once back on the main floor of the hotel, he sat her down in a quiet seating area away from questioning eyes.

"What just happened back there? Where did everyone go? They were there and then they were gone." she asked, her head in her hands.

He leaned forward, rubbing the back of her neck. "They didn't go anywhere. We did. I think you tapped into one of your dormant powers. I think you have the ability to imprint on time."

Confused, she stared at him. "What does that mean? Imprint on time?"

"It's the power to go back in time as an observer. I think because you can read minds, you can tap into their memories, like capturing a recording of something that happened in the past."

"If the walls had ears—"

"Exactly, except they have eyes and they're showing you a memory."

"Whoever he was. He couldn't see us."

"Because we weren't there when it happened. We were glimpsing through a one way mirror." Grant paused for a minute, "Except."

"Except what?"

"Except you shouldn't have been able to move that pipe. Your foot should have passed right through it."

Kate sat back in her chair rubbing the soft leather arms against the palm of her hands. She needed to ground herself with something that was real and authentic. "Great," she muttered, "The family freak strikes again. I can't even get my powers right."

"Stop beating yourself up. You've had this ability for all of thirty seconds. It will take you a while to master it."

"I guess Saffi was right. I should track down my cousin Lucy and get her to help me sort all of this hocus pocus out."

"Saffi? You mean Sapphire, my niece? When did you talk to her?"

"Just before you found me," Kate replied, holding up her arm. "She gave me this beautiful bracelet."

Grant smiled and reached for her arm, caressing it while he studied his niece's handiwork. "Sapphire's definitely a character. You must have made quite the impression. She has hundreds of these handicrafts and almost never gives them away."

Kate smiled at him, then blinked, looking wearily at Mark as he approached. "Speaking of impressions…"

Mark cleared his throat, as if he was preparing to make an announcement.

Before he could utter a word, Kate cut him off. "He wants to tell us that our presence is requested before the Council."

Grant looked at him in surprise. "Really?"

A look of annoyance crossed Mark's face. "Ya' know that trick of yours is gettin' old as dirt. Come on you two, the Council wants to know what the hell is going on."

CHAPTER 13

Mark led the way as the trio walked back through the lobby and toward the south wing of the complex. Strolling through the peaceful surroundings of the lobby did little to quell Kate's fears. She was going to stand before the Council, the original ancestors of a family chosen by Satan himself as his representatives on Earth. She felt like she was going to be sick.

Grant slowed his stride, allowing her to catch up, "You okay?"

Kate shook her head. With childhood fears flooding her head, it was all she could do to stop from sprinting through the main doors of the building. She *had been summoned.* Words to strike fear into any normal person's head. For someone who openly criticized her heritage, it was akin to a death sentence.

"Detective Morgan, Detective, a minute please?"

Kate turned to see the resort manager hustling toward her. He was a portly man, with graying hair and thick glasses. He approached her with hand outstretched, not to shake hers but to show her something on a card.

"Detective Morgan, I am so glad to have caught up with you. Might I speak with you about something?"

"Sure, Mr…" She glanced at his nametag. "Poppet. What can I do for you?"

The man hesitated, the sweat beading on his brow, his hands wringing nervously as if someone had asked him to drink poison. He glanced from her to Grant and Mark, unsure of whether to speak.

"It's okay, these are my friends," Kate added. It was somehow reassuring to see someone more nervous than she.

"Oh, yes, of course. Well, it's about your mother."

Kate bowed her head, rubbing her eyes with her fingers. Her mother was the last thing she needed to deal with right now. "What about her?"

"She left you a trunk with instructions that I am to read to you personally."

He gestured to an old steamer trunk sitting by the concierge desk. Kate stared at the unfortunate man. "What's the message?"

He looked down at the piece of paper and with shaking hands, pulled off his glasses, and lifted the card to his face. "Tell my daughter that I will not allow a child of mine to walk around dressed like a hobo. Since she will not tell me where she is staying, please see that these proper clothes are delivered to her room and inform her that I expect to see her appropriately dressed at breakfast."

She looked down at her clothes, "Hobo? These are from Macy's."

From behind her, she heard Mark's stifled laugh. A stolen glance at the men revealed a withering glare from Grant, meant to keep Mark in line. Kate sighed and pulled out a twenty-dollar bill from her pocket.

"If you could have the trunk delivered to my room, I would appreciate it," she murmured, handing him the money.

"Of course, Detective. Thank you very much."

Watching him scurry away, she sighed again and turned to the men. "What?"

"Sure there isn't a bomb in there?" Mark remarked with a smirk.

"No, subtly is more her style. If she was going to try and kill me again, it would be something tasteful, like poison."

Grant shot her a look then pulled out his phone. He

punched in a set of numbers. "Yeah, it's Grant. Kate Morgan has a trunk being delivered to her room from her mother. Can you have someone sweep it for restricted articles?" He continued on, ignoring her frantic motions to hang up the phone. "Test for everything that could kill—biological, chemical, the works…Yeah…Thanks."

Kate slapped him in the shoulder. "We were joking."

"I'm not. When it comes to your family, I'm not taking any chances."

Mark nodded. "Good advice. Here's another piece, move it. We're burning daylight."

Five minutes later, they entered the arboretum. Paths of exotic flowers and plants filled the space, giving it an ethereal ambiance. They walked down the stone path past intimate grottos with cascading waterfalls and transplanted palm trees. The heavy humidity made Kate shed her jacket but not her feeling of dread.

In addition to the trio, there were others standing there, enveloped by the enormity of the dome roof that spread above them. Two small yet distinct groups stood, silently glaring at each other. From her side, Kate saw Lucas and Leland along with Ray Morgan, brother of the now departed Gus. They were chatting with a tall man she hadn't seen before.

From the Anderson side stood Ambrose speaking quietly with two other gentlemen. A varied entourage of people lined the outer area of the circle. Judging by the mutters and whispers, their place was evident—assisting the inner circle of chosen ones from both sides of the family.

Across the center of the room, both sides of the Council sat side by side in a row. High back chairs lined up in front of the giant stone fountain that was the centerpiece of the greenhouse. With the fountain turned off, their voices echoed against the cavernous roof and rocks around them.

"Is this everyone, Alexis?" demanded Marion Anderson Lowell.

A beautiful woman with long auburn hair scanned the

crowd, before settling her gaze on Grant. After a second longer than Kate liked, she smiled sweetly and answered, "Yes, Grandmother."

Kate felt Grant stiffen. His jaw clenched and his body was poised for action. Rather than step away, however, he moved closer to her, discretely sliding his arm around her waist, as if shielding her from the woman's gaze.

"Good," Damian Morgan replied. "Ambrose Anderson. As the family member in charge of security, please step forward and give us an update on what you have found."

Ambrose stepped from the cluster of onlookers and cleared his throat. He looked around at the crowd, his disgust barely hidden beneath a veil of professionalism. "With all due respect, this information is for family ears only."

Marion Anderson Lowell pursed her lips and looked around, scanning every face in the room. "Agreed. Alexis, please clear the room of anyone who isn't Morgan or Anderson."

Kate watched Alexis wind her way through the crowd. Her grace and beautiful face reminded Kate of those models with cascading hair in shampoo commercials. With refinement and sympathy, she calmed the indignant and ushered each person out until all that remained were Kate's family and the small group of Anderson's.

"Now," boomed Damian. "Proceed."

Ambrose cleared his throat again and put his hands behind his back, adopting a relaxed military stance. "Last night a plot was uncovered, identifying the possible assassination of one or more people at this conference."

The effect of this news was the opposite of what Kate imagined. Rather than register shock, the reactions ranged from amusement to boredom. "And do we know who was involved in this assassination plot?"

"Yes sir. The suspects were Gus Morgan and Andrew Parsons."

This revelation, however, had a definite impact. A wave of whispers came at her from all directions, snippets of words and phrases, none of which made any sense. Having given up on reading the Council's veiled minds, Kate found herself distracted by Alexis Anderson and her mildly disturbing thoughts.

"And yet Gus is now dead. So who killed him?" demanded Damian

"And where is Andrew Parsons?" asked David Anderson

Ambrose raised his hand, trying to quiet the questions. "Council members, the death of Gus Morgan and disappearance of Andrew Parsons is concerning, however, there are additional factors. It also looks like 'The Sculptor' has returned."

More murmurs from the Council. Damian glanced around, looking annoyed. Muttering turned into a debate between the members, giving Kate the opportunity she was looking for. She leaned into Grant and whispered, "Why is Alexis Anderson having erotic thoughts about you?"

Grant shot a dirty look at Alexis, as if his gaze could banish her forever. He shifted slightly, emitting an exasperated sigh, "That damn power of yours is going to get me in trouble."

"You have nothing to worry about. Your friend is another story."

"She's no friend of mine." He looked down at her, his expression conflicted. "We have a history. A long time ago, she was my fiancée."

Kate's eyebrows rose with surprise. Before she could stop it, words of disbelief poured from her mouth. "You're kidding. How long is 'long ago'?"

He exhaled a lengthy breath and shrugged his shoulders. "I don't know, maybe a hundred and fifty years ago."

Kate blinked, looking at the woman who, after all this time, still wanted Grant as her own. While there was some comfort in knowing their affair was over before Kate was born, it didn't make her jealously diminish. Her rival was sophisticated, beautiful, and, most importantly, free of any Morgan blood at all.

"Isn't she your cousin?"

"Technically yes, but not unlike members in your family, she's adopted," he muttered. Trying to dispel her confusion he continued, "Both families encourage that the bloodline remain strong, however interbreeding brings its own set of problems. The newer generations have specific families to seek mates from—family lineages that parallel each of our histories and add variety to the offspring's powers. In rare cases, members of the general population show unusual abilities that can add to the strength of the family. In Aunt Hannah's case, both of her children, Alexis and Scott were adopted and their dormant genes activated to become Anderson compatible."

"So The Sculptor is back," Marion concluded, her voice cutting through the various conversations around her. "How many lives were lost this time?"

"Preliminary findings suggest eighteen bodies—all associates. We won't know until later but one of them might be Parsons."

Marion leaned over and whispered to Damian. He nodded and cleared his throat. "Ambrose, please decide which members of Zion you want to assist you. We're issuing a declaration to lock down the chateau until the conference is over. No more bridges, no one in or out until Gus's murderer and the Sculptor can be found."

"But we'll need the full resources of the government. We can't isolate ourselves from the world. Supplies need to be replenished."

"Ambrose, we both know there are people from both families who can manifest supplies if necessary."

"And what about investigative resources? We're stretched thin, just trying to keep the peace."

"This is why we are assigning a special task force," Marion said, "and why we have asked some of you here."

Damian rose from his seat. He sauntered toward them, one eyebrow raised in amusement.

"Grant Anderson, I understand that you and my great

niece were the first to stumble on the assassination plot."

"Yes, sir."

Stepping into Kate's personal space forced her to take a step back and away from Grant. Damian advanced again until he was inches from her. Inhaling her scent, he lifted his right hand and traced a single finger against her jaw, as if he were examining a prized show dog. Seemingly satisfied, he turned and refocused his attention on Grant.

"Interesting. My great niece does not disgust you, Grant Anderson."

"No sir," replied Grant stiffly. "Not in the least."

"Yes, that is evident. Your scent lingers on her."

Kate stared at the floor, horrified and desperately hoping for an end to this scrutiny. Her great uncle was the most vocal and devious in her family. Anything Grant said in his defense would not end well for him. Fortunately, before he could reply, Damian continued his remarks.

"Not enough to be a concern, of course. Morgans do not mix with Andersons." Waving his hand dismissively in her general direction, he finished his thought, "although one could understand your mistake when it comes to that. She hardly qualifies as Morgan stock."

Out of the corner of her eye, Kate could see the smirks and off-colored comments from the Morgan side of the room. Lucas especially was sending some particularly vulgar thoughts her way.

"For the purpose of this investigation only, we are recommending a partnership between the two sides," continued Damian. "Grant, we would like you to represent the Anderson side with Alexis."

Grant started to protest, but was stopped when his grandfather, Jonathan Anderson raised his hand.

Sending Grant a stern glance, Marion continued where Damian left off. "On the Morgan side, we have chosen Kate Morgan and Jake Riley to oversee the investigation for the family."

A tall man, who Kate presumed was Jake Riley, snapped

to attention. "Wait, w—what?" he sputtered through a pronounced English accent. "You're kidding, yeah?"

"Now hold on, why should these freaks represent our side?" Lucas cried.

"Oye, shut up, you Yankee moron!" Jake ordered.

"Yeah," Ray Morgan growled. "I demand justice for my brother Gus's death."

"Are you calling my only grandson, Jake, a freak?" Damian boomed.

Lucas turned red with embarrassment and looked away. Rather than offer penitence, he stood there and, after a second, puffed out his chest in defiance.

Damian glared at him. "Watch your place, Lucas. Don't think that your past accomplishments have garnered you any place of permanent significance among the Council. Protocol and tradition must be maintained. Your actions threaten to make a mockery of this family."

Leland piped up, trying to smooth over the damage caused by his son. "Councilor Damian, the boy meant no disrespect. He is just passionate about ensuring that the integrity of the investigation be maintained."

While they argued, Kate glanced across at Jake Riley. He was tall and thin with better than average looks. British born, by the accent, with the glasses and wavy brown hair, he reminded her of a college professor or someone who travelled the universe in a big blue box.

Digging through her memory didn't reveal anything about him. There were certain branches of the family tree that she'd had minimal exposure to, thanks to the influence of her mother. Of the original Morgans—Lilith, Damian, Ronin, Nero, and Ash—Damian, Ash, and Nero's offspring were raised primarily in Europe, Asia, and Australia. Kate was not privy to their lives, unlike the cousins who were a part of her upbringing.

"Ambrose," Marion said, "we will give you one hour to assemble the laypeople you need to maintain order before we close down all access to the chateau and its grounds. Be warned, we need this contained and orderly. The conference is to continue as planned, with minimal interruption to both families."

"Closing down the resort is not the wisest idea, Aunt Marion," Grant argued. "The parties responsible may lash out if they feel trapped."

"All the more reason to put this to bed, quickly and efficiently. I expect all of you to work together and solve this issue before it becomes a problem."

"A serial killer called The Sculptor isn't a problem?" Kate asked.

"He's only a problem to the associates," Marion sniffed. "He wouldn't dare touch anyone from the families." She gave Kate a cold stare then looked at Grant, addressing him as she spoke. "I assume this distraction of yours won't be an issue."

"What distraction are you referring to, Aunt Marion?"

"Your association with the Morgan girl. Don't you think you're too old for dalliances with trash, Grant? Oh, sure she appears to be different than the rest, but a Morgan is a Morgan and they never change."

Alexis looked at both of them, letting out a nervous laugh as nephew and aunt stared each other down. "They're just colleagues, Grandmother. There's nothing going on between them. Damian just confirmed it."

"Oh, you sweet, stupid girl. If you had any clue how to keep a man, you wouldn't be boring me with this conversation right now."

Bloody hell, I thought our family was bad. Kate locked eyes with Jake Riley, just long enough to catch his smirk. With an unapologetic shrug of his shoulders, he gave her a wink before turning away. Kate focused her eyes on the ancient stone floor, hoping no one had noticed her own smile.

Alexis turned red then looked down as a tight smile crossed her face. "I will keep him on task, Grandmother. You can be assured of it."

Grant glared at her then lifted his hand. A white spark

shot out of his palm and hit the atrium ceiling, sending a shower of sparks back down on him and Kate. "Listen up, all of you. No more attempts to meddle. I've linked myself and Detective Morgan to the ancients. Not a single one of you can alter either of our destinies or fates. Understood?"

A look of shock filtered across the Council's faces. Damian leaned forward, glaring at Grant. "She hasn't completed The Joining," he hissed, "She doesn't deserve—"

Lilith raised her finger and Damian stopped speaking. She stared at the pair for a moment, her eyes gleaming with interest. "Bold option, Grant Anderson. Perhaps The Joining is not Katherine's fate."

"L—Lilith, stop speaking blasphemy," Damian sputtered. "Every member of this family completes The Joining. She will complete it or die. There is no other option."

The opposing family seemed equally shocked by Grant's actions. Jonathan Anderson stood up, pointing his finger at Grant. "What have you done?"

The members of the Morgan family looked on with faint amusement. Jake Riley's eyebrows shot up and, for a second, Kate thought she saw admiration flash across his face. Marion Anderson Lowell paled, her appearance a mix of horror and revulsion.

Grant glared at Jonathan. "I made a choice, Grandfather. There will be no more interfering in my life, and this will protect her from attempts as well. If our destinies are to be determined, it will be done alone and without interference from either family."

Alexis looked at him, panic filling her face. "Grant, are you insane? You've taken at least fifty years off your life force by severing one of your ties from the family."

Grant ignored her, choosing to address his remarks to the Council. "Are we done here? Ambrose has a task force to assemble and we have a murder to solve."

"A man not afraid to stand up for his convictions. Admirable, though a bit foolish," Damian commented. He stroked his chin, looking between Grant and Kate. "Know that this declaration does not dissolve existing avowals already in play. Her mother promised her to The Joining, so his sacrifice cannot take its place." Glancing over at Jonathan, he added. "I believe there are additional intrigues on your side as well." Satisfied the business at hand was concluded, he slowly nodded. "Very well. As they say, let the games begin. We will reconvene in four days, at the end of the conference. I look forward to a welcome resolution. Petty family squabbles don't become us."

"Wait," Leland said. "Why are my son and I here? What role do you want us to play?"

"Come forward."

While they approached the Council, Kate grabbed Grant's arm. "What did you do?"

"Ended the meddling."

"They said something about your sacrifice. What did you do?"

He sighed and turned his back, partially shielding them from the Council's glare. "Our families are linked to the Council by more than just blood. They dictate our futures, in exchange for our powers and lifespan. Severing that tie means they can't come after you and you're free to live your life without their direct influence."

"And what did that cost you?"

He shrugged his shoulders, staring out into space. "No one should live forever, Kate. It's as unnatural as giving power to one group of people and letting them decide the fate of millions. I'm free and so are you. True freedom is worth taking a chance, and it's never a sacrifice."

"But why? Why sacrifice part of yourself for me?"

"Because trust begins with knowing someone believes in you. I believe in you Kate."

From the front of the room, a large chime reverberated, cutting their conversation short. Glancing back, Grant ambled over to the Anderson side of the room as Damian stood. "Leland Morgan, you and your son Lucas are in running for your grandmother's seat on the Council. Of course, this won't be officially announced until the ball tomorrow, but as contenders, we thought it best that you know the players in this investigation."

Leland paled and, for a second, Kate thought he was going to bow at Damian's feet. Clutching his son, he nodded excitedly, the jubilation on his face making her sick to her stomach. "Thank you, Uncles, Grandmother. This honor is humbling beyond belief."

The members of the Council nodded, their figures turning transparent as they faded from sight.

At the last second, Lilith raised a finger and pointed at Kate. "Katherine, do not disappoint me. I expect a satisfying resolution to this disgrace." With her final words, the Council disappeared.

CHAPTER 14

You'd better find my brother's murderer or so help me—"Ray Morgan started.

"Or what, Ray?" Kate replied. The departure of the Council ignited life in the arboretum. Birds sang again. The fountain restarted, sending a cascade of water into the granite basin that housed the majestic stone figures from days of old. She looked around the cavernous room, now teeming with the associates who had been allowed to return following the Council's departure. "What are you going to do, Ray? Murder me? Go ahead and try. I'm used to dodging our stupid family assassination attempts."

"I'll make your life a living hell."

"I was born into this family. I'm already in a living hell."

Jake Riley let out a laugh and received a dirty look from Ray for his troubles.

Kate glanced over at him then past to Grant and Alexis. They were having their own heated discussion on the Anderson side of the floor. "Or better still," she continued, "why don't you tell me who Gus was planning on killing before his demise? Perhaps his intended victim got the better of him."

"Why don't you remember who the victim is here? My brother was innocent."

"Please. Your brother was a blackmailer and common street thug. He may have worn fancy suits, but he had all the class of a schoolyard bully."

Ray sneered at her then paused, as if a great idea just occurred to him. Lifting his palms up, he aimed his hands toward the sky. There was a boom, similar to a thunderclap, followed by an unusual sound. Kate looked around, trying to find the source of the churning noise that filled the room. Slow and steady, it quickly increased in rhythm and speed. Before she could investigate further, a large sheet of water rose from the fountain. Kate let out a gasp as the tsunami crashed down on her.

She felt as if she had been plunged into the middle of a whirlpool. Tumbling around and around, she struggled against the force and pressure of the water. Ever changing in shape, it moulded itself to her movements. If she tried to swim upward the surface was just a few inches above her. Below, and it expanded to meet the pavement, never giving an opportunity for escape.

"Oye!" yelled Jake, rushing toward her suspended figure. "Let her go."

Somehow, between the struggle to hold her breath and find a way out, she felt Grant's alarm. "Kate," he yelled. "Hang on. I'm coming, hang on."

"No, that's not a good idea." Alexis extended her index finger and waved it in a circle above her head. Grant charged forward, only to be thrown back by an invisible wall. He leapt to his feet and pointed at her. "Take it down."

"No, that's a Morgan family matter, and we don't interfere."

"She can't defend herself. She's going to drown."

Alexis shrugged her shoulders. "Survival of the fittest, Grant. That's how family thrives."

Grant swore and extended his hands, trying to find a way to disrupt the barrier. His panic rose as he watched her struggling body slow, then stop.

She was trapped in the water and, no matter how she tried, it refused to let her go.

Jake glanced between Kate and the rest of the family. They stood there, mesmerized by the spectacle, yet no one thought to help her escape. He glared at his cousin. "What, are you deaf? I said, let her go, Ray."

"She wasn't kidding about being a survivor," Ray mused, looking up at her as if she was an expensive painting. It was obvious, as her body fought to expel the last of her air, she had only seconds left. He turned to Jake and smiled. "Pretty good skills underwater, but as you can see, no one can hold their breath forever."

Jake's arm shot out, catching Ray in the center of his Adam's apple. "Bloody bugger."

He dropped to the ground, writhing in pain, his hold on the water broken. With a loud crash, the bubble burst and Kate fell to the ground, gasping for air.

"Kate!" yelled Grant, sprinting to her side.

"You all right, luv?" asked Jake.

Ray let out a roar and struggled to his feet, his face red with rage. Jake rolled his eyes and flicked his hand. There was a flash of crimson light and Ray disappeared.

"Where—where did he go?" Kate gasped.

She felt Grant's hand on her back, and a tingling warmth spread throughout her body. Suddenly breathing became much easier.

"Dumped him in the lake behind the resort. The guy needs to cool off." Jake frowned, making a clicking sound with his teeth. "What kind of powers do you have, anyway? For a member of this family, you're bloody rubbish at protecting yourself."

"I—I can read minds."

"What? That's it? How the hell have you survived this long?"

With Grant's help, she staggered to her feet. "Wits and avoidance. Besides, I'm quite capable of defending myself against normal people."

"Yeah? Well, this lot isn't exactly normal, are they?"

Grant glared at him. "Give the kid a break, okay? She didn't realize until this morning that she could have more than one power."

Kate opened her mouth to object then thought better of it. Jake had the look of a man who had experienced the good and bad that life had to offer, and she suspected that Grant was the same. In the grand scheme of their families and the age of the universe, she probably was a kid to both of them.

From behind Grant, Alexis appeared with a bored look on her face. "Are we finished here? Ambrose is welcoming his team as we speak. There is forty minutes until the bridges close, so he wants us to head over to the command center."

"Go away, Alexis,"

"We have to go, Grant."

"After the stunt you pulled, not with me."

"But—"

"But nothing. You get one warning. You try to control me again, and it won't be pretty."

"The conference has begun. Any in-family fighting that doesn't result in death is fair game. Don't punish me because I'm following the rules."

"I'll deal with you later. Go away."

Alexis pursed her lips together and shot a withering look at them all.

Kate watched as she stormed out of the arboretum with all semblance of her previous grace gone.

Grant pulled out his phone and quickly keyed a message.

"Who are you calling?"

"If we're going to be trapped here, I can use a reinforcement of my own," he muttered. "Are you sure you're okay? You don't need to be at Ambrose's strategy meeting. I think you've had enough for one day."

"I'm fine, but I need to clean up first. Like I said before, this is nothing new to me." Kate pulled off her shoes and tossed them in a nearby trash can. Her wet clothes were starting to itch and all she really wanted was a hot shower to wash this latest debacle away. "Give me an hour?"

He nodded his reply. Looking at Jake, he extended his

hand. "Glad to have you on the team. Can I buy you a drink?"

"Definitely, but there's a bloke or two I need to contact before the bridges close. Rain check?"

"Sounds good." Grant turned to Kate, concern filling his eyes again. "You're sure you're okay?"

She grinned. "I'm fine, I'm fine. Just another day at the office and nothing a shower won't cure. See you soon?"

He smiled, brushing away a strand of wet hair that clung to the side of her face. Bending down, he lightly kissed her on the lips, and another surge of warmth filled her soul.

She sighed and opened her eyes as he whispered in her ear, "Just a taste of things to come."

"Hold you to that," she murmured with a grin.

With a wink and the turn of his heel, he was gone. Kate watched him leave then turned toward her own room, so preoccupied with her thoughts, she barely noticed Jake walking behind her.

"Oye, our rooms are that way."

"Not mine. I'm in the Anderson wing."

He looked at her with surprise, his stride catching for a moment. "Shacking up with the boyfriend already? Wow, you do have a death wish."

Kate slowed her pace and allowed him to catch up. Once out of the arboretum, the cool evening air was a welcome change from the warm humidity. "I'm in a room across the hall from him. Not with him. And he's not my boyfriend."

"Coulda' fooled me. So you hate the family so much you're bunking in enemy territory?"

They entered the expansive lobby, ignoring the curious glances from surrounding onlookers. "After a day like to-day, can you blame me? Two family dustups and I've been here less than twenty-four hours."

"Well, near as I see it, that smart mouth of yours is what's getting you in trouble. Stop poking the bear, and maybe it won't bite."

Kate's first reaction was to disagree but, after a moment, she conceded that he had a point. "Yeah, well, if you're such a fan of the family, why not keep the Morgan last name?"

Jake shrugged his shoulders. "Wanted a change. Was a Morgan for over three hundred years. Thought I would break with tradition and choose something different. Besides Jake Riley sounds much more exciting than Jake Morgan, and I fancy myself an exciting kind of guy."

"Well, you certainly are something."

"So are you. Something headed toward death if you don't button that trap and learn some defensive moves." He looked around, spying the manager next to the grand piano, giving the player instructions. "Oye! Innkeeper!" When the man looked up, Jake beckoned. "Yeah, you, over here!"

"His name is Mr. Poppet."

He let out a laugh as the man approached. "What? Seriously? That's a British term."

"Mr. Riley. What can I do for you?" Poppet glanced at Kate and then did a double take.

"Well, my dear Poppet, if you haven't heard, I'm on a special task force, investigating the nastiness that has occurred in this fine establishment. I need you to move my accommodations like my cousin here to a more neutral ground."

"Well, I—"

Kate put a hand on his arm. "Now hang on, Jake,"

"You see Poppet," he continued, ignoring her, "I have to try and stay impartial until we find out who is behind the mayhem and, by the looks of how things are going, it could get very ugly around here. So do a lad a favor and move me down the hall from my cousin."

The manager looked from Kate to Jake to the thick wad of bills suddenly thrust into his hand. "Yes, sir. We don't have anything in the same corridor but the presidential suite is available across the courtyard."

"Excellent, excellent, my man. Presidential suite it is.

Oh, and I will need a few spare rooms for my mates who should be arriving in a few hours."

"The suite is in a contained building with four separate rooms," Poppet replied nervously. "I'll go see to your luggage and personal effects."

"Wonderful, Poppet. I'll be in the bar if you need to find me."

Poppet stopped then turned back in their direction. "Can I have someone fetch you a towel, Detective?"

Riley shooed him away. "Oh, she's fine. Just practicing for the wet T-shirt contest we have coming up."

Poppet looked confused, then he walked away, muttering something under his breath.

Kate rolled her eyes. "Unbelievable. Asshole and saint all rolled into one. Is effortless charm one of your gifts too?"

He looked at her and, for a minute, haunting regret flashed across his face. "No darling, more like a hard-earned skill from years of dodging scrapes. Pretty soon, we're all going to be targets, and I like to know who has my back before the knives really come out."

Kate sighed. "Wouldn't we all?"

With a nod goodbye, she headed toward her room and the sanctuary of a hot shower. Almost to the end of the deserted corridor and she stopped, half wondering if her room key would still work. Taking her chances, she pulled the card from her pocket and felt it for water damage. The pliable piece of plastic didn't look any worse for wear. Absently, she flipped it between her fingers and trudged the last two hundred feet toward her room.

Ponderous thoughts filled her mind. Front and center of a murder investigation that could affect the future of humanity. She had dodged the Council and her family all of her life, only to be in the spotlight with a target on her back.

And what of Mark's revelation that she and Grant had known each other fifteen years ago? Why couldn't she remember meeting him? It certainly cleared up some of the mystery surrounding Grant. If they had known each other previously, this explained why her only thought was running away with him and never looking back.

Kate sighed and put her key in the lock. First swipe and the door remained shut. She leaned her head against the door with resignation, not having the strength to walk the long road back to the front desk.

"Come on. Open," she murmured.

Second swipe and still nothing. Banging her forehead against the solid door didn't work either.

"Why can't I have the power to pick electronic locks?" As if in response, she felt a chill run up her spine. Opening her eyes, she cautiously looked around, her body tensing for another attack. A glance to her left revealed an empty corridor and a weak smile crossed her lips. "Get a grip, Morgan," she muttered to herself. "You're turning paranoid."

"What are you doing out here?"

Kate let out a shriek of surprise and spun around, her back to the door, fists closed, and her body in defense mode. Grant leaned against the hallway behind her, his arms crossed and an amused look on his face.

She wanted to relax, but something held her back. She blinked a couple of times, willing her body to move but her legs remained planted in front of her door.

"My key won't work. I think it's waterlogged. I have to go back to the front desk and get a new one."

Grant shook his head and extended his hand. "Let me try. I'm sure I can get it to work."

Kate gripped the key, the sides of the plastic card cutting into the palm of her hand. She extended her fist then, fighting back the taste of bile in her mouth, pulled her hand back. What was she feeling? Why was she having this reaction around him? She had never felt this way before, but then could she really trust her feelings? A week ago she didn't even know him.

"Come on, baby, hand over the key. You're wet and probably freezing. Let me warm you up with my love."

He grabbed her hand, gently prying at the plastic in her fist. Kate blinked and looked away. Her mind was clouded and racing. She couldn't think straight. He was standing in front of her, wasn't he? He looked the same, but something was different. She was sure she could figure it out if she just had a minute to think.

She looked up at him, felt his hand caressing hers. He smiled as he rubbed her fingers, gently opening up her hand. Slowly his index finger shifted to her wrist and grazed the bracelet given to her by Sapphire.

He jumped back as a blue flash shocked him. Kate looked up in surprise as the memory of Saffi's warning cut through the fog in her brain. '*It will heighten your instincts and make you wary of evil's eye.*'

He let out a low whistle. "See, baby? Sparks between us. We were meant to be together. Now, let's get you out of those wet clothes."

Kate looked down at the key in her hand then back at him and smiled. The confusion was gone, replaced with one clear thought. This was not her Grant. "How about a better idea?" she replied. "Why don't we go to your room? It's just across the hall."

Grant looked around at the row of doors on both sides of the hallway. He grinned and wagged his finger at her, but before he could answer, Kate heard a voice from behind her. Grant's voice.

"Yeah, Grant, why don't you show her your room?" he said dryly "You seem pretty concerned about getting her out of those wet clothes. Wouldn't want her to catch a chill."

The other Grant raised his hands, shrugging his shoulders, and slowly backed away. Cocking his head, his expression read a combination of chagrin and delight. "She's the whole package, that she is. Can't blame a guy for trying."

"Wanna bet?" Grant replied. Lifting his right hand, he yelled, "*Verum Rev!*"

The other Grant fell backward, his body contorting and

changing before her eyes. Before the transformation could finish, the imposter raised both hands and a flash of blue light blinded them both.

Grant grabbed Kate, throwing her to the ground, absorbing the blast with his back. She tried to turn, to see who the fake really was, but all she saw were stars. The smell of Grant's aftershave and sulfur filled her senses. Blinking furiously, she sat up, trying to rub sight back into her eyes.

"Jeez, are you okay?" she asked, trying to see around him.

"Yeah. That was just a parlor trick. No harm done."

"Who was that?"

Grant stood up, brushing some kind of soot off his pants. "Don't know. Didn't get a good look at him." He walked over to the spot where the imposter had stood and bent down, touching the area with his hand.

"What did you say to him?" she asked.

"Verum Rev, it's an abbreviation for '*Verum Revelatum*.' Latin for 'truth revealed.'"

"I'll have to remember that one."

"It's an oldie but a goodie. Stops an imposter in his tracks."

Kate tried to rise to her feet, but her legs felt like jelly. After her second try, she gave up and crawled to her door, pushing her back against the hard mahogany, grateful for the solid smoothness of the wood. This felt real. She needed to feel something solid and real around her. Pulling her knees up to her chest, she rubbed her limbs with her hands, trying to inject feeling into her legs.

"I don't know what would've happened if you hadn't come along. I don't know what I would have done."

Grant looked at her, complete confidence filling his gaze. "Sure you do. You knew it wasn't me."

Kate slowly nodded her head. "At first, I wasn't sure, but the cheesy one liners gave him away," she quipped.

She'd known instinctively that it wasn't him and the bracelet confirmed it. Still, she didn't think she would be as lucky if someone else tried that again.

Grant pulled out his phone and relayed details of the encounter to the Zion team. Satisfied with the response, his mood lifted slightly. "And you know I'd never call you, 'baby.'" After a moment, he grinned. "Baby."

Kate scowled at him. "Better remember that, cupcake."

Grant let out laugh and walked over to her door, brushing the doorframe with his hand. For a moment, rows and rows of symbols filled the doorway, only to disappear back into the wood. "Protection symbols," he replied to her unasked question.

Satisfied that his charm would stick, he extended his hand. Without a word between them, she handed him her key card. He tried it in the lock a few times before tucking it into his back pocket. Reaching down, he lifted her into his arms. Striding across the hall, he opened his door and carried her inside.

Kate stood in the middle of his room. It was identical to hers with a combined living and bedroom off a large bathroom. "How did you know to come back?"

He emerged from the bathroom, the sound of a shower running in the background. "I came looking for you. You said you'd be an hour and after two had passed—"

Kate's mouth dropped open. "What do you mean an hour? Even with the walk to my room, I was only gone ten minutes."

Grant stopped in his tracks then quietly cursed. "Time and appearance manipulator. He must be one powerful son of a bitch." Shaking his head, he headed for the door. "Take your shower, don't leave here, and don't let anyone in. I'll get you some clothes and a new key for your room."

Before she could reply, he was out the door and she was alone. Kate looked around, relishing the safety and silence of his room. She sighed and padded around her surroundings. He wasn't a messy person, in fact, the room looked hardly lived in. Fresh fruit and water sat next to a paper grocery bag on a small round table. A series of large, black suitcases sat neatly in the corner. She suspected that if she opened the bureau drawers, she would find tidily folded clothes.

The large closet between the rooms contained a few suits, hidden nicely in garment bags. In the bathroom, she stripped off her clothes, tossing them on the floor and noting the designer toiletries spread efficiently across the granite countertop. Stepping into the hot shower, she sighed with relief as the pounding water soothed her aching muscles.

Minutes flew by as she let the heat and steam do their magic. The water cascaded down her body, washing away the shampoo in her hair and the lovely smelling body wash across her skin. One thing the water couldn't wash away were her memories of the last twenty-four hours. Images of mangled and desecrated bodies filled her mind. The hard facts of her stay were burned into her memory.

Her DNA, the cells that made up her body, were infused with programming from Satan and his demons. All around her, thoughts invaded her senses—unconscious confessions of heinous acts casually tossed around, as if her relatives were planning their daily "to do" lists, like ordinary people.

Instead of picking up the kids from soccer or remembering to get milk from the store, these thoughts were hideous and grotesque. '*Manipulate John X into thinking his wife is having an affair. He's a prime candidate for murder-suicide. Work on another insider trading tip and pin it on poor Sally J. She doesn't have the temperament to survive public humiliation and ten years in jail. Once she's out of the way, her family land can be sold to a developer for a hundred times its worth.*'

Kate blinked back tears, trying to turn off the images in her head. On the one hand, she had an obligation to serve and protect but, on the other hand, the onslaught of thoughts was destroying her soul—one small piece at a time.

Unable to control the tears, she slid down the marble wall of the shower, knees drawn to her chest, her body racked with sobs from all of the pain, the anguish caused by her family. How could she fight that power? The family influence was everywhere. Was there anyone in the world with the ability to stop them?

"Kate, what's wrong?" Through her tears, she saw Grant kneeling in front of her. He was oblivious to the water that poured over his shoulders, soaking through his shirt and plastering down his hair. "You don't have to worry about the attacks. I'll protect you."

Her face contorted in pain and his heart ached to see her this way.

"N—no, that doesn't concern me," she stammered. "It's those people, those innocents that can't escape my family's reach. How can I protect them all?"

His thoughts went from concern to confusion. "You were assaulted twice in one day."

She shrugged her shoulders. "Welcome to my world. For me, that's normal."

He shook his head in amazement then brushed the strands of wet hair away from her face. How could she be a Morgan when she cared more about innocents than herself? What was it about this strong woman, who could be so reckless yet so caring at the same time? Leaning into her, he kissed her hard, taking his time to explore every part of her mouth. Her selflessness and caring made his heart swell with pride. Her life was in danger every minute and yet she cared only for the chance to help others, even if it meant death for herself.

Kate responded to his kiss, pulling herself closer to him, wrapping her arms around his neck. Feeling the collar of his shirt, she tried to pull away but he would have none of it, refusing to let her out of his arms.

"Grant. Your clothes are soaked—"

"Screw the clothes," he murmured before pulling her mouth to his again.

He grabbed at the front of his shirt, pulling it open and off, oblivious to the ripping sound of buttons and starched cotton. Kate sighed her approval as the water rippled over his muscles and down the sides of his taut stomach. Dragging at the buckle of his belt, she used her legs to push down his trousers, freeing him from the bonds of his designer clothes.

Naked and caressed by steam and sweat, they explored each other through heat and haze. He started from her top and, using his mouth, gently worked his way down her neck to the sides of her breasts. Kate gasped, the ache in her building, her back arching with need for him, feeling his mouth on her, kissing her ribcage, teasing her until her breasts swelled and ached under his touch.

Continuing his exploration down her body, he slid one hand over her wrist, pinning her to the shower floor. His mouth kissing her stomach, she bucked her hips as she felt his fingers explore her. One finger, then two entered her, making her pant uncontrollably.

The need, the anticipation was killing her. Feeling his fingers caress and discover had her itching with eagerness. She needed him inside her, driving away the horror of her reality with his love.

"Grant, stop teasing—" she gasped. Her hands reached up to his buttocks, pulling down his body, beckoning his hardness toward her.

He smiled and shook his head, flexing his abs to keep his body from hers. His need outstripped hers, but the desire to see her come apart in his arms, to succumb to his touch, held him at bay. They both wanted this badly. He didn't know what history they had, but this felt right. It felt more right than anything he had experienced in his four hundred years of life upon this earth.

She gasped with delight as his fingers re-entered her, this time driving, with a purpose and determination that threatened to push her over the edge. His groans of pleasure excited her all the more as she felt his struggle to control his movements, to fight the desire to ravish her with a longing that was poised to overpower them both.

"Let's get you to bed," he said, pulling away from her and lifting her to her feet.

"No, please, I can't wait. I need you now."

He stared into her stunning blue eyes, the water pouring down her face, her expression desperate for him. A low growl reverberated from his throat and he grabbed her buttocks, forcing open her legs and pulling them around his waist. Entering her with a violence he found impossible to control, he pushed against her, driving with a force and fury he didn't think was possible. "God, you're so tight, Kate. Am I hurting you? I—"

Her moans of ecstasy interrupted him. "No, not at all. Please," she pleaded.

Her obsession for him overwhelmed her. She felt like her skin was on fire as pleasure surged over her like a tidal wave. With a murmur of agreement, his movements quickened, her body filling and stretching with a sensuous dance of hard and smooth, a rhythm of parries and thrusts that ignited her primal urges.

"Faster, harder. Please," she begged. "Don't be gentle. Take me, Grant. Take all of me,"

Feeling his lips on hers, his arms encircling her waist, heightened her passion. Not realizing that he had moved them, she felt the cold granite countertop against her bottom as he leaned her back and lifted her legs over her head, using leverage to their advantage.

Pushing her to new heights, he thrust deeper and harder. She gasped. Yes, this is what she needed, craved. Joining his rhythm, she gloried in watching his muscles ripple with each powerful motion. His hands on her made her hunger for more.

Her mind went wild with desire as she pushed herself up and onto him. She needed him more than air, more than life itself. Kate lifted her hips again, wrapping her legs around his taut waist. Pulling him to her, she raked her fingers against his shoulders, unable to contain her pleasure. His mouth on her hardened nipples was the final straw. Kate gasped then let out a series of screams. She could feel the excitement from him, the need to see her come glistened in his eyes.

"Damn it, Kate. Yes," he said, barely able to mutter the words. "Don't hold back, honey."

Grant felt her explosion crash over him. Unable to hold back his need, he let out a long moan, every muscle in his body contorting uncontrollably as he shuttered and poured himself into her. The impact of his release, the violence of pure pleasure stunned him and he gasped, drawing in long breaths, trying to get his body back under control. With waning strength, he pulled her to him and, in three strides, collapsed on the bed, his exhausted muscles barely able to hold them both upright.

For a moment, they lay together, their bodies unwilling to let go even as their breathing slowed. Kate could feel his heart pumping, a sheen of sweat covered him, despite the coolness of the room slowing their passion.

With a frown, she murmured a small complaint as he withdrew from her then flipped her around, unwilling to let her escape from the safety of his arms.

She glanced up at him, brushing away the hair that swept into his eyes. "Well, that was unbelievably—"

"Amazing?"

She grinned, nodding her approval. "To say the least."

"Too bad we have to get ready for dinner."

Kate groaned and shook her head. The pleasure of sleep beckoned. The last thing she wanted was another round of politics and bad company, despite the chateau's excellent food. One eye opened, she noticed that he had retrieved the overnight bag from her room and wisely had left the gargantuan steamer trunk from her mother alone. "No dinner. No committees. Too tired. Just want to spend the night with you and no one else."

From behind her, she heard a chuckle. Turning over, she watched as he crawled into a seated position, the silk bed sheets falling nicely around the six pack abs and sculpted chest. Grant reached over to the phone at the side of the bed and pushed a button. His conversation was short and to the point. "Yes. Do you have a tasting menu for room service? Excellent, as well as a bottle of your best Bordeaux."

Hanging up the phone he leaned over to her, giving her full view of his manliness. Kate admired the long, thick definition of his limbs, barely noticing a light tug at the sheets that had her in his arms again. "Forty minutes until dinner arrives," he told her. "Happy?"

Tracing a finger down his chest to do a little exploring of her own, she sighed, her face erupting in a big grin. "Will be after a second round."

CHAPTER 15

The morning sun brought a mixture of reluctance and resignation to Kate. Reluctance to leave Grant's bed, having found such joy in his company, and resignation because today, she would begin the investigation into Gus's death and uncover a treasure trove of Morgan secrets that would undoubtedly lead to more nightmares.

Glancing through her welcome packet gave her a wealth of insight into the Morgan agenda. Most of the senior Morgans were in closed-door meetings with the Council. For the less important family members, there were plenty of workshops for her to dig through and search for the truth.

First, she thought, as she stepped out of the shower and into a fluffy robe, was breakfast with her mother. She glanced over at Grant, sleeping peacefully while managing to hog the entire bed. At six in the morning, now was as good as ever to crack open the mysterious trunk and see what morning horrors lay inside.

Trying not to make any noise, she took the packet and softly padded over to the door, gently prying it open. The corridor was empty, the only indication of life in the form of newspapers in front of the doors. Quietly, she closed his door, noting that they had four neighbors down the length of the hallway, then walked over and jammed the new key into the electronic lock of her door.

Kate opened the door and stuck her head inside. The room was as she left it the previous morning, except the bed had been made and her mother's trunk left in the middle of the sitting room. Tossing her packet on the coffee table, Kate walked over to a small safe seated in an armoire next to the television. She punched in a few numbers, then breathed a sigh of relief when she opened the door. Her gun and badge were still there. While the FBI loaner was appreciated, nothing beat the feel of her own gun. Looking around, her anxiety eased. Nothing in the room had been touched. She reached into the safe and pulled out her weapon.

Kate walked over to the coffee table and sat on it, her gun close in case of emergency. Staring at the trunk, she wished she knew some kind of incantation or spell that would open the luggage for her. After breakfast, tracking down Cousin Lucy would be her first priority. She hadn't seen her in a while, save a chance encounter on a Manhattan street about five years ago. As far as Kate knew, they were still on good terms.

"What exactly do you think is in that trunk?" Grant was leaning against the doorway with a grin on his face. He was fully dressed, his hair wet and tousled, making him look positively boyish.

"Knowing my Mother, a portal straight to hell."

He walked over and leaned down to kiss her. Taking her mouth with his, he made his kiss deep and sensual, leaving a taste of mint toothpaste and desire that had her forgetting everything but her need for him.

"Morning. You left me in bed, alone," he murmured.

"Mmmm, hardest decision I ever had to make."

He grinned again and sat down beside her. For several moments, she stared at the trunk then sighed. He looked down at her agenda packet, now strewn on the coffee table, then back at her with a quizzical grin. "Do you want me to open it for you?"

Kate shook her head then picked up her gun and walked over to the trunk.

"You really think you're going to need that?"

She shrugged her shoulders. "Well, until I figure out some nifty powers like you, it's all I got."

Grant looped his hands around one of his knees and leaned back, an amused look on his face. "You know, Ambrose's team went through it and it came back clean. I think it's safe to open."

"Ambrose's team doesn't know my mother."

With her gun in one hand, Kate tugged on the first of four brass latches. With a dull thud, it popped open, releasing front of the trunk. Stepping back, she was pleasantly surprised to see the trunk just sit there, like any normal storage container. Latch two, three, and four undid just as easily, and the truck swung open into a small wardrobe, with hanging clothes on one side and tiers of drawers on the other.

"So any enemies lurking in there?" He was scanning the Morgan daily agenda, careful not to touch any of the papers, for fear that his find would disappear.

Kate reached in and pulled out several outfits. "Let's see. Gucci, Ferragamo, Prada."

"Some of my best friends," he replied with a smirk.

A pair of Manolo Blahnik heels and black lacy underwear caught his attention. "You should definitely wear that. In fact, I think you should only wear that. Now."

Kate held them up and feigned a look of sadness. "You don't like me in my birthday suit?"

Grant paused then casually waved his index finger. The belt on her robe came loose revealing a part of her nakedness. A satisfied murmur rose from his throat as his eyes drank in every curve. "Definitely your best look, but I'd be happy to assist should you decide to expand your wardrobe."

She walked over to him, flush with need and desire. "Why Special Agent Anderson, you failed to mention the abilities of your fingers. Perhaps we need to have a discussion about your powers."

His eyes flashed with intense craving as she stood partially naked in front of him. Slowly, he extended his finger and dragged it up between her legs. Kate gasped as a delicious pressure traveled up her inner thighs. His other hand reached into her robe and, cupping her bottom, pulled her closer to his waiting mouth.

Lightly brushing her navel with his lips, he murmured, "Discussions can wait till later."

Kate gasped in delight as he trailed a line of kisses down her stomach and toward her thigh. She pulled his head closer to her, raking her nails lightly against his scalp and through his wet hair.

"God, you smell so good," he murmured as the robe peeled off one of her shoulders, "I really wish we didn't have to work today."

Kate was about to agree when a thump at her door interrupted her. This was followed by the sound of a thud, then a rapid fire series of sounds that almost resembled knocking.

"What the hell, now?" she said with a sigh.

Closing her robe and picking up her gun, she headed for the door. Pulling it open, she aimed directly for the source of the noise.

"Oye, easy there, coz. Top of the morning to you too."

Jake was standing in the middle of the hallway with Golden Delicious apples strewn around him.

"Jake, what the hell are you doing?"

"Trying to get your attention, luv."

She sighed and lowered her gun. "Why don't you knock like a normal person?"

He flipped an apple in the air and shot her a look. "Oye. Stupid. I tried. You've got some kind of voodoo thing on your door that won't let me within two feet of it." He held up the fruit. "You must not have a grudge against produce because these sail right through that invisible barrier."

Kate turned and looked at Grant. He shrugged his shoulders. "Well, at least we know it works. Maybe a bit too well."

"Jake, come in."

"What do you think I am, a bloody vampire? You can't invite me in. It doesn't work that way." Jake took out a pocket knife. Cutting off a piece of his fruit, he popped it into his mouth and extended his hand. His palm hit an invisible wall, causing sparks to shoot in mid-air. Taking the remaining apple, he tossed it at her and smirked. "See? Here's a better idea. Why don't you come out?"

She caught the fruit and felt a surge of electricity coursing through it. It felt like the current she experienced whenever Grant touched her. The barrier that protected her was linked to him. She looked at the apple somberly and then back at Jake. If anyone else figured this out, Grant would be a target as well. "Give me five minutes."

She turned to Grant and looked at him. "Jake's right. I should get dressed and you better get to your breakfast. We're going to meet up later, right?"

He looked past her to the Brit who was pacing impatiently in the hallway. Kissing her on the forehead, he gestured toward the open door, "You sure, you're going to be okay with him?"

"Hey, he helped me yesterday with Ray."

Her reply seemed to satisfy him for the moment. "Fine. You guys follow your leads, and we'll meet up at noon to compare notes."

He turned to leave and she grabbed him by the arm. "You be careful. Not everyone on your side is thinking angelic thoughts. I'm worried someone might come after you."

He smiled and gave her a wink. "Sure you're a Morgan? You seem more like an Anderson to me."

She grinned and held up her gun. "Maybe in another life."

"Maybe in this one." Grant kissed her hard then turned and headed toward the hallway. Scooping up one of the apples, he took a bite and gestured to Jake. "She's your partner. I hold you responsible if anything happens to her. Got it?"

Jake held up his hands. "Don't judge a Morgan by his cover. She's safe with me, mate."

Fifteen minutes later, Kate emerged, dressed in a soft ensemble of trousers, blouse, and complimenting blazer. Within one of the drawers, she had found a comfortable set of flats.

Jake looked her up and down. It wasn't the bag or the shoes that interested him the most. It was the nine millimeter attached to her hip.

"You know that gun is prohibited, yeah? And, anyway, it isn't going to do you much good."

"Well, since you don't think much of my powers, for now it's my new best friend."

Jake stopped her in the hallway. "Okay, look. Neither one of us is happy with this situation. Hell, I'd rather be back slogging it as a DI than here with you lot."

"DI? Detective Inspector in Britain, right? Is that your present title?"

"No, Don't have one."

"Then what's your background?"

He grinned and shrugged his shoulders. "Just call me a man of leisure."

Kate frowned and stared at him. She didn't like to go probing into people's thoughts but when they were acting like a dick, she minded less. "You used to be with British police, then you were recruited by MI6 and your current cover is a business man."

"Hey, no fair. People's thoughts should be private."

"People should also be respectful and pleasant, so eye for an eye."

"All right, all right. Truce. I'll trust you not to go messing through my brain, if you will trust me not to steer you wrong."

"Well, that's a bold statement from a Morgan. I thought we were genetically programmed to steer others the wrong way."

"So here's a quick lesson from life. Not everything is

black and white. The Andersons aren't angels and we aren't devils. At least not all of us. I don't go around every day, void of empathy and plotting the destruction of the girl at my local chip shop 'cause she got my order wrong."

"Well, the European side of the family must have changed because the American side is downright psychotic."

"Oh, come on, that's bull—"

Jake stopped speaking when he felt her hand on his arm, pulling him to a stop. They were just feet outside the meeting room where the Morgan breakfast was being held.

Kate paused at the open doorway with Saffi's bracelet making her wrist feel like it was on fire. "Don't move," she snapped at him. "Someone's up to something."

His expression suggested she was the one who was crazy. "Like what?"

Kate stared at the banquet room. There were three entrances to the meeting space. Every door was closed except this one. Every person entering the Morgan breakfast room used every door except this one. Slowly, she approached the doorway, looking for something that wasn't obvious to an untrained eye.

"Jake, can I borrow your pocket knife?"

He whipped it out of his pocket, clicking a rather nasty blade into place. Kate cradled the knife in her hands, taking a half step toward the door. She raised the blade to neck height, running it against something almost invisible that hung in mid-air.

Jake stepped toward her, peering at the knife. She was flexing the edge of the blade against a thin wire. "Jesus," he exclaimed, "that would have decapitated us."

Kate cut the wire with the knife. Instantly the burning on her wrist disappeared. "Decapitation no, slit throats, yeah. Welcome to the way we do things in America, Jake."

Anger coursed through his eyes. Gone was the jovial side, replaced by a storm of rage. "I get it now," he replied quietly. "Can I borrow your gun, Kate?"

With a quizzical look, she handed him back his knife and her gun. The mask of a nonchalant rogue had been ripped away and he was positively livid. Kate took a step back, unsure of what he would do next. Maybe she wasn't the only one in the family who had morals.

He headed for the nearest table and, with a single leap, stood in the middle of it. A group of associates squealed as china, cutlery, and food went flying everywhere. Raising the gun, he fired off several rounds into the ceiling. Instant silence filled the room.

"Right, you lot, listen up. You want to play dirty, well, you've pissed off the wrong bloke. You insufferable gits better start acting civil, or I will personally visit each one of you and take your heads off, got it?"

Lucas walked by and smirked. "What's the matter, Riley? Can't take a joke? If you've got the audacity to investigate us, you'd better be up for a little payback."

"You self-righteous American prick," Jake fired back. "The rest of you psychos feel the same way?" He glanced around at a room full of Morgan's, challenging anyone to defy Lucas.

The family sat there impassively, looking back at him. Kate detected a slight sense of fear, coming not from their family but from the associates. One of whom had organized the trap for them.

Jake nodded. "Fine, let's do it your way." He shoved the gun into the small of his back and raised his hands to the ceiling. The doors to the meeting room slammed shut. *"Qui fallere duplica, Morgana et all!"*

A brilliant flash of red sparks flew from his hands, raining down a sparkling mist onto everyone. The junior members of the family scurried and scuttled about, trying to avoid the impromptu rainfall. The senior members of the family rolled their eyes and went back to their breakfast. Kate looked up, feeling the cool air hit her. She glanced down at the back of her hands. For a moment her skin shimmered and a wave of vertigo hit her full on.

Jake leapt off the table, ignoring the dirty looks and crass comments of those who chose to remain in the room. "That'll show those ingrates."

"What did you just do?"

"Cursed everyone here." He paused for a moment. "Well, maybe not cursed so much as unleashed a Karmic mark."

"*Qui fallere duplica.* What does that mean?"

"Latin for 'those who deceive, receive.' So anyone who tries to pull a stunt on us is going to get back double what they gave. It should make everyone here think twice before trying to kill us again."

"Great. Now we won't get anyone to talk and I just lost my appetite."

"Not me, mate. A good death dodging always makes me hungry. Where's your mum? I want to meet her."

"You sure about that? She's over there, scowling at us. Hang on, I have something to do first." Kate gestured to several of Ambrose's men and pointed to a pretty blonde. Kate walked over to her, accompanied by the men. Pulling out her chair, she hoisted the blonde to her feet. "Jennifer Johnson, you are under arrest for the attempted murder of myself and Jake Riley. You have the right to remain silent. Anything you say can and will be used against you in a court of law."

"I'm innocent," she spat, "I didn't do anything."

"Your thoughts are telling me something different."

The girl looked at her, her eyes narrowing with suspicion. "That will never hold up in court."

"Maybe not, but a search of your room probably will. Take her to holding."

The officers dragged her away. "You're making a mistake," she screamed. "Turning on your own kind. You're going to burn in a special hell for betraying the family."

"Yeah, yeah, tell me something I don't already know."

Kate waved away the empty threat and pulled out a small notebook from her pocket. She jotted down the details their brief conversation for what she suspected would be the first of many reports.

Jake reappeared beside her, holding a heaping plate of food. "She tried to kill us?"

"Yeah, some combination of her and her employer."

"Who's that?"

"Let's say a quick hello and goodbye to my mom, then I'll introduce you to the first in a long line of relatives who probably want us dead."

"Mmmm, can't wait."

Kate walked up to her mother's table and sat down, pulling out a chair for Jake in the process. As usual her mother was holding court, with her sisters Alice and Annabelle at her side.

"Katherine," she said with a sniff, "I see you opened the trunk I sent. Much better than the thrift store ensemble you were wearing yesterday. I would have chosen the Jimmy Choos, though."

Kate sighed and poured herself a cup of coffee. "Thank you for the clothes, Mother. You have great taste, as always. This is Jake Riley, my partner while we conduct this investigation at the request of the Council. His father is Cousin Charles."

Elizabeth Morgan pursed her lips, looking Jake up and down with a healthy dose of dissatisfaction. Overriding a request from the Council was out of the question, but expressing her disgust was not. "Young man, it is impolite to jump on tables and threaten your relatives. You should be ashamed of yourself."

Jake paused in surprise, a fork of scrambled eggs frozen between his lips and the half empty plate they resided on. Carefully, he put the fork down and pushed the plate away, sitting back in his chair to get a better view of her mother. After a moment of reflection, he smiled. "With all due respect, Cousin Liz, sod off. Anyone who threatens me and my partner is going to get their comeuppance and my foot up his ass."

Kate choked back her coffee, stifling a laugh. Telling her mother off was stupid but brave. Her respect level for Jake jumped a thousand fold. The aunts, however, stared at him with looks of horror. "H—how dare you speak to your elders like that?" Alice sputtered. She threw her arms around her as if her actions would ward off his words.

Annabelle flailed her arms about, threatening to hit the waiter who had come by to take Kate's order. "I'm going to have a word with your grandfather about your behavior. Imagine, British filth with a Morgan pedigree. It's preposterous they even let you into this reunion."

Elizabeth held up her hands, trying to calm her siblings down. "Sisters, this is a prime example of why we had to fight for our freedom against the tyranny and treachery of England. Clearly after all these years, they still have no class and have not advanced above their peasant beginnings."

Jake shook his head in disbelief. "Is she seriously quoting garbage from the American Revolution? It's been hundreds of years."

"And we still claim victory from the red coat scum."

Kate sighed. "All right, Mother, don't forget who won our civil war, and it wasn't the South. Enough of the history lesson," she said. "Changing the subject, do any of you have insight into who might have killed Gus?"

"That poor, poor man," exclaimed Annabelle.

"Forced to endure such a horrific death, and to do that to his remains," Alice added, "Why, it's positively dreadful."

Kate glanced from aunt to aunt. They were shaking their head in a bizarre spectacle of fake sympathy. They were pretty good at hiding their true thoughts, however, she didn't need to mind read to know this was all for show.

"So no enemies? Cousin Gus was an angel?" Jake asked wearily.

There was a pause, then all of them nodded their heads. "No, no enemies that I know of," they exclaimed, almost in unison.

Jake stood up, tossing his fork down in disgust. "Well, thanks for nothing, ladies. So glad I wasted my time."

Kate stood up, grabbing the bacon from her just arrived plate of scrambled eggs, bacon, and hash browns. "Mother. Good to see you. Thanks again for the clothes, and I'm sure we'll run into each other," she said with a non-committal lightness that promised nothing. No sense in adding fuel to the fire.

"Darling, I hope you aren't planning on bringing your horrible cousin as your date to the ball tonight. The European side of the family would not be a good match for you."

Kate cursed under her breath. Somewhere in the agenda, she had read and forgotten about the Crystallise Ball. A charade of elegance and grace where, in addition to the opening and closing ceremonies, the Morgan's and Anderson's were expected to attend and play nice together.

"No Mother, creepy inbreeding doesn't interest me. I will not be bringing Jake as my date."

"Excellent, Katherine. The first sensible thing you've said since your arrival."

"I'm going to see if I can bag an Anderson."

For the first time since she was a child, she saw her mother stunned into silence. Her thoughts, however, were flying daggers, sailing toward Kate a mile a minute. Kate walked away with curse words of indignation flashing through her mind. Regardless of the hell she would pay, it felt good to defy her mother yet again. Chasing after Jake, she was left with only one thought. Better track down Cousin Lucy. Fast.

CHAPTER 16

"Y ou must be one with the Universe. Failure to align your energy will thwart all goals, abilities and opportunities."

Kate lurked in the doorway of the small meeting room, waiting for Cousin Lucy to finish her lecture on "Chakra Dynamics and Sustained Effect on the Body." The group was small, mostly composed of associates who were at the beck and call of one Morgan or another. It explained why the crowd kept shrinking and growing in relation to the number of vibrating smart phones.

Lucy was not quite a black sheep. She was more of a dark gray color, with a healthy touch of eccentric or, in Jules's words, crazy town.

She started off her life of notoriety quite successfully, first as a French jewel thief, then as a black widow, killing off her rich husbands who literally died for her. Over her three lifetimes, she was a countess, sentenced to the guillotine as part of the Marie Antoinette affair, then reinvented as some kind of British aristocrat, having to settle for the title of Lady, instead of Princess. In her third life she was Hollywood Royalty, having embarked on a successful film career in the 1940s and was preparing to make a comeback as the "great-granddaughter" of her former self.

Kate had to hand it to her, she knew how to stave off age. Almost four hundred years later, and she didn't look a day over twenty-five.

Jake poked his head in the door, crinkling his nose in disgust. "You promised me the head of the person who almost took ours. Is that her?"

"No, Laurelle is the one you want," Kate whispered. "Apparently she's meeting Lucy here for lunch, so I thought we could kill two birds with one stone."

"And the other bird is?"

"Figuring out my third power. I have mind reading, some kind of ability to rewind time to observe past events, and some unknown third one."

"So you're on your third life then? Rotten luck, ol' mum."

Kate grabbed him by the arm and towed him to a place in the back row. "I've led a very full couple of lives. I don't need to watch the centuries creep by in some desperate quest to dodge the natural order of things."

"Oye, not fair. Some of us have a reason for kicking around."

"And what would that be? There's only so much evil a person can inflict, even for a Morgan."

Jake shrugged his shoulders, "I keep telling you, shades of gray, Kate. Not every Morgan is bent on death and destruction."

Kate gritted her teeth as another memory forced itself into her brain. "That hasn't been my experience." She paused, wondering if she should tell him a memory so close to her heart. "I can trust you, right?"

"Absolutely, partner."

She nodded and plunged into her tale. "When I was a child, I had a dog named Chester. He was a beautiful retriever, the same age as me, and my constant companion. He kept me safe and was loyal to a fault, watching over me. When I was seven, I attended my first Morgan gathering with all the other members of Grandmother Lilith's family. It was exciting for me, getting to know the rest of my family, since I was an only child. One afternoon, we were exploring the property when Lucas, Larry, and Laurelle cornered us in the barn. Laurelle took a pellet gun and shot Chester in the spine, paralyzing him. Larry tied me up and made me watch while they took turns torturing him."

She turned over her wrists and showed Jake the scars of flesh that had once been torn and rubbed raw. "It took me four hours to free myself and seconds to grab the gun and shoot my best friend in the head, putting him out of his misery. When I went crying to my mother, she shrugged her shoulders and replied, "That's what Morgan's do, darling. Now get me another sweet tea."

"Jesus fucking Christ. That's horrible."

"That's the Morgan way, Jake," she replied bitterly. "If it wasn't playing into Satan's hands, I'd kill every last one of them and not think twice about it."

"Speak of the devil. Here comes one now."

They watched as Laurelle strutted up to the front of the room, interrupting a small group of admirers who were asking questions about the lecture. Lucy shooed them away then walked over to the low stage and gracefully swung herself up to a sitting position. She clapped her hands with excitement, looking back and forth between Kate and Laurelle as if she had a front row seat to the greatest show on earth.

"Wait till you hear about my morning, Luce," Laurelle complained. "One rival out of the picture and one that will not go. Ugh, you have no idea how hard it has been to get rid of Gerry."

She reached into her Louboutin bag, pulling out a compact and a thin stick of lipstick. Flipping open her mirror, she dabbed a vibrant red on her lips and refined the matte finish to her nose and chin. "I mean, you would think the guy had nine lives or something. Impossible to kill and he doesn't even have powers. Talk about dumb luck."

"Oye, you're going to wish you had some luck, you dumb bitch."

Laurelle bristled then, with the snap of her compact, whirled around. "That's funny, I could have sworn I heard something, but then again I don't speak Limey bastard."

Jake was on his feet and half way down the aisle before Kate could warn him. Laurelle was a "respected" Morgan. Top of the class in demon spawn.

"Yeah, well do you speak handcuffs? I'm sure you're used to them in the bedroom, but let me show you what they're really for."

Kate glanced at her cousin warily. "Jake, be careful with her. She's poison."

Laurelle shot her an icy glare. "Thanks for that, Kate the Fake. I should have tried that method this morning."

Jake had a shiny set of handcuffs ready for her. "So you're admitting to attempted murder?"

"Well, sticks and stones might break your bones, but well placed words in stupid associates ears will never hurt me. Just try and prove it."

"All the same, that sounded like conspiracy and now a threat. That's enough for me. How about you, partner?"

Kate sighed, rubbing her eyes. "Sure, but Jake—"

Before she could finish her sentence, Laurelle snapped her fingers and disappeared in a flash of light.

"—she isn't going to go easy."

Jake whirled around, his eyes alight with rage. "Nice try, but that old trick isn't going to work on me." He snapped his fingers and disappeared after her.

Lucy clapped her hands again, her joyous laugher filling the room. "Well, wasn't that fun. So what about you, Kate? What's up with you, sugar?"

Kate sighed again and stood up, joining her at the front of the room. "I need your help, Lucy. Jules thinks you're just what I need. Can you give me a hand?"

"Ah, my darling Julian," Lucy replied, her voice filled with nostalgia and a lilting Southern accent. "Such a talent. Have you seen his paintings? They're positively magical."

"Yes, we toured them yesterday. He's very gifted."

"And so are you. There isn't anyone else in the family who can read minds."

Kate shrugged. "What good is that when there are people

around here who can shift appearances, teleport, and slow down time? I feel like I'm a sitting duck and I don't like relying on other people to protect me."

Lucy stroked her chin thoughtfully. "Other people like Grant Anderson?"

Kate put her head in her hands and let out a sotto voce of swear words. "Well, she figured it out and now everyone knows. Thank you, Mother, again."

Lucy laughed. "Relax, this time it's not completely your mother's fault. Handsome Grant Anderson has been the target of every girl for at least the last six Summits. His delicious hotness has united Morgan and Anderson women on that front. Besides, when you two are together, it's pretty obvious there's chemistry. No, I'd worry about jealous girls when it comes to him. I could rattle off a list who wouldn't hesitate to kill you if it meant a genuine shot at him."

"Great. I'll add that to the growing catalogue of reasons to kill me. All the more motivation to figure out my missing power."

"Power? Why, sugar, what lifetime are you on?"

Kate frowned. "My last. My third that is."

Another musical laugh from Lucy. She launched herself onto the stage and began to twirl around. "Oh, sugar, I miss the old days. I was a countess and men flocked to me. They practically threw themselves at my feet, just to feel the touch of my hand or receive a word of affection sent through one of my maids. I was always juggling two or three of them at a time. I became obsessed with secret passageways and a means to get from one place to another without my lovers noticing that I was gone. Why I remember when this chateau was being designed. The architect, Francois Le Beau had quite the thing for me."

Kate watched as Lucy clasped her hands to her chest and curtsied.

Then to the sound of music, that only she could hear, Lucy started to waltz around the stage.

Kate raised her eyebrows. Crazy didn't come close to an

accurate description. "That's all quite charming, Lucy, but what does this have to do with me?"

"You're not listening, silly. Powers are personal. They come from your natural abilities. They are a heightened response to some aspect of you that comes easily." Seeing the confusion on Kate's face, Lucy sighed and snapped her fingers. Reappearing beside Kate in a flash of light, Lucy placed her hand on Kate's shoulder and before she could react, she found herself at the driving range behind the chateau.

"Get it now?"

Kate looked at the lush fairways around her. "Why can everyone here teleport except for me?"

Lucy let out a long sigh, as if she was being patient with a small child. "I can teleport because, in my first life, I excelled at sneaking from place to place undetected."

"So you developed a power that made it easier for you to do that," Kate said slowly. Perhaps her crazy cousin wasn't so crazy after all. There was certain logic to the origin of their abilities.

"And you can read minds, because..." She paused, egging her on.

"Because I lived in fear as a child. Whatever horrific thing my family did affected me. I remember sitting in my room, trying to figure out what my mother's next move was, then suddenly one day, I didn't have to guess, I could read her thoughts." Kate sat down on the grass, stunned at the revelation. "Lucy, you're brilliant. You just fixed what years of therapists couldn't begin to understand. It makes complete sense now."

Lucy clapped her hands and thrust out her arms, spinning around like she was in *The Sound of Music*. "Yay, now what about your second power?"

Kate shrugged her shoulders. "Grant calls it imprinting on time. We were at a crime scene and, somehow, I was able to jump back in time to see the perp before he committed the act."

Lucy wandered up to a golf instructor and borrowed several clubs. While he teed up adjoining stations, she tossed Kate an iron. "So it sounds like time stamping is from your present life. You're a detective. You're trained to find clues in crime scenes."

Kate looked at the seven iron. "Time stamping, huh? That makes a lot of sense. I could go to any crime scene and know how the murder actually happened. Don't know how that will help me protect myself, though."

"Once you master the skill, you will be able to move between past and future. One quick survey of a room and you will know what's coming."

"And see an attack before it comes."

Lucy took a swing at the ball. She frowned as it sailed two hundred yards across the grass. "I can remember the days when I could swing three hundred yards with my half my clothes off. Ever play a round of Midnight Strip Golf?"

Kate sighed and took a swing at her ball. It shot out about thirty feet and hit a nearby telephone pole. "No and I never hope to. What does golf have to do with my powers?"

"Sugar, golf is like mediation and meditation is the key to everything. It's about you and the ball. You focus your thoughts, quiet the mind, and connect with the reality around you." She adjusted her stance and took a solid swing at the ball. The sound of a loud ping resounded across the driving deck, and a light at the three hundred and fifty mark lit up.

Lucy squealed and danced about, her eyes lit up with satisfaction. "Gosh I love this game. Be much more satisfying if I was naked with a hunky man nearby but hearing that ping comes a close second."

Kate sighed and looked around. While Lucy flirted with a nearby instructor, Kate pulled out her cell phone. Glancing at the missed messages from Grant gave her a reason to make a quick call.

"Where are you? Jake has been tearing up the place, trying to catch your cousin Laurelle."

"At the driving range with Lucy. She's trying to make me see a connection between my powers, meditation, and golf."

There was a long pause on the other end of the phone. "Meditation and golf?"

"Yeah, some crazy theory about being one with the ball and focusing your powers."

Another pause had Kate questioning the connection of her call. Finally he spoke. "Your cousin's pretty smart. I never thought of it that way, but damned if she isn't right."

"You like golf?"

"I'm a guy, right? Of course I like golf."

Kate sighed. "So I guess you like playing Midnight Strip Golf, too?"

This time his voice was laced with humor. "Never heard of strip golf. It sounds intriguing. Make sure you get the details from your cousin. Don't forget we're meeting at the command center at twelve."

Lucy appeared in front of her with a bucket of balls. "Was that your man?"

"He's not my man." Kate sighed. "But he applauds your teaching methods, so tell me more."

She shook her head. "You need to let the balls tell you more."

"Like what?"

"Like, you were a doctor during your second life. Could you bring people back from the dead?"

Kate crinkled her nose. "Of course not."

"Perform miracle healings?"

"Not that I know of."

Lucy wandered back to her station and started swinging her club.

Kate took a couple of shots of her own, pleasantly surprised that she could produce a decent drive.

After a few minutes, Lucy looked up. "What was your relationship like with the family back then?"

Kate fumbled her swing, sending the ball dangerously

close a group of nearby golfers. She shrugged her shoulders and mumbled, "No different than usual."

"Fine, let me be blunt. How many times did they try to kill you?"

Kate teed up her ball and swung. This time it hit true, sailing down the range to the two-hundred-yard mark. "A couple of attempted hit and runs during medical school. After we graduated, we enlisted and went to the front line of the Korean War. No one bothered us there. I guess they figured a random shelling would do their work for them."

"We?"

"James. My fiancée back then," Kate replied with a sigh. "We were young and driven to help people. It was the fifties and there was a lot of turmoil in the world."

"What happened to him?"

Kate sucked in a deep breath and swung several more times. Guilt and remorse overtook her for a minute. She hadn't thought about James in years. That was one of the problems with living a long life—after a century, the faces started to disappear. "We returned stateside and settled in a small town in Ohio. One night we were walking home from a movie and a man approached us with a gun."

"What happened then?"

"He didn't say a word, just fired the weapon. James saw him coming first and threw himself in front of me. Before I could do anything, he was in my arms on the ground."

"How did that make you feel, sugar?"

Taking a deep breath, Kate looked away into space, momentarily lost in the memory. And the anguish. "Devastated. Heartbroken. Angry. He was dying, when it should have been me," she replied, choking on her words. "He was in so much pain, but he stared at me with this expression of love. I couldn't do anything. All those years of training, and I couldn't do a thing to save him." Kate lifted her club and made a violent swing for the ball. "James gave his life for me. He knew what I was and he still loved me."

"What happened to the man with the gun?"

Kate swung again, "I don't know. One minute he was there and then he was gone."

"Sure you know, sugar. What happened to the man with the gun?"

Kate shook her head in denial. For a moment, she was on that darkened street and James lay dying in her arms. Anger surged through her—an overpowering anger that she couldn't control. Taking the seven iron, she let out a yell of frustration, tossed it into the air, and extended her hand. A shockwave shot out from her palm and blew apart the metal, disintegrating it before her eyes.

She struggled for breath and staggered back, the memories overwhelming her. "I killed him," she gasped. "He turned to dust before my eyes."

Lucy nodded her approval. Twirling her nine iron, she walked over to her cousin. "And that, sugar, is how you defend yourself."

"God, Lucy, I killed him," Kate cried. She fell to her knees in shock, trying to sort through feelings and memories that suddenly filled her brain.

"It was self-defense, Kate. You shouldn't feel bad about it."

Kate hid her face in her hands, trying to compose herself. Slowing her sobs, she drew in deep breaths. "I don't understand. Why didn't it work when Larry or Ray came after me?"

Lucy shrugged her shoulders. "Maybe somewhere in that brain of yours, you know how permanent disintegration is or maybe you just don't care."

"What do you mean?"

"Maybe part of you doesn't care enough about you to save you." Lucy paused and glanced down the neighboring fairway. Brushing the blonde hair from her face, she looked like her thoughts were a million miles away. "When enough people die for you, you start wondering if you were worthy of their sacrifice at all."

The realization hit Kate like a punch in the stomach,

knocking the wind out of her. Maybe she didn't care. Maybe part of her wanted to end it all. That had changed when she met Grant. Any death wish she had disappeared when she was with him. Looking at her cousin, she managed a smile. "Lucy, thank you. You are an angel, you wonderful girl."

Lucy blushed and looked away. "Ahh, sugar, I've been called many things but never an angel. You're too sweet. Much too sweet to be a Morgan." Spying a handsome man at the end of the range, she licked her lips and fiddled with her hair. "Now, honey, before I go, a word of advice to help you."

Kate wiped her eyes, "Of course, please, go ahead."

"Golf is like pillow talk. When men are relaxed, they jibber jabber and tell you things they don't mean to say."

"Okay?"

"So here's the thing about old Gus. Gus had a disease. The disease to please." She paused and blew a kiss to her target, catching his eye. "And Gussy wanted to please the Leland clan, so when he accidently stole something very important, he saw the opportunity to do a bit of business with them."

Kate's ears perked up, her full attention on Lucy. "What did he steal?"

"Now, if you ever flip this back on me, I *will* kill you. However, from one jewel thief to another, I believed it when Gussy spilled his guts on the golf course that day."

"Is that why he's dead?"

Lucy let out a laugh and shook his head. "Sugar, he's dead because he tried to play both sides, and when you piss off the Leland lowlifes, you better be the first with your finger on the trigger."

"I don't understand, what did he steal?"

"Ask your boyfriend. The dolt didn't realize it at the time but he stole the most precious thing to the Anderson clan. Same thing that gorgeous man stole from you."

With a wink, Lucy placed one hand on her chest and

curtsied to Kate. Snapping her fingers, she smiled, then disappeared.

CHAPTER 17

Not till you promise, you won't interrogate my source." Kate stood with the rest of the team around a table covered with images of suspects, leads, and random bits of suspicion. True to her word, she kept her promise to protect Lucy from scrutiny.

They were gathered in conference room G which had been transformed into a version of the Zion war room.

"This is ridiculous. You're speaking in riddles," Alexis shouted. "You come in here and tell us you have a break in the case, but to keep your source out of it. What if we need additional information from that person?"

"Then I will get it directly from the individual."

Alexis slammed her hand on the table. "And you can trust the source? I'm assuming it's a Morgan. Hell, Ambrose, we can't even trust her."

"Oye! That's my cuz you're ragging on."

They glanced over at Jake, the only one seated, and with a display of disrespect, his legs up on the table. He was holding a large ice pack to his face, covering a split lip and a cut above his eye.

Ambrose looked at him over his glasses. "Jake, we are extending you some leniency because you apprehended Laurelle Morgan, but if you don't get your feet off my desk, I will throw you out myself."

Jake gave him a fake salute and winced as his legs slid of the table. His soft moans turned to a manly grunt when a pretty Zion agent handed him a sultry glance and a new ice pack.

Kate smiled and patted him on the shoulder. "I hope you got her real good."

He nodded and moved his fingers into the shape of a gun. "After she stopped running, taking her down was a piece of cake."

Alexis stared him down. "Right, tough guy, and your face always looks like that."

"Look, at least, I'm making an effort, not standing around and being judge, jury, and executioner."

"Enough," Ambrose declared. He looked down at the case information and removed his glasses, tapping them on the table. "All right, Kate will interrogate her source if we need any more information. Everyone in this room has been vetted and, on pain of death, will not reveal confidences or take retribution against a Morgan or one of their associates until proven guilty. Good enough?"

"Fine."

Alexis glared at her. "Who is your source?"

"My cousin Lucy."

"The whore of Babylon?"

A round of exclamations didn't deter Alexis at all. Ambrose raised his voice above the rest and exchanged an angry glance with her. "Watch it, Alexis. One more disrespectful remark and you're out for good. You can throw around your insults in holding for the remainder of the Summit."

"You wouldn't dare."

"Say that again, young lady. Go ahead, try me."

Alexis curled her lip in distain but refrained from saying anything else. Ambrose nodded with satisfaction and looked at Kate to begin her story.

"She said that Gus had stolen something from the Anderson family. Some object that was the most precious thing to them."

Her report was met with a round of quizzical looks. For a

moment there was silence as everyone tried to rationalize her remarks.

"What the hell does that mean?" Alexis asked.

"Do we have a 'most precious thing'?" Mark asked. He pulled up his holographic keyboard and started to do a search of the Anderson database.

Grant watched a mountain of new information flash across the table top screen. "That's kind of cryptic, did she go into more detail?"

Kate turned slightly red. "Yes, she said it's the same thing that you stole from me."

Grant frowned and looked at her, searching his memory. "I haven't stolen anything from you."

There was silence again as everyone pondered what the statement meant. Finally, Jake piped up. "Oye, I got it. It's a bloody metaphor. Virginity. You stole her virginity."

"Really, Jake," Kate said, shooting him an annoyed look. Grant was looking down, but she smiled at the slight flush creeping up his neck. "You think I'm a virgin?"

"Idiot," Alexis seethed. "Put that into context. Gus stole the Anderson's virginity? It has to be something physical, like an object."

Mark snapped his fingers. "Excellent idea. What do we have that can be stolen?"

Kate's mind raced, trying to think of religious objects that might fit into that category. "The Ten Commandments?"

Grant shook his head. "Those are housed in the Ark of the Covenant."

"Great," Jake said. "Where is the Ark of the Covenant?"

Ambrose looked up with annoyance and let out a bellow. "Roland."

A geeky teenager popped his head around a corner of the office. "Yes, Grandpa?"

"Roland, where is the Ark of the Covenant kept?"

The boy pushed his glasses up over the bridge of his nose and glanced nervously around, as if he was looking for a place to hide. He mumbled something under his breath that no one at the table could hear.

"What did you say? Come here and speak up, boy."

Roland approached, kneading a file in his hands nervously. Glancing around the table, he cleared his throat and stared at a picture of the Ark positioned in the middle of the table. "Um, it's in Steven Spielberg's basement."

Jake's mouth dropped open with surprise. "What? Steven Spielberg, the legendary film maker? What is it doing in his basement?"

"Yes, Roland," Ambrose replied dryly. "Do tell."

"Well, you see he made that great movie—"

"Oye, Raiders of the Lost Ark. I loved that movie! Tops in my book."

"Me too, and so I figured he probably kept the prop 'cause they said at the time they were making it that it looked so realistic, they actually changed stuff on it as a sign of respect."

"So how did it end up in his basement, Roland?"

"Um, well, the boys and I were playing around one day and thought, hey, let's pop into his house and see what kind of stuff he kept around as souvenirs, and boy, did we find a treasure trove."

"So you decided to hide the most important relic to Jewish and Catholic history in his basement?"

"Well, the prop was just gathering dust, and we figured the security system was like Fort Knox, so, what better hiding place to switch it out?"

"Get it back. Now."

"Yeah," Grant said. "What if he decides to move it?"

"Come on, it represents one of his greatest accomplishments. Did you see that movie? He's not going to get rid of it. Besides there's an alarm that signals on our database if it ever moves."

Ambrose glared at Roland. "Make the necessary phone call and move it now. Go, before I lose my patience and make you attend public high school."

Grant glanced at Mark, who was apparently thinking the same thing. Mark pulled up the alarm database and table lit up green, showing no movement on the Ark. "Well, that rules out the most famous one. Anyone got anything else?"

"Oh, the Holy Grail!" Jake exclaimed. "The cup that Jesus drank from?"

Mark rolled his eyes. "The Holy Grail is not a cup, it's a myth. The cup, the pieces of silver, and anything left from The Last Supper are housed at the Vatican. How about something not from an Indiana Jones movie?"

Kate snapped her fingers. "How about the Spear of Destiny?"

Mark shook his head. "That's under Morgan control, not ours."

Kate glanced at Jake, who shrugged his shoulders. "I didn't know we had any relics."

Mark switched databases. "Yup, you should have that, the crown of thrones, and the cross that our Lord was crucified on."

"Why would we have those items?"

"Because it required Satan's work to kill the Son of God. Those artifacts are laced with his power and would corrupt anyone on our side."

Kate shivered at the idea of something so evil in object form. "Anything else that you know of?"

"Numerous books of the dead, stuff associated with Satanic rituals. I'm sure there is a lot more than we have access to. You would have to ask the Council."

"No thank you. I am quite happy not to know."

Grant walked around the diameter of the table, looking at images of various artifacts, all accounted for in the database. "Okay, we're going about this all wrong. We know it has to be capable of being stolen, and it's precious to us. I just don't know why she would mention me. Kate, can you run through her account again?"

She nodded, looking at the faces around her. "Lucy said and I quote, 'The dolt didn't realize it at the time, but he stole the most precious thing to the Anderson clan. Same thing that gorgeous man stole from you.'"

Silence filled the room again. Finally Grant spoke. "And he was in league with Leland's offspring. Probably Larry, if one of his associates was with him the night we overheard them speaking."

Kate nodded. "Larry, Lucas, Lee. It could be any or all of them. Lucy mentioned that he was playing both sides. Pit brother against brother and that's reason to suspect them all."

"Well, at least we know where to start drilling for information," replied Grant. He glanced up and frowned. "Kate, what is it?"

She looked at him excitedly, a light bulb going off in her head. "I think I know what she meant. Lucy's a romantic. As she was leaving, she put her hand on her chest and curtsied. Do you get it?"

"Doesn't she have a reputation for being crazy?" Alexis asked. "This could be a wild goose chase, after all."

"Maybe, but I know what Grant stole from me."

The rest of the table stilled and looked at her. She smiled shyly, feeling slightly embarrassed. "He stole my heart or, if you like, the keys to my heart."

"Aww, pumpkin, that's so cute," Jake replied, adding a retching sound. "So you have a bloody heart somewhere that's the most precious thing to the Anderson family?"

Grant paled and looked at Ambrose. "No, but we have a key." He shifted uncomfortably. "It's not possible, is it?"

Ambrose stared down at the table then slammed his hand against the surface. "Mark, who has possession of the keys? I need to know now!"

Mark looked wildly at his keyboard. "What keys? I need more information than just the word 'keys.'"

All around them, the activity in the office ceased. Everyone stopped in mid-motion, looking shocked at Ambrose's outburst.

Grant pulled over a chair and gently pushed Ambrose into it. "Mark," he said quietly. "Punch in the Keys to the Kingdom of Heaven."

There was a loud gasp and suddenly everyone in the office was hunched around the table. Mark entered the command then shot a panicked look at Grant. "It's a restricted database. I need a code."

A path was cleared and Grant walked to the keyboard, punching in a series of commands. There was a collective cry as the table changed from green to red and an alarm sounded throughout the office.

"Call the Council," Ambrose said hoarsely. "We need to inform them."

Kate's knees buckled under a new chorus of voices exploding through her head. Grabbing onto the table for support, she struggled to stay on her feet. "No need," she gasped. "I can hear the outrage. They already know."

CHAPTER 18

"I can't believe they just bloody well threw us out."

Kate and Jake were sitting in the hallway outside of conference room G or the Zion Room as it had become known of late.

From her seated position on the floor, Kate watched him pace up and down the hallway. "Can you blame them? I'd be freaking out too if you told me someone from Satan's family had carte blanche to kick in the front door of my house."

"So I've heard the phrase before, but are there physical keys to get into Heaven?" he wondered. "If so, then how the hell did Gutless Gus get a hold of them?"

"Shhh, don't announce it so loudly. We don't need all the relatives playing scavenger hunt in a locked-down building."

He nodded and sat down beside her. "Right, right. Would be like advertising a free buffet to a room full of fat people."

Kate rolled her eyes at the crassness of his comment but, secretly, she had to admit, the metaphor was right. "Yeah, if the people were all power hungry psychos bent on destroying the world."

She put her head in her hands, relishing the relative silence of the deserted hall. First, Gus was murdered, and now, a serial killer called The Sculptor was on the loose. As if that wasn't bad enough, Gus had stolen something that threatened everything this Summit stood for. Her head was pounding but, more importantly, the lack of answers was killing her. Pulling out her phone, she texted Lucy a few questions.

Jake leapt to his feet, dusting off his jeans. "Right, this is stupid. We're investigators. We still have a murder to solve. Old Gus may have been a crook but he's dead and someone has to be held accountable."

Kate glanced at the return message from Lucy and flipped open her notebook. Jotting down her response, she tapped it absently against her leg. "Grant told us to wait here."

"Is this the way it's going to be? Just because you're shagging him, you do whatever he says?"

"I wish that were the case," Grant replied.

Jake turned around and leapt back in surprise. Grant and Alexis were suddenly standing there. "Gad blimey, where did you come from?"

Alexis rolled her eyes and pointed to the door over her left shoulder. Kate wearily looked up at them. "What did they say?"

Grant knelt down. "Are you okay? You look exhausted."

She nodded. "There's much more chatter in my head than usual and trying to block it is draining me dry."

He gently placed both his palms on either side of her face. Kate felt a surge of warmth and the roar was reduced to a dull but manageable noise. "Better?"

"Yes, much better. Thank you."

A gagging sound from Jake interrupted their moment. "Right, so what now, peeps? Do we charge down that hallway and start arresting everyone in sight?"

Grant shook his head, helping Kate to her feet. "How about lunch? We should eat and there's a lot to discuss."

A short time later, they were sitting in Borealis, separated from the other diners in the VIP section at the back of the restaurant.

"So what the hell happened in there?"

Grant put his hand up, stopping Jake from speaking further. Reaching into his pocket, he pulled out a ball point pen and clicked the end of it. "It's a scrambler, in case anyone is trying to listen in."

Kate took a sip of water, suddenly feeling more like she needed a nap than fancy French food. "What did the Council say?"

"Some changes in our directive," Grant replied. "Obviously solving the murder is important, the Morgan side demands nothing less, but we need to find those keys as soon as possible."

"What are the bloody keys to the kingdom of Heaven?" Jake demanded. "You can't tell me there is a door out there that connects directly to God?"

"There were three of them, created at the beginning of time," Alexis explained. "It's a triad of symbols etched into a solid gold physical object. The keys don't unlock anything, it's the symbols that are important. Utter their meaning and the bearer can control what happens in Heaven from Earth."

Kate looked down at the linen table cloth. Tracing a pattern with her finger, she followed the woven gold threads to a matching mixed bouquet of flowers as the centerpiece. She sighed. "Matthew 16:19."

Alexis's eyebrows rose in surprise. "You know the Bible?"

"And I will give unto thee the keys of the kingdom of heaven. And whatsoever thou shalt bind on earth shall be bound in heaven and whatsoever thou shalt loose on earth shall be loosed in heaven."

Grant looked at her strangely. "You memorized the Bible?"

Kate shook her head. "I keep hearing that passage. It's been randomly running through my mind for the last few days."

"Is it a male or female voice?"

"Male."

Grant looked around the restaurant. "Is he here?"

Kate heaved another sigh. "No, I can't pinpoint the source directly. This voice is different, it's just floating out there in the air, like it's not connected to one person."

"If you've been hearing it, why didn't you say anything before?" Alexis asked. She sat straight in her chair, as if taking time to eat was a major inconvenience for her.

"Why are you always in such a pissy mood?" Jake replied in between bites of the French bread and cheese plate that had been placed in the middle of the table.

"Have you any idea how many verses from the Bible are floating through people's heads?" Kate said. "Between prayers, quotes, and running commentaries of everyone who passes by, it's hard to keep track of who said what, never mind anything that might be suspicious."

"All right, look." Grant raised his hand to stop the debate. "The Council has asked us to investigate Gus's activities leading up to his death and where he might have hidden the keys. Now that the stakes are higher and the balance is in jeopardy, they want checks and balances too."

"What does that mean?"

"It means we switch partners. One Morgan and one Anderson to keep each other in check."

Jake snorted and threw his hands up in the air. "Oh, for crying out loud, you two go off and play snuggle bunny while I get stuck with the ice queen."

"Believe me," Alexis replied as a Cobb salad was placed in front of her, "I'm not happy about it either."

"It won't be just us, there are others on standby in case either team needs backup. Right now, we need to make sure the Summit runs as normally as possible. Jake, I understand you have some people we could call on?"

Jake nodded, attacking his Kobe steak sandwich as if he hadn't eaten in days. "I have a couple of MI6 associates of mine, chilling in my Presidential Suite. They've worked on the strange and unusual with me back in London, so they're no stranger to our background."

"Good, can you have them start doing a background check into Gus, his associates, and any suspects you think, might be a factor."

"What about Zion?" Kate asked. "Isn't that what they are for?"

Grant glanced down at his untouched haddock with rice pilaf, before reaching for a handful of French fries from Kate's plate. "I think we should run our own investigation and keep as much as we can between the four of us."

Having lost her appetite, she pushed her hamburger in his direction, "You don't trust either side right now."

Grant looked around. "Right now, I trust the people at this table. Until we have more information about motives and alliances, we need to treat everyone as a suspect. How did the keys end up in a position to be stolen? How, of all people, did Gus manage to get his hands on them? That relic holds the most power of anything on Earth and, if we don't get it back, no one will be leaving this conference alive."

"Well, firstly, mate, thanks for the vote of confidence. Not sure about frostbite here, but I'll trust you for now. Secondly, don't you think you're laying it on a bit thick? What do you mean, 'no one will leave this conference alive'?"

"The Council was very clear about that point," Alexis reported. "With this breach of trust, no one from either family can be trusted. Unless the keys are recovered and those at fault held accountable, they will destroy the chateau, all of its occupants, and everything within a hundred miles."

Kate blinked. "Wow, when that leaks out, we're going to have herds of people lying to our faces."

Alexis reached for her wine glass again. "Someone will buckle, especially with those odds at stake. Anyone who walked through those doors yesterday morning is trapped here until eight a.m. on Friday morning. Both families and their collateral damage either live or die together and if the Morgans are like the Andersons, their survival instincts will send us a whole list of suspects."

"Well, today's Tuesday, so we have two solid days and minimal leads," Jake said. "What's the plan? Flog and quarter everyone at the Crystallise Ball tonight?"

Kate stopped picking at her plate, abandoning the last of her French fries. With everything to keep her occupied, she had forgotten that about that damn ball again. Ambrose's comments about her and Grant made her stomach drop and her anxiety rise again. "Why don't you guys go to the ball, and I can do some sneaking around? It will give me the chance to practice my powers and hopefully find some kind of lead we can use."

Grant looked at her strangely. "You don't want to go with me?"

She looked down and mumbled, "Well, I wasn't completely sure. You never asked."

"You're right," he replied. He leaned over the table and plucked a white rose from the middle of the centerpiece. "Katherine Morgan, will you be my date to the Crystallise Ball tonight?"

She accepted the rose and smiled. "I'd love nothing more."

Jake nodded his approval. Turning to Alexis, he extended his hand. "How about you, my ice princess? Care to be my date tonight?"

Alexis glared at him. "I thought you hated my guts."

"Nah, I just like to have a good tease. Besides, you're drop dead gorgeous and I'm sure there's something interesting beneath that glacial surface."

Grant took a drink from his water glass. "It will strengthen our front if we all go together."

Alexis hesitated, then shrugged her shoulders with resignation. "What the hell, why not? I used to slum it when I was much younger. I'm sure I can do it again. It's a double date." Glancing at Kate, she looked her up and down. "Size four? I think I have a dress or two that will fit you."

"Oh, that's very kind, but I'm sure I can rustle up something to wear."

"No, don't be silly. We want to look good for our dates." Alexis reached into her purse and sent a quick text. "There, my cousin Cori has added you to our appointment at the salon. If the boys can let us slip away at seven, we'll be ready for the dinner at nine."

Kate hesitated, then slowly nodded her head. "Okay, but until then, what is the plan?"

For a second, a shadow of annoyance crossed Grant's face. Clearing his throat, he said "First and foremost, if Lucy is right, then Gus had accomplices, so it will be an interrogation of Leland and his children."

"All of them?" Kate looked at him with surprise. "They won't reveal anything to me."

"Yeah, they aren't exactly friends," Jake added.

Grant frowned at the subtle glance between the two of them. Standing up from the table, he put the scrambler back in his pocket. "That's why we aren't conducting the interrogation. The members of the Council have decided to do it themselves."

"Rotten luck for them, but what are we supposed to do in the meantime?"

"Kate and I are going to observe the interrogations." Grant put up his hand to silence the retorts from Alexis and Jake. "You two are going to go and drill into Gus's timeline. We need to know when the keys were stolen, where they possibly could be stashed, and who else Gus met with besides the Leland siblings and Lucy who might have information."

"Grant, that's bullshit," Alexis declared. "Any Zion dumbass can handle that assignment. Why can't we see the Council in action?"

"Because the Guardian of the Keys is being difficult and will only talk to a member of the original Protector clan. Your passion and charm have been your strengths, so I want you to take the lead on this one."

Alexis stopped dead in her tracks, her eyes growing as large as saucers. For the first time since Kate had met her,

she looked genuinely happy. Letting out a squeal of excitement, she leapt at Grant, wrapped her arms around his neck,
and kissed him soundly.

"Thank you, you darling, thank you for remembering,"
she cried breathlessly. "Why didn't you say so in the first
place? Of course, I'll get whatever information we need."

Grant turned red, clearly not expecting her reaction. He
took a step back and gently pushed her away.

Kate watched the pair together and felt her stomach drop
as the old remnants of their relationship hit her full on.
Strong thoughts of their time together overwhelmed her,
melting the tiny sliver of confidence she had in her and
Grant's relationship.

The awkward pause that followed was made only more
uncomfortable when she realized there wasn't going to be
an explanation from Grant. After a moment of silence, Kate
turned and walked down the hall.

"Where are you going?" he yelled. "Holding is that
way."

"I'm not going."

"Why not? We need you there. Once they break, you'll
be the only one who can tell us what they're really thinking.
Come on, Kate, why are you angry? We promised that you
would talk to me."

"Talking goes both ways, Grant. What just happened to
her? What did you say to make her so happy? Why was I
just bombarded with a million memories of the two of you
together?"

"Is this a jealously thing, because we haven't got time
for petty stuff like that."

"Yes, Grant, it's a jealously thing. I'm a girl and, as
much as I try to push that away, right now, I hate Alexis and
I hate that you were ever with her!"

He stilled, his piercing gaze drilling into her. "What do
you want me to do, Kate? Apologize for a relationship that
happened before you were born? 'Cause that's not going to
happen. I'm a lot older than you, and I have a history.

That's something you're going to have to deal with because there is nothing that I can do about it."

"Don't tell me how to feel."

"Then don't judge something you know nothing about and does not concern you."

She knew that she was being illogical and irrational, and he wasn't the person she should be angry with. Part of her just wanted to run. Escape her history, her responsibility, and run away. Her other part wanted to dash into his arms and apologize for overreacting, but all she could do was stand there, silent and unyielding.

"Besides," he continued, "you and Jake seemed to have had a moment back there. Alexis caved pretty easily. Maybe she's not the only one warming up to him."

A wave of anger smacked her so hard, he might as well have physically hit her. "What?" she whispered.

"You heard me."

"You son of a bitch, now who's judging?" she said then turned and walked away.

She ignored his calls, desperate to escape this situation. Wiping her tears, she replayed the last few days. How could she have been so stupid to think they could make this work? She let her guard down, all but declared she loved him in front of a room of strangers, and now her heart was in pieces, and there was nowhere for her to run.

She couldn't go to her room. He would find her there and, as she had predicted, the chateau had become an inescapable nightmare. The chapel was out of the question. That was his sanctuary, but there was one place, though. One place where she felt like she could be herself.

CHAPTER 19

Grant barrelled down the hallway toward holding and the interrogation of the Leland clan. For the sake of expediency, the members under suspicion—Larry, Lucas, Lee, and Laurelle—were being questioned in tandem, their questioners each a different member of the Morgan Council. Far above them, the sessions were recorded and monitored by Ambrose and Mark as witnesses for the Anderson side.

Grant walked through the threshold of a smaller conference area and immediately felt the vertigo of a transformed room. All around him, beige walls and crystal chandeliers morphed into a black room filled with monitors and a futuristic computer system. The room had changed into a three level command center—cold, metallic, and octagon in shape. Below each of the eight windows was an adjoining interrogation room and, as he wandered from window to window, he looked down on the different suspects enduring a bombardment of questions and torture techniques.

Ambrose glanced up from a computer meant to act as a high-tech lie detector and gave Grant a quizzical once over. "Where's Kate?" he asked casually.

"She's not coming. We had a fight."

"Family matter?"

"Sort of. Alexis matter."

"Ah. Too bad, we could have used her ability."

Grant clenched his jaw and positioned himself above the

window to Larry's interrogation room. "I'm sure I'll get along just fine without her."

Ambrose glanced sideways at Mark, who was flipping between the interrogations of the suspects and a rough time-line of events from the last few weeks of Gus's life. He glanced back and let out a low whistle. "After what she did, you chose Alexis over her? Wow, man, I didn't think you were that cold."

"I didn't choose Alexis over her," Grant snapped. "We were done centuries ago."

"Does she know that?"

Grant shifted uncomfortably. "Of course, she does. At least, I think she does. She's just being jealous and irration-al." Irritated by the question, he changed the subject. "And what the hell do you mean, 'after what she did'? What did she do?"

Their conversation was temporarily interrupted by the screams of pain coming from the rooms below. Mark winced and turned off the sound. "Damn, those Morgans. They don't mess around. At this rate, the suspects will be dead before we can get anything useful out of them."

"Sure would help to have a mind reader here, right now," Ambrose drawled, not bothering to look up from the moun-tains of files around him.

"Well, tough. She stormed off and I don't really care where she is right now."

Mark tapped his pen on one of screens. "She's practicing her powers at the driving range. Must be mad because she destroying an awful lot of premium balls."

Grant glanced at the security camera. It was a grainy shot, but he could see her move her club then extend her hand as something in mid-swing ignited and made a tiny explosion in the air. "So she finally figured out her third power," he grunted. "Good for her."

"I think senility is catching up to you, Grant," Mark said absently. "She had that power in Texas. She used it when she saved our asses."

Grant stilled, a look of surprise crossing his face. "What?"

"Yeah, she used it to obliterate her serial killer cousin Rocco. Kate Morgan is one impressive girl. Tortured for days but still found something inside of her to pull off a miracle before she died."

"What?" he repeated, hoarsely. "What are you talking about? Torture? And what do you mean, she died?"

Ambrose looked at him sternly. "Mark, enough. His memory was wiped for a reason."

Mark flipped through another screen, jotting down notes as he went. "Yeah, but if they're done, and she ends up dead for good, he should at least know why."

Grant dashed across the room, pulling Mark out of his chair and pushing him against one of the observation windows. "You're going to tell me everything," he said, his voice laced with quiet fury. "And don't leave out a single detail."

Mark pushed him away then held up his hands. "Easy, partner. No need to get madder than a wet hen. I'm on your side."

"Yeah? Prove it."

Mark straightened his tie and pulled up his chair, leaning back against the wall. "What you know so far is the truth. You two hit it off like nobody's business, however, as the case went on, it became clear that the person we were looking for was a relative of hers."

"Who is Rocco Morgan, anyway?"

"He was an illegitimate brother of that bunch down there, but because he wasn't formally part of their family, he was out drifting and killing on his own."

"So they don't know about his death?"

"Not who killed him, but they know he probably departed this earth. That's the thing about these Summits—if you're not in this hotel, then you have to be dead."

"So what happened?"

"We tracked him through Texas to an abandoned warehouse outside of San Antonio. He had kidnapped Kate and was using her as bait to get to you. When we reached the warehouse, she was bloody, beaten, and almost unrecognizable from being tortured for days." Mark cleared his throat, a haunted look filling his eyes. He wasn't the only one. Flashes of grief appeared on Ambrose as well. Mark looked away for a minute, as if trying to dull the memories before continuing his story.

"For some reason the guy had an obsession with our family. Being rejected as a legitimate Morgan made him determined to prove himself and the best way he knew how was to kill Andersons as proof of his loyalty to his clan."

"So why go after her? Why not leave her out of it?"

"He knew of her history with Lucas and the hate his siblings had for her. She was also an easy way into our circle. Before he kidnapped her, he had been stalking the two of you for weeks. He knew that you had probably told her family secrets, both of you being so over the moon in love."

Grant clenched his hands and bowed his head. "I don't remember any of this." It was hard, but he needed to hear it all.

"She never broke," Mark reported. "Refused to say one word about you or your whereabouts. By the time we got to her, she had only minutes left. We figured if we combined our powers, we had one shot to save her."

"And?"

"We were ambushed by a dozen hired guns, determined to make sure Morgan succeeded with his plan. Fell right into the trap, although you would have killed him if it weren't for his men getting the upper hand. Morgan put four slugs into me and dumped me for dead. For you, he knew you were too powerful to be killed any ordinary way so he gutted you to keep you down, then started to drain your energy. I vaguely remember Kate screaming your name. There was a loud boom and a shockwave ripped through the walls of the warehouse. When I managed to lift my head again, all that was left was the smell of burnt flesh and charred piles of dust where Morgan and his men had stood."

"And Kate?"

"She was dead. Your dad, Chase, and Uncle Jonathan arrived, but there was nothing that could be done. You were out of your mind with rage. They knew she would come back for her final life in seven days, so they felt it best to erase both your memories, implant false ones, and pretend it didn't happen."

Grant's voice was low, barely above a whisper, as if he was reliving the incident, instead of hearing it for the first time. "But they must have known about the reunion. That we were going to bump into each other again."

"Kate has been the target of her family for years," Ambrose cleared his throat, looking embarrassed with his explanation. "No one really believed she would live to see this reunion. Your mother hoped that finding someone else would settle you down and, if you did happen to meet up again, not remembering would do no harm. Of course, that little stunt you pulled with tying your fates to the Universe, means that we're prevented from interfering again."

Grant turned his back to both of them, watching impassively as Damian inflicted horrific pain on Lee Morgan. His voice was tight with strained emotion. "You just need to know who was involved with Gus, right?"

Ambrose nodded. "Yeah, she can probably tap in from the golf course. No need to be here in person."

"Fine." Grant turned and threw open the door.

"Grant," Ambrose called out.

Grant paused at the door, not bothering to turn around.

"Filling in her blanks will only cause her psychological pain."

"I know. That's the last thing I intend to do."

The door slammed shut with a bang and Ambrose sighed. "I hope he keeps his word."

Mark shrugged his shoulders. "Well, we'll find out soon enough. If we can't find those keys in two days, any number of secrets and lies aren't going to matter."

CHAPTER 20

Kate had a pretty good rhythm going. Hit the ball, hear the "ping," and destroy it before it had a chance to hit the green. All the while, she muttered unpleasant things about Grant, peppering in the occasional swear word to make her feel better.

After about fifteen minutes of grumbling and repeating their encounter out loud, she found herself alone, most of the other golfers choosing to relocate to the club house on the far side of the eighteenth hole.

In between her swings and her running dialog, Kate heard a low whistle. She had passed enough building sites in New York to recognize the call of a horny construction worker, so when a voice from behind her whistled and yelled, "Hey baby," she was fully prepared to use her club on something other than expensive golf balls.

"Hey, baby," repeated the voice. It was low and raspy and good fuel for her anger. "Come on, baby, come over here. Let me soothe all your worries away."

Kate gripped her club and tried to ignore the voice but it was relentless. After the third cat call, she whirled around then stumbled back, gaping at the massive beige and white cabana that had appeared a few feet from her tee station.

It billowed in the wind, open flaps revealing a large platform settee and matching living room. To the left, a seating area complete with stylish rattan furniture and a wet bar, to the right a massive California King divan overflowing with soft linens and pillows. In the middle of the refined elegance, sat a familiar face surrounded by fresh fruit, buckets of ice, and lots of liquor.

"Jules, what the heck? What is all this and where have you been?"

"Welcome to fantasy cabana," he declared in a cheesy Spanish accent. Letting out a peal of laughter, he waved his hand at her. "Oh, I've been so busy, doing deals, making new friends, and taking a page from your book, Katie. Engaging the enemy."

She rolled her eyes and turned back to her driving practice. "Not some of my best advice. Believe me."

"What, trouble in paradise already? It's only been two days."

"Well, with so many distractions, I think he's just not that into me anymore."

Julian flipped on the blender, adding liberal doses of fruit, ice, and tequila. "Now come on, Katie, you can't expect a guy to come sans baggage. After all, he *is* over four hundred years old."

"Ah, surprise, you know about Alexis."

"Darling, who doesn't know about her and Grant? She flashed the ring in everyone's face about three reunions ago. You have no idea how many jealous girls were after her when she announced their engagement."

Kate gritted her teeth. "Yeah, well spare me the details. I've had enough fighting for one day."

The sound from the blender got louder with her every word. "What?" yelled Julian. "Can't hear you above the self-pity spewing from your mouth."

Shooting him a dirty look, she turned back to her practice, collecting a few errant balls that had managed to escape her frustration.

"Come on, don't be mad. Have you told him about Danny, Andrew, or James?"

She centered a ball then shook her head. "No need to, they're all dead."

"What about Devon? What if the Baron of Wall Street, in his ten thousand dollar suits and chiselled physique, came walking back through your door."

Kate paused mid-swing. "He's no match for Grant. Not even half the man."

"That's not the point. Point is, that you haven't mentioned your baggage, and just because his ex has to be here, you're holding it against him."

There was a long moment of silence as she considered his point of view. "Maybe." She leaned against her club and rubbed her eyes. "Okay, so you're right, but she's beautiful and powerful and...and..."

"Not a Morgan?"

She hung her head in defeat. "Yeah. Not a Morgan."

"Look, Katie. You can't change your genes, any more than you can change your personality or the color of those beautiful blue eyes. What's done is done, and the more you try to disown your past, the less control you will have over you."

She sucked in a deep breath and winced. "Guess I have been a bit of a drama queen, huh?"

"A Morgan quality I admire in us all."

She smiled and gazed out to the setting sun. "Speaking of, you haven't seen Lucy, have you? I have a couple of questions for her."

Julian took a sip of his drink and stretched out on the sofa. "Oh she's long gone. Beat a path out of here after she spilled the beans about Gus."

"How? The place is in lockdown."

He laughed and a large box of chocolates appeared on the table in front of him. "You're a funny girl. She knew the architect. There are secret passageways that the Council is blind to all over the place. I'm telling you, if I had known what Gus was up to, we wouldn't be in this situation right now."

Her head snapped around, the driving range long forgotten. "What do you mean?"

"I mean I was there. Well, not for that conversation, but as part of the group that day. It was me, Lucy, Gus, and Lucas, all playing a game of Round Robin."

Kate searched her memory for the rules of that game. More than a few hospital meetings during her past had ended up on some golf course or other. "Round Robin…everyone switches partners at several points in the game. When you partnered with him, what was he like, did he say anything?"

Flipping chocolates into his mouth, he pondered her question. "Gus was in a great mood. Kept talking about some big business deal with a partner that would change the world. We made a wager on the round, which I lost. Never was very good at golf."

"What was the wager?"

"He was buying a new penthouse in Florida and wanted a painting of mine for the great room. Said it had to be large and majestic enough to show the world he wasn't gutless anymore."

"What about the painting, did you give it to him?"

"Never had the chance. He stopped by the studio and looked at some of my new work, but he wasn't happy with anything he saw. He only stayed a few minutes then received some kind of phone call that put him into a terrible mood and he left."

"Did he mention who his business partner was?"

Julian looked past her and smiled. "Darling, it's starting to get late. The ball is in a few hours, you should probably think about getting ready."

Automatically, Kate glanced at her watch. It was close to seven. So much for the salon. "I'm not going. I don't want to talk to him tonight. We both need some time to cool down. Now about his business partner?"

Julian grinned and shook his head. "Didn't say but seemed awfully eager to talk to Lucas in private. Sure you're not going to be there tonight?"

"No, now stop asking me."

"All right, but just in case you change your mind, I'll have the staff put a little something in your room." He grinned and stretched out his arms. "Enjoy the cabana, my little gift to you both."

There was a flash of light and he was gone. Just as the sunset ended, candles ignited across the interior of the cabana, giving the space a romantic feel. Frowning, she pondered his final remark and turned back toward her tee. Annoyance turned to shock when she saw Grant heading toward her.

Part of her wanted to hide. He looked so determined, so conflicted, like an angry parent intent on instilling a lesson with his delinquent child. Kate lifted her chin and held her ground, prepared for round two. If he wanted to pick up where they left off, she would be more than happy to oblige.

"What do you want?" she asked angrily, not sure if she could handle the answer.

Grant charged up to her, grabbing the club from her hand, and tossing it to the ground. Before she could respond, he slid his hand into her hair, pulling her mouth to his, crushing her lips, and forcing his tongue into her mouth. His passion was overwhelming, the possessiveness poured from him. With a small cry, she let his yearning overpower her and succumbed to his need, yielding to the depth of his kiss, and matching his desire with her own.

"I want you. I'm sorry," he replied, his voice low and filled with a need she had never heard before.

Kate blinked and, for a moment, saw a flash of guilt so strong it scared her. "I'm sorry too. I was being stupid," she cried, running her fingers through his hair.

She didn't know what had happened but he looked like a broken man. Her heart shattered for the ache he felt and she pulled him to her, hoping to kiss away his pain.

Grant lifted her off the ground, carrying her toward the opulent bed. His fingers spread beneath her shirt, peeling away her top to reveal her black lacy bra.

Kate tugged at his shirt and released his belt. He paused

at her skirt to cross his arms and grab at the soft cotton of his shirt. With a single pull it was up and over his head. She ran her fingers over the ripples of his taut waist, never tiring of his naked body.

"You're so beautiful," he murmured as he trailed his hands up her breasts, releasing the clasp to her bra. Stripping her down, he caught her hands with his own, pushing them through the layer of pillows to the luxurious divan below.

She smiled, rejoicing in the way he took command. His emotion was so great, she couldn't block out the thoughts that rang through her head.

"Yes," she gasped as she felt him ready himself to enter her. "Do that and everything else."

'*You're reading me?*' His thoughts floated to her.

"Not by choice. Your thoughts are so powerful, I can't block them out."

Grant smiled and pushed himself up on his forearms. He slammed into her with such intensity that she cried out, begging for him to never stop, demanding all that he could manage and so much more.

The fire in her built and, suddenly, all she could feel, hear, was the intensity of his love. With all the power she could muster, she forced her thighs together, feeling a surge of pleasure from him as she rolled him over. Straddling him, she joined his rhythm, and together they rode the crest of raw emotion.

Desiring more, she pulled away and flipped herself onto all fours. Happily obliging, he entered her from behind, their bodies joined with such force that she cried out with happy abandon. His hands were everywhere, trailing pressure on her soft skin that ignited her and drove her to new heights of rapture. Again and again, he drove deep into her, cramming her with such fullness that her moans of ecstasy pierced the night.

"Come for me, Kate," he rumbled. "I need to hear you come."

She nodded, unable to utter a word. Her world was spiraling out of control, her body felt like it was pure flame. Clenching herself to him, she felt him flip her again.

"Grant, yes," she panted.

His skin glistened with sweat. The delightful muskiness swept over her, followed by wave after powerful wave of vigor and power. She gloried in his need to possess her as she arched her back and screamed his name.

Her exclamations shredded his self-control, seizing him and making him her own. Grant let out a moan as his body shuttered in release and shattered its earthly bounds.

She gasped as a wave of power flooded her senses, pushing her back into ecstasy like it was her first time. Kate cried out again, unable to stand the beauty of the man within her. He looked like pure light, captured in a god form. Grant was the piece of her soul that yearned for freedom and sun. He filled her with such joy, she didn't know how she existed before he came along.

Lying beside him, their bodies languishing in the cool evening breeze, she wondered about his sudden need to possess her, to express in actions how he felt. She resisted the desire to read him, respecting the complexity and privacy of the man who had chosen her to be at his side.

Grant stirred and opened his eyes. A satisfied smile came over his face as he felt her fingers splayed in his own. Flipping onto his back he slowly panned their surroundings. "So do I want to know where this traveling bedroom came from?"

Kate smiled then crawled over him toward a glass pitcher of strawberry margaritas. Pouring a large glass, it was all she could do to keep it upright as he pulled her back by her ankles.

"Accommodations are courtesy of Julian. A bit over the top, but much better than sand and grass stains."

Grant took a sip of her drink and propped himself up on his side. "Remind me to thank him when I see him, though I don't know how he figured this would be needed out here."

"It's one of his powers. He can manifest objects, teleport, and has limited intuition about the future."

Grant lazily ran his fingers up and down her thigh. "Lucky him. If we can't find the keys, he might need some of those powers to survive."

Kate smacked her head and quickly relayed her conversation with Julian. With the sudden distraction, she had forgotten about her cousin's interrogation and this new piece of the investigation. Watching Grant hunt through the bed for his cell phone made her mind snap back to reality. They couldn't just hide away. They were the best chance to close the case that threatened to destroy them all.

"So Lucas is the one that the Council should focus on?"

Kate closed her eyes and tried to pinpoint the thoughts of her cousins in interrogation. She gasped as a bombardment of information hit her at once. Between the wails and cries came heinous confessions but nothing that got them any closer to the keys.

Focusing on Lucas gave her the best advantage. "He did play golf that day, just as Julian and Lucy mentioned," she said, scanning through his memories. The torture made his thoughts scattered, and she was bounced between past and present, trying to sift through the mud, back to the days that mattered.

"How much does he know about the keys?" Grant asked. He held up the speaker on his cell.

Around her, the cabana disappeared. Suddenly she and Grant were on the golf course, pulled by one of her powers into watching the four of them at the ninth green. She was almost to the memory she needed. "Have an incredible proposition for you, Lee," she recited slowly as the images in front of them slowed to a crawl. "Stumbled across something that will make Leland and your brother top of the Morgan family."

"I think we're working you too hard, Gus. You're delusional. We're already at the top of the Morgan family."

"Lucas, I'm talking about owning the whole world. Each

one of you with a place on the Council."

Lucas hit the ball, easily beating Gus's last swing. "Gus, your powers include reworking objects—which doesn't include turning lead to gold, so of no use to me. A three-second ability to see the future, also totally pointless, because what does a three-second head start get anybody? And teleportation—the most common and boring power in the whole family. None of those talents have the capacity to overturn the Council. How in your deluded mind do you think you can pull this off?"

Gus pulled him to the side and watched as Julian and Lucy took their place on the green. "By unleashing Hell in Heaven and on Earth."

Lucas snorted his distain. "Earth, no problem, but Heaven? The only way to do that would be to eliminate every Anderson along the way."

"And I've started on a plan for that, but what if there was a way around the Anderson family?"

"Woo Hoo, Gussy, let's go. There are drinks to enjoy and men to blow!"

Gus waved at Lucy and turned back to Lucas. "If I could pull it off, would you support my plan?"

"If that pea brain of yours figured a way around the Anderson choke hold, then I'm all in. Tell me more."

Gus shook his head. "Can't. My partner warned me not to say even this much. Will fill you in at the Summit. Just be ready to follow."

Kate gasped as another wave of memories overtook her. The scene around her changed and she was back at the cabana. "That's all he knows. He was supposed to meet with Gus after the opening ceremonies but something scared Gus off. He doesn't know what Gus was really up to and neither do the others."

Grant nodded and picked up his cell phone. "We just saw the whole thing." He nodded his head at the response. "Right. Right. Okay." He glanced at his watch and hung up the phone. "We better get going. We'll probably miss the dinner but there's still time before the Council declarations."

Kate groaned and pulled the sheets over her head. "Can't we skip the ball and stay here?"

Grant reached over, pulled the sheet back, and gently kissed her. "We'll get an update from Alexis and Jake then speak with Gus's siblings and see if they can give us any insight into the mysterious partner."

Kate sighed and started to gather their clothes. Hesitating slightly, she started to speak then shook her head.

"What?" asked Grant.

"Why did you and Alexis break up?"

He looked down at his shirt, pulling at the buttons. "We were part of a chosen team called The Protectors. It was 1800s and a delicate time for industrial development in North America. We were heading into a future of war and tried to stop enemies from creating additional problems."

"Like the Morgans?"

"Mostly them, but there were other factors involved. Alexis was driven, confident, and passionate about her beliefs." He paused, pulling on his pants. "Back then, she was a lot like you."

"Explains why I don't like her."

He smiled but there was sadness in his eyes. "Something in her altered and, as her life extended and her power grew, she started to change. She began to get these grandiose ideas about eliminating all evil and bringing back the golden age to humans. She wanted to create a perfect world, full of the right people who would only live with the purest intentions."

Kate stood up and slipped on her sandals. "Can that even be done? I'm no fan of evil but everyone has a dark side to them. How could you create a society with only good intentions? That would be taking away free will."

"The Elders felt the same and ordered us to rework the team, feeling there was too much concentration of power in too few hands. We had huge fights about us, our beliefs, and the direction of the organization, until I broke it off, left the group, and joined the BOI, which eventually became the FBI."

Kate glanced at him with embarrassment. "I'm sorry about overreacting before. I don't know why I was being so stupid."

"No, I'm sorry. I should have been clear. Alexis and I are done. Forever. I don't ever go back. I focus on the future. You can trust me, okay?"

She nodded. "Same with me and, whatever happens next, I'd die before I let anything happen to you."

Before he could answer, his cell phone rang. "It's Ambrose, he has a couple of questions for you."

She took the phone and he watched as she happily chatted up a storm. Guilt filled his mind as he replayed Mark's story about Texas. She had died for him once and, now that he knew the truth, he would make sure that it would never happen again.

CHAPTER 21

Kate glanced at the dresses that hung before her then back at her watch and swore. The walk back to her room had taken slightly longer than she expected and now she was showered, naked and really, really late for the ball.

Grant had left on the way back from the driving range, citing a couple of loose ends and a promise to meet at the front doors of the chateau's grand ballroom. That was twenty minutes ago and his texts started as casual, then as the minutes passed and she failed to show, changed to mock threats, citing he would come and break down her door.

True to his word, Julian had sent three stunning dresses with explicit instructions. "Do not touch any of them until you have made up your mind. Just like the night ahead, once you set your mind to something, you must adhere to only that path."

She bit her lip and looked at the options again. The first was a stunning, off the shoulder, green satin and chiffon. She couldn't tell but it looked vaguely reminiscent of eighteen hundreds, complete with a cinched waist and light bustle of taffeta. The second was a deep plum strapless, with tiny crystals and a dramatic plunging back. Attached to the front of it was a crystal peacock pin, which she remembered from a painting as being one of his logos. The third was a stunning work of metallic silver and gold. Intricate threads of gold were woven into a silver bodice, and the silver skirt flowed like mercury, reminded her slightly of Sapphire's gift.

Her cell phone vibrated again and she sighed, letting fate make the decision for her. Kate squinted and reached out, unsure of which one she would touch. Her hand barely graced the fabric, when a bomb seemed to go off around her. She shielded her eyes but it was too late. The light of a thousand flash bulbs blinded her, leaving her unable to see beyond the stars that filled her eyes. Amidst the chaos around her, she felt a cool mist spray her skin, quickly followed by intense euphoria. Kate fought to stay on her feet as vertigo hit her and the room began to spin. Then as suddenly as it began, it stopped and she stumbled forward on legs that felt like they belonged to someone else. From out of her blindness, she felt an arm around her waist, supporting her.

Kate's sight returned and she looked around at the faces that smiled back. She was outside the ballroom and the arm she felt was Grant, supporting her.

"Where the heck did you come from?"

She shook her head, just as surprised as he appeared to be. "One minute, I was choosing a dress, and the next minute, I was here." She focused on his face, unsure of what was going on. "I'm not naked, am I?"

He smiled and let his gaze linger, looking her up and down. "Quite the contrary, you are stunning."

He swiveled her hips around so she caught a glimpse of them in a nearby mirror. In his black tie, her breath caught at how handsome he looked. She gaped in surprise as the image that looked back couldn't possibly be her. Dressed in deep plum, her dark hair was a sea of curls and crystals, cascading down her naked back. In place of her cell phone was a dark purple and black crystal encrusted clutch, with a peacock logo popping out of its center.

"You look amazing," she breathed.

"I'm a vagrant next to you. That's quite the dress, Detective. It's getting me all hot and bothered."

"It's a gift from Julian. In the 'forties, he was a stylist before the word was even born."

"Hmm, that's twice I owe him," Grant murmured as they moved toward the entrance of the room.

"Maybe I should go back and change," Kate whispered, looking a bit uncomfortable. "I'm not wearing any underwear."

Grant moved his hand up her back, holding her firmly by his side. Under his gaze, she flushed with excitement. "Make that three times, and you're not going anywhere."

They entered the ballroom, transformed into a palace of heightened decadence, making the name Crystallise Ball appropriate indeed. The centerpiece of the room was also the backdrop for the Council's seating area. An enormous freestanding waterfall of flowing crystals cascaded over a precipice of large cut blocks of smoky quartz. Enormous arrangements of white flowers sparkled at the center of each table.

In the middle of the room and directly in front of the eight thrones that made up the Council's seating area was a large dance floor, currently occupied by couples from both families.

The tables from both sides seemed to blend into each other, a mixture of silver and gold tablecloths, decorated with overflowing centerpieces of pale flowers and bottles of pink champagne.

"Wow, this is—"

"A magnificent piece of art, not unlike you, my dear Katie!" proclaimed Julian. He walked toward them with two flutes of champagne, giving them his nod of approval.

"Jules, why am I not surprised you had a hand in this? It's incredible!"

"As are you, looking fabulous in one of my original creations."

Reaching out, he offered his hand to Grant. "Julian Morgan, that chance encounter in the gallery didn't give me the opportunity to formerly introduce myself."

"Grant Anderson. Thanks for looking after my girl. I think I owe you a few."

To Kate's surprise, Julian blushed, waving objections away with his hands. "Oh, no, not at all. Well, if we survive the Summit, then sure, I might come a calling, but everything in its own time."

"Speaking of, can you direct me to Gus Morgan's family?"

Julian frowned and shook his head. "Business later, Agent. Dinner's almost over and you both look famished. Why don't I show you to your table?"

Kate looked around. Half of the patrons were sitting at what appeared to be a never ending feast of courses. The others were milling about in small groups or dancing to an eclectic variety of music from the small orchestra to the right of the dance floor. "We have a table? Please tell me it's not with my mother."

"Oh, she tried, darling. Of course, she refused to have an Anderson sit with her, so best not to go and introduce yourself."

"Noted. I'm sure we can find a place with my family," Grant replied, scanning the floor.

"No need, come with me."

Julian led them to a VIP table across the dance floor. It was off to the side for privacy but closer to the front for a clear view of the Council, once they decided to arrive.

With his usual flourish, Julian deposited the couple there then disappeared to continue his hosting rounds.

"So is this the outsider's table or special privilege for law enforcement?" Kate joked.

"After today's festivities, I'm willing to bet the former," Ambrose said dryly. He was sprawled back in his chair, tuxedo bow tie askew, and looking suspiciously around the room. Beside him, a distinguished lady, reached up her hand toward Kate.

"You'll have to excuse my husband. He doesn't know how to separate work from play. I'm Gloria Anderson."

"Yes, I know who you are," replied Kate. It wasn't every day a Superior Court Justice sat in front of her. "Judge Anderson, I had no idea you were Ambrose's wife. Kate Morgan. It's a pleasure to meet you."

"The pleasure is mine, my dear. Anyone who can put up with Grant is stellar in my books."

Grant leaned over and gave Gloria a kiss on the cheek. "Whole heartedly agree, Gloria." He glanced over at Mark, who was sitting next to a half-eaten plate of salad. "Lose your date, Mark?"

He grunted and looked away. Kate sat down on the other side of him and glanced at the two place cards beside her. "Where are Jake and Alexis?"

Mark shrugged his shoulders, "I figured they were with you guys. I haven't seen them all afternoon."

Watching Grant in conversation, Kate smiled at his relationship with the rest of his family. They had a comfortable banter that she envied. It was the conversation of a real family that didn't just make the effort on occasions like funerals and weddings. They shared their lives with each other.

While the waiter filled her wine glass, she looked down at a small box sitting adjacent to her plate. Pulling off the ribbon, she dumped a small crystal cube and a handful of sparkles into her hand. On its face, the etching was simple with two words, *Summit 2018*.

"Oh, Julian, always the eye for detail," she murmured as she placed the box in her purse.

From across the room, the orchestra struck up a rousing polka, making it almost impossible to hear. With salad, a filet mignon, and a hearty piece of cheesecake placed in front of her, Kate took the break in conversation to skip the salad and dive right into the main course.

Two bites in and she felt the plate pulled to one side. Jake appeared from the dance floor and proceeded to devour her meal without as much as a word.

"Hey, give that back," Kate exclaimed, putting the cheesecake in front of him instead. Looking down at the leftovers of her steak, she sighed and pushed it away, reaching for her salad instead.

Grant shifted to the seat beside him. "Where have you been and where is Alexis?"

Jake finished the cheesecake and gestured at the waiter to bring a second plate. "Well, let's just say, we nipped away for a bit of afternoon delight. When I left, she was looking quite relaxed and content."

Grant looked at him suspiciously. He was acting almost manic, as if he had a hundred too many cups of coffee. "No offense, Jake, but you're not exactly her type. What happened with the Guardian of the Keys?"

"Oh, that was great, interesting bloke, I must say."

"Well, what did he say? What happened to the keys?"

Jake reached for a second plate of steak, cutting into it with such force that he almost broke the plate. A light sheen of sweat covered his brow, and his gestures became more and more erratic as the story went on. "Nice chap, said he was cleaning out his house and must have accidentally discarded it, mistaking it for a worthless artifact. Can you imagine, just tossing it by mistake?"

"Jake, what's wrong with you?"

Kate's question didn't even cause him to pause. "Nothing, luv, feeling great," he said, his voice rising in pitch and level. "Haven't felt this good in years."

Everyone paused their conversation and stared at him. Grant leaned over to Ambrose. "I think he's been memory jacked."

"Memory what?" asked Kate. "What is that?"

Grant's mouth set in a firm line. "Someone has altered his memories and he's having a bad reaction." Looking at Jake, he spoke to him very clearly and slowly. "Jake, who initiated sex, you or Alexis?"

"Why me, of course. I've wanted her since I set eyes on her yesterday."

"Uh, huh. What positions?"

"Grant!" Kate exclaimed.

She quieted when he held up his hand. "Top, bottom, front, back? Give me details." Grant grabbed him by the arm. "Remember the officer in New York?" he asked Kate. "People who have been memory jacked can't remember specific details, only feelings. The person who did this would have filled in only minor blanks."

Jake seemed the opposite of offended. He paused from eating to sit back and puff out his chest. "Why, it started on the floor—no, on the bed. I—I don't actually remember, but it was great."

"Son of a bitch," Grant swore.

Ambrose rubbed his eyes, echoing his sentiment. He picked up his cell phone and starting barking orders to the person on the other end.

"What's going on with him?"

Grant shook his head at Kate then stood up and pulled Jake out of his chair. "I'm going to punch you in the face. It's going to hurt but you'll feel much better in a few seconds. Mark, grab his arms. I don't need him falling into the next table."

"Grant, are you sure this is necessary?"

Gloria, caught Kate by the arm and pulled her back from the men. "Don't worry, dear. He'll be just fine."

Mark grabbed Jake and steadied him as Grant drew back and threw a right cross. At the last minute, Jake ducked, leaving Mark to receive the punch. Swearing and thrown off balance from the impact, Mark caught himself on the chair, swiveling it around, and doing a full three sixty. Throwing the chair aside, he hit Jake in the jaw, knocking him to the floor.

"Jake!" Kate yelled.

Curiosity from the opposing tables was quickly quelled. Ambrose raised his hands at the adjoining tables. "It's all right folks, just police business."

"Ow, Grant, what the hell?" Mark said, rubbing his jaw.

"Sorry, cuz, didn't think he had the sense to duck."

"Really? Look at the guy. Does he look like the type to leave a bar on two feet?"

Kate rushed to his side. "Jake? Can you hear me? Are you all right?"

Jake pushed himself into a seated position, staring up at the people above him. "What the hell are you lot looking at? And what am I doing on the bloody floor?"

Kate smiled, glad that he was returning to his old self. "Jake, we think you were under some kind of memory spell. What's the last thing you remember?"

He looked at her and then did a double take. "God, you look beautiful."

Irritation crossed Grant's face as he balled his fists. "Maybe he needs to be hit again."

"Oye, cool your jets, mate. The last thing I remember was you and her staring each other down while Alexis prattled on about some old mission." Jake glanced around. "Where is she anyway?"

"That's a good question. Do you remember anything about your meeting with the Guardian?"

"The who?"

"The guy who lost the keys, think Jake."

Jake shrugged his shoulders and slowly climbed to his feet. "Got nothing for you. I can't remember a thing, other than that I feel great."

Grant swore and spun around pointing his finger at Ambrose. Kate watched the two men exchange a heated conversation then Ambrose shook his head. "We don't know where she is at the moment."

"She?" Kate exclaimed. "You mean Alexis?"

Jake grimaced. "She did this to me? How do you know?"

"'Cause she's done it to me in the past," Grant replied grimly. "Besides, with your strong personality, she's one of the few who could have pulled it off successfully."

"Thanks, I think. But why? Why whammy me into thinking we slept together. She could've just asked."

"'Cause, my old partner knows more that she's letting

on, and she needed you out of the way." Grant stared across the dance floor, scanning the crowd for any sign of Alexis. Pulling Kate to his side, he shot her a look, silently asking if she could read Alexis's thoughts.

"Nothing that I can get a read on but, to be honest, there's too much interference here," she said. "Maybe if I leave and try from a quieter part of the hotel."

She felt his arm encircle her waist, pulling her closer to him. "You're not going anywhere." Feeling him stiffen, she looked across the crowd to see Lucas and Laurelle approaching. Their act in front of the entourage gave no indication of their interrogation at the hands of the Council members. The poisonous thoughts were a different matter and chilled Kate to the bone.

"What the hell do you want?"

"Family matter, Anderson. We need to have a chat with our cousin."

"Not without me, you're not."

"Thought you might see it that way," Lucas replied. A bolt of energy flew from his hands, hitting Grant in the side. The blast caught him off guard, sending him crashing into their table. Mark leapt up and deflected the rest of the blast, creating a large hole in the wall behind him.

"Grant!" Kate screamed. She tried to turn and run but Lucas grabbed her by the wrist, holding her close to him.

Around them the hall erupted in screams and shouts from both families. Kate watched as a small army of Morgan's rallied behind Lucas and Laurelle.

Behind her she felt the rustle of skirts and suits. Glancing back, she saw Ambrose to her left and a dozen men behind him.

"Give us back the keys and maybe we'll forget this indiscretion," Ambrose yelled, staring Lucas down.

Kate's arm shot out, punching Lucas in the stomach. With his grip released, she rushed to Grant's side, helping him up from the floor.

"I'm okay," he said, but the wince in his expression gave her cause for alarm.

"You don't look okay," she replied, her voice filled with concern.

He gave her a quick kiss on the lips, "Just knocked the wind out of me." Stretching to his full height, he walked toward Ambrose at the front of the line.

"What the hell do you want, Lucas?" Kate spat. "Don't think for a minute, you can play innocent in all of this."

He scanned her body, a smile creeping across his face. "Quite the right jab, Katherine. My baby girl is growing up. Your mother said time is up. Come and rejoin the family."

"Go to hell."

Kate joined Jake, her eyes scanning the crowd for her mother. She didn't immediately see her, but that wasn't a surprise. Elizabeth Morgan was the type to observe and criticize from a distance. A wave of anxiety washed over her. Confronting her cousins didn't concern her. It was the look of victory on their faces. Like she had been played and the rules of the games were deciding how badly she had lost. The band had fallen silent and the crowd stood at attention, anxious to see what would happen next.

"Give them back the keys," Kate said angrily.

"We don't have them," Laurelle replied.

"But you know about it, and you're wishing you had them now."

Laurelle laughed, her perfect face changing into a grotesque sneer. "The chance to create Hell on Earth and see it duplicated in Heaven. Who wouldn't want that opportunity? I'm just sorry Gus didn't act sooner."

"What are you talking about?"

"Don't be stupid, Kate. Gus was an idiot but he has some common sense. You don't think he would have arrived at the conference and not brought such a precious commodity with him?"

"You know where they are?" Grant challenged.

"Of course we do," Lucas replied.

He raised his arms and his army took a step closer. The crowd of tuxedos and finery seemed split down the middle and Kate could feel the animosity coming from both sides. She blocked out the thoughts that bombarded her and focused on Lucas. He was hiding something big and it wasn't the lies. The keys were still missing but there was something else…something that he had managed to conceal even during the interrogation session earlier.

"Lucas," she demanded. "What have you done to the Council?"

A hush fell over the hall as all eyes turned to him. He raised his finger and shook it at her. "Naughty, naughty, baby girl. You know it's impolite to read other people's minds."

"Stop calling me that."

Lucas turned and leapt onto the stage that housed the Council thrones. Pulling a microphone from a nearby stand, he sat down in the middle chair and addressed the crowd. "My baby cousin is right. We have relieved the Council of its duties. The time has come for a new Council and a new age. For too long we have sat in the shadows and allowed history to unfold without us. We are immortal, we are superior, and we are the evolution of the human race."

The crowd murmured, though, Kate noticed, not opposed completely to his reasoning. She could hear outrage combined with applause. It was clear that his comments were not foreign to the families or their way of thinking.

"Families, we have the power to rebuild the earth and advance it farther than modern man can even fathom. Why not use to the keys to break the walls down and merge the good and the bad to make Earth a better place to live."

"But what about the balance?" yelled someone from the crowd.

"Ah yes, the balance. Haven't we been maintaining the balance for millennia? So we shall continue to maintain the balance, just at the hands of a new Council. A Council that isn't afraid to challenge its makers and do what is right for the good of everyone involved. A Council that understands the necessity of evolution and change in a modern world."

"You mean a Council ruled by you," Grant said. "Nice speech, but at the end of the day, you want the power for yourself."

"Interesting words, from the heir apparent to the next Council."

Grant bristled. "I want no part in creating a new Council."

"Oh, but you don't have a choice."

Kate turned to him. "What's he talking about?"

Ambrose leaned over and quietly filled in the gaps. "It's an old failsafe from the time of the crusades. If the Council ever becomes incapacitated, their power transfers to four members for safekeeping. Two members from each family and for the Andersons it was two members of the Protectors."

"Who are the recipients from our family, Lucas?"

"The first born son of a first born son, assuming no original family members exist," Lucas replied.

Julian stepped forward. "My grandfather, Alexander, was the only one not on the Council but he died under mysterious circumstances. Lucy's father Harold was the first born of Nero and he was murdered as well."

Jake stepped forward. "Hang on, my father Charles also died under mysterious circumstances, so that leaves Leland—"

"And me," Lucas said with a smirk, "his first born son."

"You planned this," Kate yelled. "You murdered Gus and you murdered the Council!"

"The Council's not dead, baby girl. They're just learning a lesson. And, as far as Gus is concerned, well, I wish I could take credit for that one."

Lucas smiled and gestured to his right. From behind one of the thrones, a vision in red sequins emerged.

Grant sucked in his breath. "Alexis," he snarled.

"We were supposed to be the future, Grant. Husband and wife and a face of the new Council."

Grant stiffened, watching as she stepped from the stage and toward him. "We are the last of the protectors and, in an hour, when the Council is fully seated in their new resting place, we will be the beneficiaries of half their power. The transformation of the world can begin." Her hand stretched up to graze his face but he smacked it away.

"In an hour," he replied in a menacing tone, "I'll have found the Council and you'll suffer for your betrayal."

She nodded sadly. "I thought you might feel that way. Especially after taking up with a Morgan whore." Before anyone could react, she pulled a dagger and plunged it into his side. Kate screamed his name but the damage had been done. He slumped to the floor, clutching his side. Kate stretched out her hand and Alexis flew across the room, propelled back by her power.

The crowd surged forward, forcing Lucas to jump on stage, waving his hands. "Family members, I offer you a unique opportunity. The keys to the kingdom of heaven are hidden somewhere on the premises. Bring them to me and I will give you a place on the Council. Join us in the creating the future, or do nothing and perish at your neighbor's hand."

His words created panic. The crowd erupted into chaos, some tearing apart the hall, searching for the keys, while others took the opportunity to address old grudges. Fights began to break out everywhere. Ambrose rushed to Grant's side. "We have to get him out of here. this is going to turn into a blood bath soon."

"Not going anywhere," Grant panted. "She has to be stopped."

"Grant, you're hurt and you can't be hurt," Ambrose said. He grabbed the hilt of the dagger then pulled back yelling in pain.

"What? What is it?" Kate cried wildly as Gloria rushed to Ambrose's side.

Flipping his badly burned hands over, Gloria closed her eyes and chanted something under her breath. His hands illuminated and, when the light disappeared, he was fully healed.

"You cured him, can you do the same for Grant?"

Gloria shook her head. "Kate, that dagger has evil in it. It took some kind of a hex to burn Ambrose that badly."

Kate stared at the handle. Judging by its size, she knew the blade couldn't be more than an inch in length. With her knowledge as a doctor, and a quick assessment of Grant's injuries, it looked as if it had hit just below his lung and it could be safely removed.

"Gloria, hand me those cloth napkins, I'm going to pull it out."

"But the blade—"

"I don't care what kind of hex it has on it. It's killing him." She looked around and spied a drink on the table. "Jake," she barked, "That glass of alcohol. What is it?"

He stumbled to the table, narrowly avoiding a fist fight between his cousins Glen, Sophia, and her date. Grabbing the glass, he took a quick whiff, "Ugh, bourbon, I think."

"Give it here." She grabbed the drink and poured half of it on the napkins. Handing the glass to Grant, she watched him down it. "Ready? This might hurt a bit."

He nodded and she quickly pulled at the handle, switching it for the alcohol infused cloth. He grimaced a bit, then nodded his relief.

Kate stared at the knife. It appeared to be made of a single shard of transparent crystal with an ornate silver handle. Inside the blade were tiny shards of black and red all pointing downward, burrowing toward the tip of the dagger.

"Are you okay? Is it hurting you?" asked Gloria

"It can't hurt her. She's a Morgan."

They looked up to see Sapphire standing there. "Saffi, you need to leave," Grant gasped. "It's not safe for any of you here."

Sapphire nodded then pulled at Kate's left wrist with her

hand. "Uncle Grant can only be hurt by something so evil, just to look at it would kill a normal man,"

Bending over, Sapphire removed several anklets from her leg and tied them around Kate's wrist. Just for a second, the delicate strands of thread swirled in a sea of colors, then settled onto her skin, not unlike the etching of an ornate tattoo.

Oblivious to Sapphire's actions, Kate stared at the blade. Artifacts, supernatural powers, and theories swirled in her mind. Making an educated guess, she shared her hunch with the crowd, "These shards are from the Spear of Destiny. If it could kill the Son of God, then it can certainly kill Grant."

Jake looked at the blade in horror. "Are you kidding me? How the hell did Alexis touch it?"

"I don't know or care," Kate replied, tucking the dagger into her purse. "We need to get Grant to safety."

On the other side of the ballroom, crowds of people panicked as the lights dimmed and fireworks erupted from crystal sculptures around the outer perimeter of the dance floor. Kate looked around for signs of Alexis but in the chaos of bodies she was nowhere to be found.

"Jake, grab his arm, we have to get him out of here." She grabbed Sapphire by the hand gave her a quick hug. "I'll protect your uncle. You need to get your family together and get out of here. Find a safe place to hide."

Pointing to Ambrose, she pushed Sapphire in his direction. Lifting Grant up, Kate motioned to Jake. "Come on. I need to find a place to operate."

Together they supported his weight, pulling him outside of the ballroom. "Where are we going to go?" Jake asked, looking around.

"My room. At least it's protected against Morgans."

They dragged him down the hallway and cut across the back half of the courtyard. Jake propped Grant between Kate and a stone sculpture then crept down the garden path to get a view of the North wing from the garden's flip side.

Kate gently lifted Grant's head, her alarm growing by the second. He was slipping in and out of consciousness and, despite her pressure on the wound, every step seemed to result in a bigger blood stain.

"How's he doing?" Jake asked breathlessly. He had his pocket knife in one hand and had sidled up to the cold stone around them.

"Not good. He's losing a lot of blood. How clear is the way?"

"It's not. They're starting to erect some kind of cheesy barricade. Larry, Lee, and a bunch of associates. I think they're trying to corral people to certain parts of the chateau."

"What do you think they're up to?"

"Wide scale massacre? Who knows? One thing's for sure, I don't think they counted on ol' Gussy making them go on a scavenger hunt."

Kate stilled, reaching out to try and read her cousins minds. She was petrified for Grant but for everyone's sake, she had to focus. She had pushed away her fear before. Separating her love for him and the need to survive would be their only way out of this nightmare. "Jake, you have to find the Council. They're the only ones who can stop this rebellion."

"What about you guys?"

"Help me get him to the gallery. There are a couple of alcoves hidden away and the room only has two exits. If I have to, I'll make my stand there."

He rubbed the back of his neck, his distaste for her plan clearly showing in his face. "Any suggestions for where the Council might be?"

"Trust only Ambrose and the people you brought with you. I don't have a clear answer, the Leland clan are doing a good job at hiding their thoughts, but there's a fear of claustrophobia and being buried alive coming from a couple of them."

Grant reached up and pulled Jake to him. Whispering

something in Jake's ear, Grant slumped back when Jake nodded.

"What did he tell you, Jake?"

"The name of someone who can help me, but don't worry about that. Where the hell could they hide eight bodies?"

He paced around then suddenly snapped his fingers. "I remember reading something about a family crypt on a part of the grounds. Didn't see any graveyards when I was casing this place so maybe it's underground."

She nodded and motioned to Jake. Together they carried Grant though the back door of the gallery. Passing Julian's dragon painting, they dragged him onto a bench in front of the large canvas with a pastoral scene.

The atmosphere was almost reverent, the quietness of the gallery a welcome distraction from the anarchy they had just come from. While Kate attended to Grant's unconscious form, Jake ran the perimeter checking the doors and windows of the building, the sound of his footsteps echoing throughout the hall.

Kate bit her lip and pulled off the blood soaked cloth napkins. She gasped as memories of triage during the Korean War flooded back. He looked like he had been hit with shrapnel. The blade had done more damage than she'd initially thought and, through the blood, she could see the ripped and torn remnants of skin and muscle.

"Damn it, I wish I had a trauma kit."

Kate cried out in pain as her left wrist spasmed and a feeling like fire coursed through her veins. She grabbed at her arm and gasped as one of Sapphire's wristlets burst into flame.

"Jesus, Kate, are you okay?" Jake cried. Rubbing his eyes, he stared at her. "For a minute there, it looked like your arm was on fire."

"It was, but I'm okay." She caught her breath as a large duffle bag appeared at her feet. Bending down, she started to cry in relief when she saw what was inside.

"It's got everything. A full supply of surgical tools,

bandages, and saline." With shaking fingers, she grabbed a syringe and a large bottle of morphine.

"Have you got any guns in there?" Jake asked. A loud boom, shook the room and he swore under his breath. "I sealed the doors but that won't last long. We're going to have to move you. This space is too open for you to protect him."

She shook her head and injected the morphine. "He's too critical to move, Jake. Besides you need to go."

He looked up as another blast rocked the building. "You can't fight them off by yourself." Gesturing to the door in frustration, it was all he could do to keep his balance against the rattling shocks. "If Alexis is part of that mob, she'll kill both of you just to get Grant's share of the Council's powers."

"And if you're dead, there's no hope to find the Council. Then what? Someone finds the key and it's not only our families who will be wiped out of existence."

He paced around, watching her set up an IV bag of saline. "I just don't feel right leaving you."

"You don't have to worry, Jake. Not at all." They turned to see Julian hurrying toward them. Another gigantic explosion rocked the building and he tottered to the side, almost falling against one of his paintings.

"Jules, you should get out of here. Whoever's on the other side of that door is going to bring down the entire building."

"Katie, please, this building has endured multiple attempts to breach its walls—from kings, popes and one bonafide wizard. Better people than Morgans or Andersons have tried without success."

"So the doors are safe?" Jake asked, looking a little more confident.

"Well, I didn't say that. A barricade is only as good as its designer and, to be honest, Jake, putting up walls is not your specialty."

"Fantastic. So we just sit here and wait until they break down the doors?"

"Not really. We have a Council to find."

"But, Kate—"

Julian raised a hand. "Jake, you are aware of my specialties, my gifts for the strange and unusual?"

Jake shook his head, as another shockwave sent a light rain of four-hundred-year-old dust showering down on them. "No, but I'm sure you're going to tell me," he said with a sigh. "Right, get on with it then. You obviously have a plan and I'd like to hear it before they turn us into a big pile of bones."

"Yes, well, I am heralded throughout the world for my paintings. Some people say they are absolutely magical." Julian gestured to the painting of the knight fighting a dragon. "Take Hubert for example. He's a positive party starter." He turned around and waved his hand. The painting started to shift and Hubert the Dragon came to life, shooting out flames into the walkway of the gallery.

"What the hell?" Jake blurted as he stumbled backward. The heat from the flames temporarily took the chill from the room. "You can make things come alive?"

"Oh, heavens no, my boy. That takes true gifts that I just don't have."

"Then how?"

"Well, it's a simple matter of understanding the right combination of time dilation and time travel. Once you know the formula, you trap a moment, add a bit of paint for sharpness and color and voila, a masterpiece that's not only functional but portable."

"Right, so my understanding of...oh...five words in that statement draws me to the conclusion that the bloody dragon is real?"

Another blast interrupted their conversation. This time, voices could be heard heading toward them. Kate glanced up from her work, a tiny piece of shrapnel in between her fingers.

"That's a great story, Jules, but a stationary dragon isn't going to ward off a mob of Morgans."

"No, but like I said, time dilation." Julian pointed to the pastoral painting at Stonehenge. "Two days in there equals two hours out here," he replied hurriedly as a window across from them blew apart. "That's all the time you get, so he had better be healed by then."

Before she could reply, the space around her went dark. She lifted her bloody hands to her face as a bright light encompassed them both and temporarily blinded her. When she opened her eyes, she was standing next to a harvest table, with Grant's unconscious form next to her.

"What the—Julian?" She glanced around the decrepit kitchen that looked like something out of the dark ages. A large stone hearth encompassed one wall. Instead of a stove or sink, there was a series of rickety tables and what looked like a hand pump for water in the middle of the clay floor. In the corner of the room was a small cot made of stretched leather and ratty blankets overfilled with bits of straw.

Kate checked Grant's vitals before putting down her scalpel and walking to the door. She gasped as the sunlight caught her off guard. She could feel the wind on her face and hear the rustle of the long grass around her.

Staring down, she noticed her clothes had changed as well. Gone was the evening gown, replaced with a dress that looked like it belonged in a Renaissance fair.

"We're in England," she said, trying to remain calm. "No, check that, we're in a picture set in England in what looks like, the 1600s." She walked back into the building and shut the door firmly behind her. Panicked thoughts were quickly replaced by logic. "Well, on the positive side, at least no one's trying to kill us here."

She checked on Grant. His color had returned and he was breathing easier. Picking up a set of tweezers, she continued to remove the tiny shards from his wound then, satisfied with her work, quickly stitched him up. Unsure of the safety of the water pump, she rooted around the kit until she found a bottle of sanitizer. Disinfecting her hands was only the beginning. She sighed and looked around. Sterilizing this room would take more than a small bottle of chemicals. "No water, no plumbing. Well, I can't expect much for being in a painting," she moaned. "I just wish the house had modern, working amenities, like a bathroom, running water, and maybe something to eat."

As soon as the words left her mouth, she regretted it. From her side, a sharp pain ripped through her. Screaming, Kate dropped to the floor, clutching her stomach. Her wails were enough to wake Grant and he weakly sat up, looking down at her.

"Kate?"

The pain was so strong, she couldn't answer him. Looking up, she stretched out her arm and watched as a second set of bracelets melted away. "Don't move, just stay there," she panted.

Another blinding flash of light, and she was hit with a wave of vertigo. Grant grunted something unintelligible and slumped back down on the table. Lifting her head, she watched as the scene around her changed. The tables reworked themselves to soapstone countertops with a farmer's sink and various pieces of stoneware. A professional range manifested at the far end of the room with a stainless-steel refrigerator next to it. The large stone hearth shrank to a something out of a country inn and the cot in the corner changed to a comfortable-looking queen sized bed.

Kate closed her eyes as the last wave of vertigo passed through her. Looking down at her arm, her fingers clawed at the remaining set of bracelets but they were attached as if tattooed to her wrist. Slowly she climbed to her feet and, steadying herself, leaned over Grant.

"Kate, what happened? Where are we?"

Smiling, she leaned over and kissed his forehead. "Hey, stranger, long time no see. Believe it or not, we're in one of Julian's paintings. How are you feeling?"

"The pain is gone, so better."

"That's the morphine talking, but you're healing quicker than I expected." She checked his wound and was surprised to see the bleeding had stopped and a pinkish glow was returning to wound site.

"Morphine? Where did you get morphine?"

She held up her arm. "Sapphire and her wrist bands. I asked for a trauma kit and got everything I needed."

He gently pulled her wrist and stared intently at the design on the bands. "Is that why the house just changed?" She nodded and he scowled. "Those are wishing beads in there. You can't use them again."

"Whatever trinket Sapphire gave me, it saved your life."

He groaned and started to sit up. "No, you saved my life. Again." Pausing as another wave of pain overtook him, he gritted his teeth and continued his explanation. "Wishing beads manifest your desires, but at a cost. Energy can't transform into matter without coming from somewhere. In this case, the objects, like the morphine, are made by sucking the life force from you."

"Well, a little lost life force was worth it."

Grant slowly slid off the table and tested his ability to walk around. Ignoring her objections, he pulled the IV out of his arm and flexed his hand. "You need to stop doing that. Stop putting your life in danger for mine."

She bristled at his response. "I'm fine."

"Are you?" Before she knew what was happening, he grabbed her and pinned her against the front door of the cottage. "Fight me off, come on."

The sudden onslaught of anger caught her by surprise. "Grant, this isn't like you. What are you doing?"

"Trying to prove a point. You know karate and I'm wounded. This should be a piece of cake for you."

Kate grabbed at his hand. Fueled by rage and confusion, she moved his arm from the top of her chest. He reacted quickly, pushing her back against the door and holding her in place with one hand pressed against her stomach. She gripped his wrist with both hands, the need to prove him wrong stronger than the erotic pull of his body pushing against her.

Pulling at his fingers felt like moving steel. Her breath became labored as she tried to dislodge him. It was no use, even in his weakened state, he easily overpowered her and she slumped against the door, tears rolling down her face in frustration.

"I—I can't. You're too heavy."

Slowly he lifted his hand, wiping her tears away. "I'm not too heavy. The beads have taken a piece of your life-force and drained your energy from you."

With one hand on her waist, he pulled her to him and fitted his mouth over hers. Carefully he kissed her, pushing away her initial resistance and opting to take her more fully with his mouth. She felt a surge of electricity race through her and before she could stop herself, pulled him closer, hungrily, silently begging for more. She felt his response— felt him harden and throb—as he captured her tongue with his and she flattened against him, molding her softness to his body.

Kate felt like she was a flower, basking in the morning sun. From the depth of his kiss came a surge of power, and she felt renewed, intense warmth overtaking and energizing her body.

"What is that?" she murmured, breaking off the kiss. "Why do I feel like I've been drugged? I feel so good."

Grant caressed the side of her face. His eyes were bright with a passion and desire that took her breath away. "You have a piece of me in you now. A tiny bit of my soul to re-place the parts you gave so selflessly away."

She felt her insides melt. The love she felt for him over-whelmed and filled her with fear at the same time. "But in your weakened state—"

"Around you I have the strength of Atlas. That's what you do to me."

A flush of embarrassment filled her. She looked down and tried to conceal the worry that had to be clouding her eyes. "Well, enough talk. We need to get you to bed, Special Agent Anderson."

"Exactly what I was thinking."

The faint stain of red under his bandages snapped her back to reality. "Not that. Not as long as you're injured. We only have a small window to heal you before we rejoin the battle out there."

Her reminder of their reality shattered the moment and he nodded wearily. He gingerly sat on the bed, slowly lowering to a lounging position. "How much time do we have here?"

Kate started exploring the kitchen, opening cupboard doors, and testing appliances. "Julian said something about two days equaling two hours out there."

Grant pulled a pillow under his head. "Your cousin is very clever. Time dilation mixed with a fluidity particle enhancer and he's managed to isolate a moment of space time hiding."

Kate stared at him, dumbfounded, a tea pot in one hand and a kettle in the other. "Wow. Gorgeous with a great body and a big brain. Suddenly, I feel very dumb."

She was rewarded with a mischievous grin. "Don't be ridiculous. When you've lived as long as I have, you pick up knowledge and expertise along the way."

"And understanding the secrets of the Universe is one of them?"

"Well, Doctor. Get me off bed rest and I'll be happy to show you what other skills I have hidden away."

CHAPTER 22

"Where the hell did they go?"

Julian brushed away the falling dust then, with raised brows, watched Jake search the gallery, as if Kate and Grant were hiding behind the nearest potted plant. "You know, for MI6, you really are quite skittish."

"Sod off. Where are they?"

Julian pointed to the Stonehenge picture. "In there."

Jake gaped at him then turned and looked at the picture. "What you mean? They're frozen in there?"

"Not frozen, the picture is a gateway. They've been transported back in time to a set moment from my memory. If I'm not mistaken, they are somewhere in the 1530s."

"What? Why? Bring them back!"

Echoes of voices interrupted the conversation. Julian waved his hands nervously, gesturing for Jake to be quiet. "Not with those people around. You know where the Zion room is?" When Jake nodded, Julian grinned. "Then meet me there."

With a flash he was gone. Jake threw up his hands in frustration and disappeared just as a mob of people entered the room. Alexis led the charge. She darted around the deserted gallery, barking orders to everyone around her.

"They must be around here somewhere. Check every room and get a set of blueprints. Grant's wounded. He can't have gotten very far."

Laurelle sauntered up to her, a look of distain on her

face. "There's no one here and certainly no keys." She turned to peruse the paintings around her and called out haughtily. "I want you to burn these. Julian always had such gaudy taste."

"Don't make me tell you, again, how important it is to focus on the prize," Alexis snarled. "In an hour, the Council will be fully incapacitated and their power will be ours. There will be plenty of time to redecorate after we've won."

"And the keys?"

Alexis shrugged her shoulders. "Your sad-sack cousin was your problem. It's your fault they're missing right now. Fix the problem and find the keys. They should be your only priority."

Laurelle glared at her and turned to walk away, "Fine."

Alexis grabbed her by the arm and swung her around. Her fingers closed around Laurelle's throat, pushing her against a nearby column. "Don't make me regret this pathetic alliance with you and your siblings. We both have something to gain, so be a pet and do as you're told."

"I had to endure torture for your cause."

Alexis rolled her eyes. "Please spare me the martyr act. You got back a fraction of what you've given out. Don't think for a second that you're a victim in any of this."

In the hallway outside the Zion ballroom, Jake appeared, his body tensed and ready for action. Much to the surprise of a couple of guards, he raised his hands before anyone could fire. "I'm a friend, don't shoot. I'm looking for Ambrose Anderson."

One of them spoke into his radio and nodded, escorting him inside. The war room was a flurry of activity, as people in suits scurried around. Jake saw a blueprint of the chateau projected across one wall. Across the way, a series of tables housed some pretty serious artillery. His eyebrows rose as everything from modified hand guns and grenade launchers to something that looked like a full-out bomb were the focus of a number of people.

At the back of the room he spotted Ambrose speaking

with Julian. They seemed to be involved in a fairly heated conversation.

"Jake. Good to see you're in one piece. Come with me."

Jake nodded to Mark and headed in their general direction. "How bad are the causalities?"

Mark shook his head, his tuxedo ripped under the arms from a number of well thrown punches, "Still too early to tell. At least several are seriously injured from attacks at the ball and dozens more as collateral damage. Have you seen Grant?"

Snippets of conversation involving words like 'Armageddon' and 'apocalypse' floated by the two men. Jake shook his head, his mind grim. "Last I saw, Kate was patching him up but he was still out cold."

"So he's alive then?"

"Far as I know."

"So where are they—"

Ambrose interrupted. "Need to know, son. Julian says they're safe and I doubt that Kate is focused on anything but getting him well. We have bigger problems to worry about now." He ushered them over to the blueprint on the wall. "Our first priority has to be on getting the Council back and, if what Julian says is correct, they should be hidden somewhere under the main building's floor."

A secondary map of the tunnels appeared next to the floor plan. "In the area where the victims of The Sculptor were found is a set of steam tunnels that connect the old and new parts of the property. We should begin our hunt there and spread out."

"What about going after the assholes that started this whole thing?"

"There are groups of people from both sides eager to see Alexis and Lucas apprehended. We've already sent a special team to attempt an arrest."

"Pawns," Julian remarked, looking at the wall.

"Excuse me?"

"It's a clever idea, this scheme of theirs. Murder poor

Gus, knowing the Council would lock down the building. Now we're got limited resources and multiple big problems to solve."

Mark smacked his forehead. "He's right. We've sent men to find Lucas and Alexis, while our people are trying to restore order and our strongest asset is missing or, worse, dead. We're beyond spread thin and they know it."

"So while we're running around like chickens, those buggers are getting stronger by the minute. Kate was right," Ambrose stated. "We need to find the Council before they figure a way to kill them off."

"Of course, if they get to the keys before we do, then who cares about the Council? They'll be powerless to stop them from destroying civilization as we know it." Julian stroked his chin, deep in thought. "Not enough men, too many obstacles to stop. Really is a lose-lose situation." He stopped talking when he realized the others were staring at him. "Well, just playing devil's advocate. After all, I am a Morgan."

Ambrose grumbled something under his breath, then added, "All right, smart ass. What do you suggest?"

Julian winked at him cheekily and blew a kiss. "Well, for starters, get the right tools. This equipment is so 1990s and your map is all wrong." He walked over to one of the room's blank walls and raised his hand, sweeping it through the air. A portrait of a much different blueprint painted itself on the wall.

"Wow, that's bloody amazing," Jake declared. After staring at it for a few moments, he turned back. "What is it?"

"It's an accurate floor plan of this property."

Jake turned around to study at it again and, this time, cocked his head, looking at the picture upside down. "Really? I mean don't get me wrong, Jules, it's pretty and all, but it looks like a bunch of colored lines."

"Troglodyte." Julian sighed. "Like all of my artwork, you just need to look at it the right way." He snapped his fingers and a tall metal post appeared in the middle of the room.

Raising his hand again, he swiped at the painting and threw the image at the post. In a swirl of color, it repositioned itself as a three dimensional holographic floor plan, showing four different layers of the chateau.

"All right, I stand corrected. This is bloody awesome." Jake walked over to the floor plan and pointed his finger at the green colored first layer. "So this is the hallways and rooms, yeah? What's this blue layer here?"

"It looks like secret passageways," Mark, replied excitedly. "If you squint, the blue intersects with green and shows back ways into each of the rooms."

Julian clapped his hands in delight. "Excellent work, my boy. Looks like the rangers can show MI6 a thing or two, after all."

"Oye, what happened to family loyalty?"

"I'm loyal to my fans and my reputation. Neither of which will exist if the world goes to hell." Julian checked his watch then pointed to the layer of red at the bottom of the diagram. "The bits in red, below the steam tunnels, are the original family crypts. I think if we search there, we'll probably find the Council."

Ambrose snapped his fingers and conversation ceased, everyone looking in his general direction. "Listen up, people. Right now we have two priorities—finding the Council and the keys. Alpha, Beta, and Omega teams, see Mark for reassignment."

There was a sudden shuffling as hundreds of people gathered around the holographic floor plan. Ambrose gestured to Jake and Julian then snapped his fingers again and turned to the crowd. "Just a reminder, people. This is a sensitive issue and unless you are forced to, we refrain from using lethal force. Arm yourselves with Shockers and remember our motto."

As if on cue a unified chorus of "protect the balance" rang out from the group.

"What's a Shocker and where can I get one?" Jake asked as he rubbed his hands together.

"It's a stun gun. Not a Taser, something a bit more high tech," Ambrose replied grimly. Shooting a glance at Julian he smirked. "Still think we're too 1990s?"

Before Julian could reply, Jake grabbed a nasty-looking handgun from a passerby and started waving it around. "Right. Fully armed and ready for battle." He threw his free arm around Julian's shoulders. "Where do you want us? Leading the charge of this light brigade?"

Julian blanched and removed his cousin's arm. "My darling boy, I am a lover, not a fighter, and if you are going to reference military assaults from history, don't jinx us by referring to one who had their asses handed to them on a platter."

Ambrose grabbed the gun back from Jake. "He's right. Besides, I have another task for you two. My teams will rescue the Council. I need you both to help me interrogate one of your own."

"Well, if that's the case, Grant gave me a name of a friend who will give your teams a hand." Jake leaned over and whispered instructions to Ambrose.

Ambrose looked at him with surprise. "Really? Are you sure?"

"Just the messenger, mate."

Mark looked at the two of them suspiciously. "What did he say?"

"Need to know, mate. Sure your pops will share eventually."

Ambrose nodded. "He's right, but first, your assignment." He led them past the war room and into the upper deck to the interrogation observation room. There they stared down at the lone occupant of all eight interrogation rooms.

"Sophia Morgan, twin to Gus and, as far as we can figure, his nearest confident. If anyone knows about the location of the keys, it's her."

CHAPTER 23

To the left, no a little higher. Yes, that's it. That's perfect. Push hard, just right there."

Kate squinted at the pile of rock in the distance and
let a shockwave from her hand fly. It hit the stones head on
with such velocity that they disintegrated into dust and sand.
She sighed then, pulling up the hem of her skirt, trudged
back to where Grant lay in the middle of their impromptu
picnic lunch.

"I'm useless," she grumbled. "Unless you want piles of
cremated relatives, I can't draw on this power." She flopped
down on the blanket, promptly becoming tangled in the
folds of her dress. "And this Renaissance garb is ridiculous.
It took me twenty minutes to get dressed this morning. I
think I'm going to wish us some practical clothes."

Before the words were out of her mouth, she found herself pinned to the blanket with his hand over her mouth.
"You will do no such thing," he warned. "I'm not letting
your life force drain because you don't like what you're
wearing."

With a glare, she silently nodded. Feeling the pressure
alleviated, she slightly opened her mouth, capturing Grant's
pinkie and sucking it hard.

He groaned and moved his hand, exchanging his fingers
for his mouth. Shifting his weight, he pushed her into the
long grass. She reciprocated by running her fingers down
his back, pulling his hardness toward her. She loved the way

he kissed her, taking his time and building up her need as if he was expertly stoking a fire. Soft, yet demanding, his mouth devoured hers, pulling her into ecstasy and driving her into a frenzy of desire.

After a few moments of fumbling with the layers of her skirt, he broke the kiss and pushed himself away. "So maybe you were right about the dress."

"So that means I can—"

"No. That means it's a sign that you should be practicing and not seducing me in the middle of an open field for any Englishman to walk by and discover us."

"So what's the worst that can happen? We get chastised for public indecency."

Grant reached for the stone pitcher of water they had procured as part of their picnic lunch. "Try this scenario. You get publically flogged and I'm imprisoned for taking your virtue." He gestured around with the small stoneware cup, "Besides, this is technically a graveyard on some Earl's estate and we shouldn't be here."

"And Stonehenge looks like that?"

He glanced back at the elaborate circle upon circle of rings made of stone and timber and shook his head. "Julian must have pulled that version from a much older date. Still to the natives, it would look like it did in the 1600s."

"Which is?"

"Not much different than it does today."

Kate leaned back and breathed in the cool air, closing her eyes for a second to absorb the warmth upon her face. "There's something magical about this place. I can feel the love radiating from here, as if this was a special meeting place. Grant, it feels like paradise. I can smell lilac and roses and taste…" She paused for a minute, trying to find the words. "This is going to sound crazy, but I can taste Ambrosia so thick, if I didn't know better, I would be able to scoop it out of the air."

Grant's eyebrows rose in surprise. "Really? You can sense all that?"

"You can't?"

"No, no I can." He looked puzzled for a moment. "I'm usually the only one who can."

She opened her eyes and exhaled a long, satisfied sigh. "What is this place? What was its real purpose?"

He shifted his body over, pulling her into his arms. "Well, legend has it that Stonehenge was the original meeting place of angels."

She gazed off at the stones in the distance. "Really?"

"After Adam and Eve were kicked out of Eden, the door to paradise was lost to humans forever. As the human race began to populate the Earth, God took pity and sent down angels to guide the faithful and punish those who failed him. They came and returned to Eden through a door in that circle."

"So I'm sensing and smelling paradise?"

He kissed her hair. "Possibly. Of course, it's possible this is one big hallucination courtesy of your crazy cousin."

She looked down and laced her fingers through his, nestling closer to him. "Let's come back here and find out."

"What do you mean?"

"If we survive the Summit, let's go to the real Stonehenge. Next month on my birthday."

Grant glanced down at her with surprise. "I should probably know this but when's your birthday?"

"October twelfth."

He nodded in agreement then slid to the left and stretched out his hand. A powerful beam shot out and hit the bottom of one of the largest stones. The sound of thunder echoed through the sky. She sat up and looked back at him. "What did you do?"

"I etched something that only you and I will recognize. If this place is a real moment in time and not an illusion, if your cousin Julian is really that powerful and able to get us out from lockdown at the chateau, then my symbol should be there next month."

Hopeful thoughts crossed her mind. If they truly were

free, they could disappear into history and live out the remainder of their lives, liberated from the Council, spending a happy life, quietly watching history go by. Kate glanced around at the sunny, blue sky and guilt filled her heart. There would be no world if they didn't solve this mystery. As much as she wanted to be selfish and run away with this man, she realized that, like it or not, they had to see this through to its end. Smiling, she leaned over and gave him a passionate kiss. After a moment of whipping him into a frenzy, she pulled away and shot him a devilish grin. "For that, do I get a hint of what the symbol might be?"

With a grin he shook his head then pointed to another monument of rocks in the distance. "You'll get a spanking if you don't get over there and master your skills."

Pouting, she stood back up, squared her shoulders, and whipped her hair back, holding it against the wind.

"Good girl," he said. "Now, focus your power and push the stones over, gently."

Kate extended her arm toward the stones. Clearing her mind, she channelled just enough power to knock them over. Turning back to Grant, she grinned as she got the thumbs up. Over the next hour, she repeated the movements, managing to take the level of intensity up and down.

With the sky turning cloudy and the wind picking up, she decided she had practiced enough. Turning back to Grant, she stopped as a sharp pain coursed through her head.

Concern filled his face and he pushed himself to a sitting position. "You okay?"

"I think so, just a bit of a headache." She paused then heard the voice so loudly, its volume seared a path of pain through her head. Kate dropped to her knees, grabbing the sides of her head, trying to stop the agony.

"Kate, what's wrong?" Grant was at her side in a minute, kneeling down but unsure of how to help.

"Someone is trying to contact you. I'm being flooded with thoughts and memories."

He reached out and grabbed her hands. "Channel the

thoughts into a time imprint. Just like at the golf course. Use your powers to divert the dosage into a memory of reality."

She nodded and shut her eyes, squeezing his hands as she wrestled with the voice in her head. It was so powerful, it was all she could do to funnel the influence out of her mind. She drew in a deep breath and screamed, using all of her energy to push it away. Then as if a large door had shut, there was silence in her head.

Kate released her grip on Grant's hands and opened her eyes. They were still in the field but everything around them was silent. No birds chirped in the surrounding trees. She couldn't feel the wind on her face or the intermittent warmth of the summer's day. Instead, she stared at a lone figure who was standing in the grass near them.

He was dressed down yet distinguished in his khaki pants and button down shirt. Polished yet casual, came to her mind. She barely recognized him without the suit and tie.

"Grandfather?" Grant asked, stunned.

He gave Grant a warm smile. Hands in his pockets, he walked toward them, deep admiration in his eyes as he surveyed the surroundings.

"Grant. I'm glad to see that you're all right. Miss Morgan, it's nice to see you again."

"Council member Anderson. It's a relief to see you aren't dead."

He rewarded her with a warm smile. "Call me Jonathan, please. We're not in session here. There's no need for formality."

Grant strode up to him and gave him a hug. "Where are they keeping you? As soon as we're released, we'll come and get you."

He raised his hand as if shooing away a fly. "No need. Ambrose and Kate's cousin Jake are close to finding us. This mutiny won't last very long."

Relief flooded his face. "Don't worry, Grandfather. I'll make them pay."

Jonathan shook his head. "Quite the opposite, Grant. I want you to save Alexis. Help her to find her way back to us."

Grant stiffened, shaking his head in disbelief. "She should get the punishment she has inflicted."

"Grant. That is not our way."

"She doesn't deserve forgiveness."

"Everyone deserves forgiveness. Even the Morgan family."

Grant let out a long sigh and looked to the heavens. "I don't think I can."

"You loved her before. Very deeply. I need you to find that love again."

Kate felt her stomach drop, his words cutting into her. She didn't feel the right to intervene but she couldn't listen to any more of their conversation. The cottage was a short walk away and she was too tired to defend her right to mean something other than her lineage, yet again.

"Kate?"

She turned and smiled at him. "It's okay, Grant. You two look like you have lots to talk about. I'm going to get dinner started."

She stopped briefly at the cabin door, watching Grant's body language and desperate to know that they had a future together. He wasn't one to walk away from a fight. She just hoped he was fighting for her.

Grant swore lightly under his breath as he watched her walk away. "That is the woman I care about. Not Alexis. She and I are finished."

Jonathan shoved his hands deeper in his pockets. "She's a Morgan."

"Kate's different than the rest of them."

"And after she completes The Joining? Will you still be in love with the woman who is left?"

"She won't complete it."

"She doesn't have a choice."

"And there's nothing you can do?"

Jonathan sighed and shook his head sadly. "You know we can't interfere, Grant. You made that point very clear when you separated your destiny from the family line. A foolish act, by the way. We can't protect you if the Universe determines your time is up."

"I don't care. I love her." He stared at the cottage wistfully before turning back to his grandfather. "She died for me once. I'd gladly do the same."

"Have you told her that?"

"No. When this is all over, perhaps. But for now, it's better that she doesn't know." Grant knew that she needed to be protected, even if it was against her own will. They were in such a perilous situation that telling her how much she meant to him, that he loved her, would only make her sacrifice herself faster. He needed her to fight him, to be confused about her feelings because, if the moment ever came where she was forced to choose, he wanted her to see the worth in saving herself.

He was annoyed that his grandfather seemed pleased with that response. Grant could see his image fading, returning to the chateau and the place where he was temporarily a prisoner. Hating the words that came out of his mouth, Grant issued a reassurance. "About Alexis. I will do what I can."

"You promise?"

"If she can be saved, I'll make every effort. If she has chosen a path with no redemption, I won't sacrifice myself to save her."

"But our ways—"

"Our ways are not my ways. You should know better than that. I am my own man."

Out of respect and courtesy, Grant waited until his grandfather's image disappeared. He walked back to the cottage, wondering what he would say. Perhaps she already knew. She could easily have read his mind. Somehow, he doubted this, but telling some form of the truth would still be the best plan.

He opened the door and found her sitting at the harvest table. He could smell a stew simmering on the stove and fresh bread cooling on the counter.

She was staring at the contents of her clutch—the souvenir from the ball and the crystal knife that had started all this trouble.

"Is that a dagger that I see before me?"

She groaned at the obvious reference to Shakespeare, yet appreciated the irony of his statement. "Lady Macbeth went insane with guilt. Don't think for a second that Alexis will feel the same."

He sat down on the bench beside her and reached for the dagger but she smacked his hand away. "It burned Ambrose when he tried to pull it from you. See how the tip has disintegrated and those shards are lined up at the end? It's pure evil, itching to kill you and I'm not letting it try again."

Grant held up his hands in resignation. Instead, he grabbed the crystal cube and began to spin it on the table. "Summit 2018, huh?"

Kate smiled and stood up, taking the weapon and her clutch with her for safe keeping. Putting them on the counter, she tasted the stew and, after adding additional salt, turned off the stove. The silence between them, quickly became unbearable.

"So you're going to try and save Alexis?"

Grant let out a sigh and continued to spin the crystal. "I don't know what I'm going to do."

She reached for a knife and began to cut thick slabs of fresh bread, relishing the smell with every slice. "What do you think turned her to my family's ways?"

He turned the cube more slowly, watching as its prism cast tiny rainbows in the evening light. "I wish I could say she was possessed or influenced, but the truth is she has been pushing for this kind of change her entire life."

"Creating a perfect society is admirable idea. I don't know how realistic it is, though."

"It's not. History tells us so." He sighed and pushed himself up from the table, wincing a tiny bit as a dull pain travelled up his side. Bored and restless, he wandered around their small world.

"We're born and all we want is to be loved and to love others." Kate sighed. "Then we learn and grow and something changes in us. When did it become so easy to hate and lie? To cheat and steal?"

Grant eased himself back on the bed, kicking off his shoes and unbuttoning the front of his shirt. "Humanity has been that way for thousands of years. Whether a person chooses to murder others or save them is what will change the face of the world. I just hope we can cultivate a future where more people want to help than hurt. You want to save the world, Kate. You can only do what you can do. Sometimes you have to let the world save itself."

She spooned the stew into bowls and moved them to the table. "How do I do that?"

"Start small. I know the NYPD has a youth outreach program. Start mentoring kids who want the direction. Change lives one by one and, hopefully, they'll pay it forward."

She poured water into both of their cups and sighed. "My life in New York seems so far away. A week ago I was chewing you out on a street corner."

He chuckled and patted the bed beside him. "And now you're my doctor and housekeeper."

She frowned and put her hands on her hips. "I'm no one's housekeeper. I pay someone who has talent to do that for me."

"Noted. Then why don't you come over here and let me explore your talents?"

"Dinner's getting cold."

"It can be reheated."

"We don't have much time before we have to go back. We should be strategizing and putting together a plan."

He sighed and cocked his head with annoyance. "Are you going to make me get up and come after you?"

Kate smiled then wiped her hands on a tea towel and walked slowly toward him. With every step, she removed another layer from the dress she wore. With only her shrift left, he reached up and pulled her down on top of him, caressing her face with his hands.

"God, you're so beautiful," he murmured, pulling her mouth to his.

She let out a moan of delight as he captured her, first with the soft pressure of his lips, then as his tongue twinned with hers, deepening the kiss and making her shiver with need.

Kate pushed his shirt off, running her hands down his powerful back, skirting the smooth muscles of his six pack abs. Her fingers found his waistband and she pushed his trousers away, grateful to have his hardness finally released.

Grant slid his hands down her soft skin, pushing the thin layer of cotton dress up so he could admire her nakedness and memorize the fine curves of her body.

She trembled at the way he pushed the dress over her head and, with a swift knot, tied her hands. Sinking back to the bed, he pushed open her thighs, cradling and gently kneading her buttocks with his hands. The fire within her heightened and her need started to grow. He smiled as he dove down, deep between her legs, kissing, then exploring every womanly fold.

She felt herself going insane with need as his tongue thrust back and forth, filling her, then taking away the pleasure she desired the most.

"Please, Grant…"

"Not just yet. We have hours ahead of us. I want to make it last."

Disappearing between her legs, he started his torturous pleasure again, exploring her with his tongue, his fingers, and finally the thick head of his hardness. Just an inch, then he was gone and her frustration built to a frenzy. She felt overwhelmed with need, obsessed with having him inside her, filling her until she felt like she would split in two.

When he entered again, desire took over and she thrust her hips up, capturing him, enjoying his moan of surprise as his will broke and he thrust hard into her again.

"More, please," she begged.

He withdrew again and increased his power, slamming into her with such force that she cried out his name.

"Come for me, Kate," he said between gritted teeth. Pulling her fully under him, he released her bonds, splaying their fingers together. His words were her undoing and she screamed as his pummelled her over and over again.

With her tightness around him, her desire, her need hit him head on. Like a surge of power, he felt her love filling his soul, pouring light into the dark corners he worked so hard to cover and absolving him of the guilt he felt. In that moment of exquisite release that overwhelmed him, he felt whole and filled with a joy that took his breath away. She radiated beauty and love and gave it to him so innocently that, in that moment of bliss, he made a silent promise to them both. No matter who or what happened in the next few days, no one would take her away.

CHAPTER 24

Sophia Morgan sat in her interrogation room, looking more like an Upper West Side socialite than a mob mom. Dressed in a matching black cashmere sweater and skirt by Chanel, she nervously picked away at her hundred-dollar manicure before grabbing at her Italian black leather and gold tote. "Why isn't there a signal in here?" she exclaimed to the walls of her temporary cell.

Slamming down her phone, she stood up and tested the door. When that refused to budge, she started walking the perimeter, raking the walls with the tips of her long, fake nails.

"You might as well sit down, luv. We're going to be here a while."

Sophia whipped around and looked coldly at Jake, who was seated in front of her.

"Teleportation, huh?" she smirked with her Long Island accent, "You must be a riot at all the strip joints in England."

Jake laughed and slapped his knee. "Good one. With that expensive dye job and tight little ass, I bet your clients love you."

"How dare you?" she hissed, chanting something under her breath.

"I excel to dare, darling. And don't forget, I gave you a Karmic Mark at breakfast, so whatever you hexed me with, you can expect twice as bad back."

She paled and sat down, some of the bravado draining from her face. "So what do you want anyway?"

"Take a guess, sweetheart."

She sniffed and gazed at the ceiling. "You want to know about Gus. Everybody wants to know about Gus. My poor brother is more popular now than when he was alive."

"Well, old Gus was up to naughty things. So why don't you tell me about them?"

"What makes you think I know anything about his plans? I'm just a poor Jersey housewife."

"With two dead husbands and a third one away on business for the past year?"

"He's scouting out new oil wells in the Middle East."

"Mmmm, right in the heart of all that fighting." Jake flipped his pen between his fingers. "I'm willing to bet that if the bloke is alive, he's into illegal arms or terrorist activities."

"Well, if you get me a signal, we can call him right now."

Jake leaned back in his chair and started to doodle on Ambrose's file. "Not necessary. We're here to talk about Gus after all. So why don't you tell me, for starters—"

"Where are the keys? Right?" She threw up her hands, then reached for her bag and pulled out a package of Marlboro's. Before he could say anything, she flicked a crystal-encrusted lighter and drew in a long drag. "I don't know where the stupid keys are. He didn't tell me about them." She took another pull and pointed her finger at him. "If I did, I certainly would have told him not to bring them here. Christ, with all the hiding places in the world and you bring them right back to the enemy? How stupid could you possibly be?"

"Actually, I was going to ask if you knew who he was going to kill."

"Oh? That?" she replied, looking surprised. Taking another long drag, she paused to smooth down a bit of her hair. "That I know. It was supposed to be goody-two-shoes

Kate and the hunka, hunka burning love."

Jake blinked a couple of times then casually rubbed his neck and looked up at the invisible panel of observation glass. After the disbelief passed, he leaned in toward her and asked, "Why?"

"Oh, that's an easy on," she clucked. "'Cause he saw they were going to be trouble."

"Excuse me?"

Sophia smiled and lit up a second cigarette. "Yeah, you see Gus was all into this new age meditation thing. He was trying to improve his power. You know the one where he can see three seconds into the future." She tapped her temple with finger while her cigarette sent ash everywhere. "He thought he could get an advantage, 'cause with three seconds of premonition, it really doesn't get you anything, unless you're walking under a swinging piano and can tell if it's going to be dropped on you."

"Like in the cartoons?" Jake asked weakly. He gestured to the cigarette pack and she happily handed him one. Lighting it, he wondered how he could be related to so much crazy.

"Exactly!"

"So meditation gave him enhanced sight?"

"Not at all."

"Oh, okay."

"But he did get a flash of a vision. He consulted someone very close to him, who told him what it meant."

Jake pondered this statement for a minute, resisting the urge to shake the information out of her. "So let me get this straight," he said slowly. "Someone in the family interpreted a random, obscure vision to mean that Gus needed to kill Grant Anderson and our cousin Kate?"

She nodded excitedly. "Now you got it. I must say, Jake, I was told your side of our family was stupid and crazy. You're smarter than I thought."

"Gee, thanks, Sophia. I really like you too."

She blushed, missing his sarcastic tone. "Such a handsome boy. After all this nonsense is over, you'll have to come on down to Jersey. I have a daughter who is single, you know."

Jake cleared his throat uncomfortably. "That's very kind, Sophia, I think I'm too old, and too related for her...um...so who told poor Gus to take out our cousin and her, um, friend?"

"Oh, I can't tell you that. But rest assured it was someone very important."

She offered him another cigarette, which he happily accepted. "Come on now, Sophia, you can tell me. Hell, I'm not really a part of this investigation. They're just spread so thin, they needed some kind of Morgan to speak with you."

She nodded knowingly. "You seem different than the rest of them. Such cretins those Andersons. It's no wonder she offered her seat to him."

"I'm sorry, who?"

Her eyes opened wide and she let out a squeal of laughter. "Oh my, look what I've done. I've gone and spilled the beans. Must be the cigarettes. I laced them with too much of the good stuff!"

Jake looked at the cigarette in his fingers, knowing now why he felt so relaxed. Marijuana in his interrogation room. Ambrose was going to have a field day with this one. "Good for you, Sophia," he said, playing along. "You rebel, you. Go ahead and tell me everything, darling."

Her demeanor changed and she lifted her chin, pride getting the best of her. "She said Gus was her favorite one. That her grandchildren had disappointed her and he was the only one who she could see secede her."

"And she is..."

"She saw into the future and said his was very bright. If he brought her the key and killed those troublemakers, he would be the chosen one."

"Did he bring her the key?"

She shook her head sadly and started to cry. "Someone else got to him before he could. My poor brother, just trying to get ahead and look where it gets him. Strung up a god-damn flag pole." Sophia leaned in close to him. "She was so angry, she handed over fifteen more associates to The Sculptor."

Jake felt his mind reeling. Between the smoke and her gibberish, he didn't know what to believe. "So fifteen more people are dead?"

"Oh, they're not people, they're associates."

"Okay, forget about the people and the serial killer," he said with an exasperated tone. "Blimey, who is she?"

"Why Aunt Lily, of course."

Shock filled Jake's mind. He glanced up at the concealed window where Ambrose and his team were watching. Lilli-an Morgan, one of the original Council members was be-hind the stealing of the keys, hits on his team, and mass murder. Could this get any more unbelievable?

"Thanks Sophia, you can go," Jake said, waving at the door with his hand. There was a quiet clicking sound and it opened behind her. Placing his head in his hands, he gave up a weak groan as she left the room. "Have a nice reunion and try not to end up dead, yeah?"

He heard the quiet tapping of the glass above him and snapped his fingers. Up in the observation deck, he leaned against the wall, rubbing his eyes in frustration. "What the hell is going on here?"

Ambrose tossed down his pen. "I don't know. We solve one mystery and another one pops up." He looked over at Julian, who had manifested a small living room and was dozing in a nearby recliner. "We have twenty minutes be-fore Grant and Kate, reappear. What do we know so far?"

"They accidently overhear a murder plot, which turns out to be about them."

"Then the murderer, Gus is killed, by whom we still don't know, but we presume it's because of the keys he stole."

Jake wandered over to Julian's impromptu living space, grabbing a half bottle of wine and an elaborate cheese and cracker plate from his lap. Making himself comfortable on a nearby couch, he took a swig. "Well, mate, my guess is that Alexis tapped him when he wouldn't tell her where the keys were."

"It certainly looks like that."

"And then my evil cuz, Lucas, hatches some plan to hijack the Council and steal their powers, which has thrown both families into chaos."

"And now it sounds like one of the Council members is behind it all." Ambrose let out a long sigh and started to pace the floor. "This doesn't make any sense. The Council has powers beyond anything we are capable of understanding. They see past and future and how it links to Heaven and Hell."

"Well, why would they allow themselves to be captured?"

"They wouldn't, unless—"

"Unless what?"

"Unless one of them wanted something so badly, they would be willing to overpower the others."

"So Aunt Lily *is* behind all this? What about Alexis and Lucas?"

Ambrose paced madly, trying to put all of the pieces together. "Julian talked about pawns. Gus, Grant, Kate, Alexis, Lucas, you, me, we're all pawns."

Jake sat up in his seat. "How so?"

Ambrose picked up a piece of paper and rolled it into tube. He absently tapped it against his leg as he paced. "A criminal wants to commit a crime but he is surrounded by hundreds of people with different powers who could possibly affect the outcome. Even if he has control of the situation, there are always unknown factors. People who might be more observant, who could possibly thwart the plan."

Jake leaned forward. "Okay, so the crime is stealing the keys. You would want a patsy you could control. Someone who would do your bidding without question."

"Right. That's Gus."

"But they didn't expect him to grow a backbone and involve other members of the family."

"The Leland clan." Ambrose switched from tapping his leg to tapping his hand. "Lucas and his siblings are expendable, though. Knowing who the Morgan's are, you would expect there to be some collateral issues, especially dealing with a family who are preprogrammed to only look out for themselves."

"So that accounts for half of us, what about your side?"

"Murdering Gus would send us in the wrong direction. Look for the murderer, then the missing keys, but you would still need to account for any loose cannons."

"Yeah but you didn't even know the keys were missing."

Ambrose shook his head. "Every reunion there is an inventory of all artifacts and papers kept by both sides. It was only a matter of time before the loss would have been discovered."

Jake nodded. "So talking about loose cannons. You mean someone who might see through the murder?"

"Someone who is more powerful than all of the other family members combined," Ambrose replied. His eyes darkened. "Like my nephew, Grant."

Jake popped a piece of Brie into his mouth. "So if Grant's on his game, he solves Gus's murder and throws a monkey wrench into the plan for escaping with the keys. So how do you throw off such a smart guy?"

Ambrose lifted his eyebrows and stared at Jake.

"Bloody hell, are you talking about Kate?"

"Why do you think she's still alive?"

"Do you really think the Morgans are so hell bent on getting rid of her? Yeah, she might be the only one who's got a conscience but, come on. Use her relationship to distract him?"

"In a thousand years of Morgan history has anyone ever dodged The Joining?"

Jake chewed thoughtfully on a whole-wheat cracker. "Well, yeah, I can think of a couple of Morgans who objected. After all the ceremony is pretty crappy. That's why most of us go through it as kids. A kid can't fight back."

"Are the ones who objected still alive?"

"Well, except for Kate. That would be a no." Jake glanced down at his watch and swore. Lifting his foot, he gave the back of Julian's recliner a solid kick. "Oye, Jules, wakey, wakey, old man. It's almost time to get Grant and Kate from that painting."

Standing up, he walked over to an adjoining table and started loading up his pockets with guns. "Time to end this, Ambrose. We get the love birds and go after Alexis and Lucas. If anyone knows about Aunt Lily's ultimate plan, it's one of them."

CHAPTER 25

Ambrose, Jake, and Julian hustled down the deserted hallways. Evidence of Lucas's rebellion was everywhere. The hallways looked like the aftermath of a war. Blood spattered the walls and floors. Furniture had been overturned and pillaged while paintings were ripped out of the frames and their pieces scattered around the floor.

Julian pointed to the floor, outrage filling his eyes. "Some of these were masterpieces. Those ignorant assholes!"

Ambrose slid around a corner, pointing his gun down the deserted corridor. "That's why we use the Shocker and enlist a curfew. Anyone we come across is stunned and locked in their hotel room."

They made their way down corridor after corridor and into the expansive lobby. "Blimey," Jake whispered. He cautiously side stepped broken glass and expensive china. The front desk was empty, its beautiful wooden carvings chipped and defaced. The front entrance was open but they weren't fooled. Anyone in attendance of the Summit was prevented from exiting those doors.

Julian turned to face them, holding up a piece of stained glass from the overhead skylight. "Twice, this gem of architecture was moved and never the damage done that happened tonight. Whoever ruined this place will pay!"

"Yeah? Well, I hate to see what they've done to your paintings."

Julian's eyes widened and he let out a scream of panic. Waving his hands in front of him he darted around the others, past the front desk, and toward the connecting corridor.

"Julian, wait," Ambrose angrily yelled. "It might not be safe."

Seeing the uselessness of his words, he muttered something then angrily gestured to Jake with his gun. At a fast jog, they quickly joined up with Julian.

The gallery resembled the rest of the chateau. Torn up carpets, overturned and dug up plants. Julian's screams echoed through the expansive space. All of his paintings were in disarray, some of them face down, others on their sides. Only two remained intact and in their frames. The pastoral sixteenth century Stonehenge and his retelling of *St. George and the Dragon*.

"Hubert! Hubert! Are you all right?"

"Is he all right? Look at the scorch marks and the burned bodies littering the place," Jake replied. "I'd say he more than defended that excessive painting you put him in."

Ambrose glanced down at his watch. "Julian, it's time. How do we get them back?"

Julian looked up from the painting that he had been hugging. "What?"

"Grant and Kate? We need them more than your dragon."

Wiping the tears from his eyes, he nodded. Turning toward the painting, he raised his hands and commanded, "Open Sesame!"

"Really?" Jake scoffed. "Can you get more cliché?"

"Actually, no. There are no magic words. They'll just reappear with the two hours is up. It's a feature I built into most of my paintings. Otherwise, I would never be able to get back out."

As if on cue, there was a loud pop and they reappeared, dressed as before with Grant in a blood stained tuxedo and Kate in her plum-colored dress.

Jake grinned and practically pounced on Grant, shaking

his hand. "Well, aren't you a sight for sore eyes, mate?"

Ambrose smiled, giving both of them a big hug. He squeezed Kate's hand. "Thank you for looking after my nephew. He looks much better than the last time I saw him."

Grant leaned over and kissed her forehead. "What can I say? She's an excellent doctor." His expression grew concerned when he glanced around the room and surveyed their dishevelled state. "Want to fill us in on what we've missed?"

Jake pulled out two extra Shockers and thrust them into their hands. "Well, short form, Council's still missing, Alexis and Lucas are somewhere on the prowl, and everyone is either incapacitated or locked in their rooms."

Grant glanced at his gun and pushed a small button on the side. "So nothing's changed from two hours ago."

"Actually, that's not true. We think we know who Gus was planning to kill before he was offed."

"Great, who was it?"

"Err, well, you two."

Kate rubbed her eyes with her fingers. "Of course, why not?" She fiddled with the modified gun, before throwing up her hands in defeat. "Julian, can you zap us into more appropriate clothes and replace my clutch with some kind of tote or large messenger bag?"

"Oh, of course my darling. Something trendy yet appropriate?"

"Something comfortable and practical. Jeans and a shirt with sneakers will do."

He nodded and snapped his fingers. Everyone's wardrobe changed to variations on business casual. Breathing an audible sigh of relief, Kate deposited her gun into the Italian leather and canvas Tory Burch messenger bag.

"So what's the status of the council?"

Ambrose sighed. "Mark's coordinating five different teams but so far we haven't found anything. The catacombs are much more extensive than the diagram on Julian's map."

Kate watched Grant's body language, his fidgeting a cause for concern. "You can feel their power, can't you?"

Grant stared into space, trying to reconcile the effect this influence had on him. "It's joyous and terrifying at the same time." He struggled to find the words. "I can see the world in such amazing color. The best way to describe it is like staring down at an ant hill from a great height then looking beyond it to what is really in the Universe."

"That kind of power could be very addicting," Ambrose said quietly.

Grant nodded, partially lost in thought. "All the more reason to find the Council and put a stop to this immediately."

Jake polished one of his Shockers then rooted around his leather jacket, finding a second one. "So that's the plan? Join in the hunt for the Council?"

"For you and Ambrose, yes. My grandfather foresaw that both of you would be the ones to find them, so that's what you are going to do."

"Well then, what about the rest of you?" Ambrose turned to Julian. "Perhaps the artist could rally some members of both families to start putting this place together? Grant's brother Chase, is a good person to contact on the Anderson side and I'm sure you know a few Morgans who might be willing to help with the restoration?"

Julian gave him a wink. "It's the middle of the night, but I can con them into thinking they might find a pot of gold at the end of the rainbow." He glanced over at Grant and Kate. "What about you two? Are you going to search for the key?"

"I'm going to hunt down Alexis and Lucas. Kate is going to her room."

She shot Grant a look, her face filled with disbelief. "What? No way."

"It's the only place you will be safe."

"I'm not sitting this one out so don't even try and make me."

Jake rolled his eyes and grabbed Ambrose by the arm. With a quick salute they disappeared in a flash of light. Sensing the imminent fight, Julian also turned tail and quietly scuttled away.

Grant pulled out his gun and pointed to it. "Do you know how to use this? In case someone breaks through my barrier?"

"I'm not sitting in my room."

"Yes, you are, end of discussion."

"Perhaps the enlightened Grant, doesn't get it. I'm going with you."

He sighed and put his gun away. "Both Alexis and Lucas have the same enhanced powers. I can't fight them both and keep you safe."

She shook her head in disbelief. "I'm not asking you to."

Anger flashed in his eyes. In two strides, he pulled her into his arms, one hand in her hair, forcing her to look up into his eyes. "You can't fight them, they're too strong, Kate."

"So you expect me to let the man I love be out matched in a possible fight to the death?"

His eyes softened at her words and a boyish smile crossed his face. She was undeterred, however. Taking his face in her hands, she repeated her words. "I love you, Grant Anderson, and whether we are meant to live or die, I want it to be together."

Guilt flooded his eyes and a feeling of déjà vu swept through him. They were replaying Texas, only this time, she didn't have a final life to fall back on. "I don't want to lose you, Kate. I lost you once and it would destroy me to watch you die again."

Questions filled her mind, but they would have to wait until a more appropriate time. Kate lightly caressed his face. "I promise you, I'm not going anywhere."

He started to speak but she stopped his words with a passionate kiss and he aggressively complied, devouring her mouth in a way that almost brought her to her knees. After a few moments, he released her and turned away, pacing in circles as he thought.

She could see by the expression on his face that realization was setting in. Even if he managed to subdue her, she would find a way. She excelled in finding a way.

She watched as his eyes scanned the floor, quickly moving back and forth as if he was reading some vial document. "I can't see a way out," he muttered, his fingers tapping anxiously on his leg. "Every scenario of the future I can see ends in your death. Alexis and Lucas are too powerful and we can't win."

Kate watched the agony cross his face, as if he was losing her again and again. She had never prayed in her life but just this one time, she asked for a miracle. For Jake and Ambrose to find the council and for Grant and her to make it out of this situation alive.

She grabbed his hand, pulling him to her. "What if we don't win?" she asked quickly. "What if we can just hold them off until the Council is found? You said it yourself, sometimes we need to set aside our ego and not worry about winning. What does the future tell you about a stalemate?"

For the first time since returning, she saw a glimmer of hope in his eyes. He paused for a second, and she could see the weight of the Universe in his gaze. After a long moment, he looked down at her and smiled. "You amaze me Kate Morgan. I don't know what I'd do without you in my life."

Grant leaned down and pushed his hands into her hair, holding her to him as he kissed her. She let out a sigh, reaching up to clasp her hands behind his neck. Before she realized it, she felt one of the pillars at her back as he trapped her between cold stone and the warmth of his body. His kiss was unyielding and demanding, taking every part of her mouth as if it was his own.

Kate felt overwhelmed by him, trying to break the kiss to catch her breath, but he was too strong. Her body screamed to be touched, to feel his strength inside her, the heat of desire building within her. His fingers moved to her stomach and breasts, leaving a trail of raw want in his wake. Within his kiss, she felt a strange energy surge, as if the chemistry between them had caught on fire. She couldn't control the needs of her body as she felt herself building toward a crest of desire and need. What was he doing to her with just a kiss? She felt overwhelmed, his passion making her feel the exhaustion of a long night of love making combined with the euphoria of desire and release.

Unable to stop herself, she felt the ache between her thighs grow and the exquisite feeling of fullness overtake her. She felt gloriously naked and exposed, as if the world had disappeared and there was only her and him, joined in an infinite space of time. Kate's skin felt like it was on fire, every touch of his was like he was inside her. Breaking the kiss, he pushed her arms above her head, pushing her to new heights, his clothed body, fully upon her. "Come for me, Kate," he murmured. "I need to see you go crazy in my arms."

His words were her undoing. Any shred of self-restraint exploded as she cried out his name, unable to see or think of anything but him.

"Yes, Kate, that's exactly what I need." He kissed her once again, this time taking her euphoric screams into him.

She repeated his name over and over again as he shielded and tempered her. Opening her eyes, she stared dazedly into his handsome face and sensed something different about both of them. He looked positively angelic, as if a ray of sunlight burst forth, filling them both. Kate gasped, feeling the barriers between them disappear. They were two halves, eager to unite as one person. She felt the joy of his successes and sorrow for the past burdens that he claimed. Her surroundings seemed crisper and alive. Touch, smell, hearing, vision, and taste were ignited with fifth dimension clarity.

His leather jacket felt softer than snow. The tiniest noise didn't go unnoticed and the gallery looked clearer and sharper, as if her entire world had become focused and clear.

"What just happened?" she said with a gasp. "I feel different."

He cocked his head to the side and gave her a boyish grin. "You're feeling the power of the Council coursing through you. For the next few hours, you'll be sharing some of my powers."

She looked at her hand, able to see the imperfections in her skin, the blood coursing through her veins. Suddenly, she knew the location of each member of Anderson and Morgan families. Lifelong insecurities and regrets disappeared and, for a split second, she understood everything that had ever been a mystery in her life.

"How long will it last?"

"Hopefully, long enough to help me capture our cousins."

Kate nodded and looked around the room. She understood the reason behind everything, from Julian's choice of color pallet on his paintings to the medieval architecture that held up the roof. In seconds, she could comprehend the fervor that infected Alexis and her misguided possibility of a better world. She could feel the Morgan rage and desire to use destruction as a drug. She gasped as the events of the last three days suddenly made sense.

"Grant. I think I know where the keys are."

"What, really? Where?"

Kate shook her head, knowing that the knowledge had to remain with her. "For your safety, I don't want you knowing. It's just one more thing they can use against you."

He started to argue, but she stopped him. "Please, just trust me. The time isn't right and, in your heightened state, Lucas will be able to sense what you know."

She could see the struggle, the effort it took him to agree with her. Still second guessing the decision to keep her by his side, he sighed. "Okay, are you ready to do this?"

"They're still in the armory?"

He stared off into space for a moment, gathering context before they confronted them. "Apparently, Gus used to go on and on about the chateau's armory. He was something of a history buff and loved that they turned it into a museum. They probably think the keys are hidden there." He grabbed her hand, lacing his fingers through hers. "They're going to try and trick us. Make us see things that aren't there as a way to slow us down. Don't fall for anything you see, okay? Promise, you won't let go of my hand."

Sensing his apprehension, she smiled, trying to calm his nerves. "Don't worry, there's no place, I'd rather be."

They headed out the back doors and crossed the large courtyard to a retrofitted stone building that looked like it once housed stables. They crossed the threshold and immediately felt a powerful wave of vertigo.

Kate shut her eyes and when she opened them they were in the middle of a small forest, with a meadow to the left of them, a bright red barn in the distance and to the right a path that continued into the wood. It felt real, but deep in her heart she knew it was an illusion. Lucas was powerful but not even he could break the Council's decree that bound them to the chateau. Still, it was shockingly real. She could feel the warm summer wind on her face. The sun was shining but the air had a chill to it. Beneath her feet, fine gravel crunched and, in front of them, a crudely painted sign indicated a choice. The traveler could go to the main house or the barn.

"Kate, what's wrong? You recognize this place?" Grant said. He looked around, taking stock of their surroundings. He could smell the dampness of a nearby pond and the gently wafting fragrance of Magnolia trees.

"We're at a location from my childhood. It's the Morgan family farm in Georgia."

He watched her stare at the sign, stunned by her flood of memories from this place. With his new power, he could feel everything that she felt, could hear every thought that filled her mind, and it scared him.

"What's at the barn, Kate?"

"Me. Chester, my dog. Lucas is torturing the both of us, as we speak."

Grant felt the taste of bile in his mouth. "What?" he replied hoarsely.

"I'm eight years old and, in that barn, they're holding us prisoner. Chester is barely alive and judging by the position of the sun, it will be another two hours before I can free myself to put him out of his misery."

Grant could barely speak, the rage inside threatened to overtake him completely. "And Lucas is with you?"

She stared at the sign, repeating over and over that this was a trick. That they couldn't actually go back in time to her childhood. "Lucas, Laurelle, Larry, Lee, Lila and Lesley. The whole gang is there. Six against two and today my younger self finds out what being a Morgan is really about."

Grant gritted his jaw, barely able to speak his thoughts. "I'm going to kill that bastard."

She shook her head, surprised at how calm she felt. "House rules, remember? We can't kill a member of the other family without consequences. Lucas is playing with me. Trying to push me by triggering all the reasons why I hate my family."

"I don't care."

She gently squeezed his hand and then cleared her throat. "It's not going to work, asshole," she yelled. "If anyone kills you, it's going to be me."

The reply was merely a whisper, a seductive drone. "You think you can stop me? You have no idea of the power coursing through my veins."

The picture around them changed. The trees thickened and the ground felt spongy beneath their feet. His voice continued on, an amusing query as, if he relished the outrage of their tone. "Hundreds have fallen before me and you will be no different." Around them bodies began to appear. Hanging from trees, breaking through the boggy ground. All mutilated, their dead eyes and hollow faces frozen in fear and sorrow. Kate gasped as the full onslaught of his crimes presented themselves. She felt their final thoughts, their fear and sorrow for the ones they would leave behind. She heard his threats and felt their fear, as they lay dying, that the ones they loved would be next.

Grant watched the scene around him impassively. She had seen his expression before, when they were chasing Junior Malone through that New York alley. His was the face of justice and determination. There was nothing in hell itself that could stop him from accomplishing what was on his mind. "When this Summit ends," he said quietly, "If by some miracle you're not dead, I'm going to make sure every victim gets justice for what you've done."

Lucas chuckled and made a chiding sound. "Such a gentleman to the end, Special Agent Anderson. My partner and I will rewrite the laws of society and they will bow to us. Come now, we are intelligent men. There is no need to have lies between us."

Grant inhaled a deep breath and clenched his free hand into a fist. "Which partner is that Lucas?" Kate frowned but a reassuring squeeze of his hand, told her to keep quiet. "You know you can never have her, because she's mine."

Kate felt her stomach drop. Jonathan Anderson's words wormed their way into her mind. Grant was trying to save Alexis and presented his case with an intense possession that made her soul ache. She wanted to be the recipient of those words, not Alexis.

Curiosity must have gotten the better of Lucas. There was a flash of light and he stood before them with Alexis at his side. "Why, you must be mistaken, I already have my queen. She's been mine for quite some time and there is nothing you can do or say that will take her from me." His eyes turned to Alexis and she smiled back. She radiated joy as he grasped her hand and pulled it to his mouth, kissing it like a model Southern gentleman.

"I'm talking about Kate. You've wanted her all along and it eats at you that she will never want you back."

Lucas faltered slightly and, with it, the mirage around them. "What are you talking about?"

Grant's eyes glistened with interest and Kate felt the sickening realization that his hunch was right. "You want her badly. I felt it in the New York alley and I'd bet money that was you in our hotel hallway. That's why you couldn't kill her when she was young, that's why you keep trying to impress her now."

Alexis froze, her eyes locked on Kate. "Lucas, tell him he's wrong."

The slight pause spoke volumes and gave Grant the final nudge he needed. "Is this what this power play is all about? Take over the Council to impress the one person who could never tolerate, much less love you?"

A panicked look spread across Alexis's face. This time she begged for the truth. "Lucas, please. Tell him he's wrong."

"He used you, Alexis," Grant continued. "He used you to get poor Gus to steal the keys. He doesn't love you. He loves the one thing that he can never have and who will never, ever love him back."

Kate saw his reasoning but the impact had its blow. He was correct, but the raw truth paralyzed them all. They were suspended in a minute of painful realization, stripped bare and, for one of them, humiliated to the core. "Grant," she whispered. "You need to stop talking. He's going to kill you. Please, stop talking now."

The words were barely out of her mouth, when a maelstrom of hate burst from Lucas. The energy charge blew them both to the ground, the mirage dissolving around them, replaced with the reality of a museum floor.

Kate felt herself propelled backward into a wall. She covered her face as display cases exploded and shattered around her. She heard his yells, his rage at being humiliated. Staggering to her feet, she pulled out shards of glass from her left leg, her fear for Grant overtaking the intense pain of her wound. Lucas was fighting him with the strength of a hundred men, driving him back through blind fury and the hatred of a broken man.

"Grant," she cried. Lifting her hand, she focused on destroying the walls behind them, hoping desperately that the destruction would throw Lucas off his concentration.

They were trading blows, their bodies so close together, she couldn't risk her aim missing Lucas and hitting Grant by accident. She looked around and saw part of the museum collection lying on the floor. If she could move a sword in his direction.

'*I've given you some of my powers.*' His words floated through her mind. What his exact powers were, she didn't completely know, but one that she had experienced was levitation.

She focused on a tarnished sword with a strip of jewels on its handle. Her first swipe sent the sword two feet across the floor. Kate glanced down at her pant leg, seeing only her clotting blood. She knew the glass had missed a major artery but the injury was slowing her down.

Lifting her hand again, she felt an arm around her neck, pulling her backward and down.

"You've taken everything from me. You're not going to rob me of this opportunity," Alexis hissed.

Kate flipped her body around, relying on martial arts to pin Alexis to the ground. "The very idea of Lucas makes my stomach turn. You can have him."

"We were together for fifty years. Grant and I. Fifty years. He asked me to marry him and you come along and think you can destroy that in three days?"

Kate could sense Alexis's emotions taking over. She was losing focus. Kate punched her in the stomach, knocking the wind out of her. With an open opportunity, she refocused her sights on the sword and flicked her wrist. The blade flew across the room, landing in Grant's right hand. Satisfied he had an advantage, she turned back to Alexis.

"You're trying to destroy the balance. Using those keys will only devastate the world."

"No," she spat. "You and your family are destroying the world. We can right the Morgan wrongs and finally bring about God's plan for humanity."

"You're crazy. That's not for you to decide. That's what the Council is for."

Alexis slowly climbed to her feet. "They've been dragging their feet for millennia, claiming their actions are for the good of the balance. She confirmed it and said this was the only way."

"She. You mean my grandmother Lily?" Kate shook her head, tossing her hands in the air. "You just don't get it. My grandmother, Lucas, and every Morgan alive, manipulates. That's what they do. They play people and my grandmother is the worst. She played you."

Alexis screamed obscenities and attacked her. Grabbing at her necklace, she pulled it off her neck and flung it at Kate. The necklace stretched and lengthened, catching Kate around the waist. Quickly it expanded and crept across her body, pinning her arms to her sides.

"Alexis," Grant yelled. "Let her go." With a strong uppercut, he smashed Lucas across the jaw, sending him flying across the room.

Alexis manipulated the chain, dragging Kate toward her. She stepped in front of her, pulling her to her chest. "You stole my soul mate and wormed your way into our family." She held up Kate's wrist and looked at the last band of Sapphire's bracelets with distain. "Wishing beads from my own cousin, given to the enemy."

Kate struggled to move but the chains strengthened with every jerk of her body. Stilling her movements, she sensed a bit of play and slowly moved her right hand to the opening of her messenger bag.

"Alexis, Grandfather forgives your actions. He asked me to do the same."

"Don't lie to me, Grant," Alexis screamed. She gripped Kate's arm with both hands, sliding her fingers beneath the strings of her wishing beads.

"Alexis, stop. Those beads will hurt both of you."

She turned and looked at Grant, her eyes glistening with tears. "She's a parasite to our family. You need to be free of her, Grant. Once you are, you'll see."

Panic filled his face. "Alexis, I'll do whatever you want, just stop. Please, stop."

"Alexis, do it," Lucas yelled. "Our family will be indebted to you forever. Come back to me and we will set the world on your path."

"Shut up!" Grant let out a yell and thrust his hand forward. The sword flew from his hand and caught Lucas in his shoulder, pinning him to the wall.

Alexis grasped the beads and closed her eyes. "I wish this world was free of Kate Morgan. I wish that she had never been born."

"No!" Grant yelled.

Kate gasped as the effect hit her dead on. She dropped to her knees, unable to sustain the energy to support her. Alexis screamed in pain as the beads caught on fire and their flames exploded, charring the skin on her wrist.

For Kate, the nausea was overwhelming. She watched as her skin turned gray. Instead of tears, she tasted the blood that flowed from her eyes. Her skin was a canvas of fire as burning flames swept through her body. She felt her lungs shutting down, unable to get any air. Kate drew in one last breath and, using her remaining strength, grabbed the dagger, and plunged it up into Alexis's chest.

Across the room, Grant paled as he watched Kate collapse with the pallor of a corpse. He heard himself screaming her name, knowing even as he did that by the time he reached her, she would be dead.

Alexis looked down and screeched as the dagger caught fire, exploding in her chest. Staggering back, she fell to the floor, watching in horror as her skin shredded and stripped away.

"What have you done?" she shrieked and then she was gone.

Kate tried to call out but she couldn't remember how to inhale air. She heard his shouts, but she was unable to see through the blood that filled her eyes. Alexis was dead and, with her death, the intense pain that consumed Kate, subsided. For that, she was eternally grateful. From somewhere she felt hands lift her up then warmth as she lay in open arms. From her place on the floor, she was powerless. Only with her last bit of strength, could she blink away the blood and watch as the last of the wishing beads disappeared. They sparkled and glowed, but as they disappeared, so did the world around her.

CHAPTER 26

She was back in the English countryside, walking through the lush green grass and relishing the cool wind on her face. In the distance was Stonehenge—the Stonehenge she remembered, not the one from Julian's painting. On the wind, she heard a deep voice call her name.

Kate frowned and walked toward the monument. She knew she was forgetting something and it bothered her that she couldn't remember.

"Kate," said the voice. "Kate, come back to me."

The voice was warm and soothing but unfamiliar to her. She turned around, expecting to see someone there, but finding nothing.

Turning her attention back to the stones, she reached up and felt the roughness of the rock beneath her fingers. "What am I forgetting?" she murmured to herself.

"Kate, you need to wake up."

She winced at the sound of the words. The volume suddenly hurt her ears. The rock face changed and she pulled her hand away, its rough exterior unexpectedly bruising her fingers. Everything hurt her. The brightness of the sun, the wind on her cheeks, the touch of her clothes against her skin. She felt like her body was being ripped apart in a sharp burst of pain.

"Kate, wake up!"

She opened her eyes and looked up at the ceiling. She was in a bed surrounded by stained glass windows, rich mahogany wood bookcases, and the smell of fresh flowers. Shifting her body weight, she groaned as reality hit and her memories flooded back. Every muscle hurt and she had a splitting headache. Exhaling a loud groan, she immediately felt a hand grasp hers. A blanket of warmth flooded her body, chasing away the aches and pains.

"You're going to have to tell me how you do that someday," she said weakly, turning her head to the right.

Grant was sitting next to her, looking every bit like he had fought a big battle, with his ripped shirt and pants, blotchy with blood.

"Welcome back," he murmured. "I think you lost one of your nine lives back there."

She smiled weakly, struggling to control her grief as guilt flooded her face. "I'm sorry about Alexis."

He shook his head, barely restraining his anger as his jaw tightened. "I'm sorry she did that to you. You did the only thing you could do."

"Unfortunately, you still have to be held accountable to the Council," Jake said. He sauntered up to the end of the bed, his hands in his pockets and a huge black eye. "Do you feel up to it now?"

"Now?" Grant protested. "She's just returned from this side of dead. Why now?"

Jake rubbed the back of his neck as a look of chagrin filled his face. "She's been asleep for over twenty-four hours and the conference is due to end soon. Besides, mate, if she knows the location of the keys, the Council wants them back to their rightful owners or we all go boom." Glancing around, he leaned in close to them. "Don't know about you, but the sooner I leave this retched place, the better."

"He's right, darling, so up, up, up," Julian added, clapping his hands. He breezed into the room, his forced enthusiasm evident to them all.

"Okay, okay," Kate grumbled. "But you're coming with us."

"Me, Katie? Why?"

She groaned and sat up, throwing her covers to the side. "Because I think you know more that you realize." She waved away his protestations and declarations of innocence. "I don't think you're guilty, Jules, I just think you played the part of an unwilling participant in an elaborate scheme of deception."

"Oh, well, in that case, tsk, tsk," he replied, raising his eyebrow disapprovingly. Glancing between Grant, Jake, and Kate, Julian shook his head then raised his hand and snapped his fingers. There was a flash of light and their clothes changed. "From tattered rags to designer glam. Now you're ready to appear before the Council."

The catch in his voice killed his attempt at a lighthearted atmosphere. There was no disguising the sombre mood. Even his choice of dark-colored clothes betrayed the seriousness of their situation.

From across the room, a polite cough caught their attention. A distinguished man with slicked back hair and glasses was waiting for them. "On behalf of the Council—" he started, only to be interrupted by Ambrose.

"Let's get this over with." He sighed. Turning to the man, he dismissed him with the wave of his hand. It was obvious by his weary look that the fallout of the rebellion had far-reaching consequences. Pausing for a moment, he looked Kate up and down. "You okay?"

She nodded, unsure of what she should say next. In the morning light, family lines were painfully obvious and Ambrose wasn't a Morgan. She might have had reasonable cause to kill Alexis, but her death was still a loss to his entire family.

"Ambrose, I'm—"

"It's okay, kiddo. Sometimes we're put into impossible situations." He gave her a reassuring smile and gestured down the hallway. "After you. The Council is watching. When you arrive at the hiding place of the keys, they will join us there."

She smiled shyly and bowed her head. Before she could take a step, Grant grabbed her by the hand and whispered to her. "No one blames you for what happened."

"I do. There should have been another way."

Squeezing her hand firmly, he stayed fastened to her side, past the army of staff, family members, and associates cleaning and repairing the chateau. Kate walked them quickly though the lobby, trying not to gasp at the destruction. There would be plenty of time to reflect later. Jake was right. The faster they left the chateau and returned to a normal life, the better for them all.

She stopped at the gallery which, compared to the rest of the resort, looked practically untouched. A few random dirt stains and a large piece of burned carpet were the only indication that a battle had taken place here. Even the worst of Julian's paintings had been rescued and restored to their rightful places on the walls. She nodded to Ambrose then nervously cleared her throat.

"It's here."

"How can you be so sure?"

The voice came first followed by the Council members. They appeared in the open center of the space, surrounded by their entourage. In addition, Leland and all of his siblings stood surrounded by guards. Mark and the Zion team appeared, as well as the VIP members of both families, brought there to bear witness.

Kate lifted her head, no longer afraid of the Council or its powers. She was beyond caring what anyone thought, especially the members of her family. "It's the only explanation after examining Gus's timeline." She turned to Mark and the Zion team. "You accounted for all of Gus's whereabouts from the time the keys went missing. Was there any opportunity to hide them?"

Mark shook his head. "Through cameras, we can account for every minute. Nothing gave us reason to believe that he hid the keys anywhere."

"And a search of his room and belongings?"

"Nothing."

Kate nodded. "As I suspected. Gus was smart enough to know something as important as the keys could not be left on their own. We also confirmed he had plans to meet with his co-conspirators at this conference, so he would have brought the keys here."

Damian leaned forward, fascination in his eyes. "So where are they, if you're convinced he brought them here."

Kate pointed to one of Julian's paintings. All eyes turned to the winter painting of snow and crystals, showcasing three crystal cubes, suspended in mid-air. "I think he hid the keys in there."

Marion Anderson Lowell looked at the painting with skepticism. "I don't see anything that looks like a key."

"I think that's the idea," Grant replied. He turned to Julian, gesturing for him to join him. "When Gus joined you, he wasn't there for very long, correct?"

"Yes, only about twenty minutes, then he received a phone call and he had to leave."

"Did you show him this painting?"

Julian slowly nodded, confusion still filling his face. "I showed him all of them. Said they weren't for sale until after the reveal at the conference, not that he seemed interested in acquiring any of them."

"But you must have talked to him throughout the years about your paintings and how realistic they are. 'Why, just look at the dragon. He comes alive if you get too close,' that kind of thing."

Julian looked a bit more relaxed, puffing out his chest with pride. "Yes, Hubert is one of my greatest creations."

Grant nodded. "And this painting is no different, it looks almost three dimensional."

"And that's his secret," Kate added. "It looks three dimensional because it is."

Damian frowned. "So we have to send someone into the picture to get it?"

Julian shook his head. "Not possible. I didn't incorporate that feature into this design."

"This makes no sense," Marion argued. "If the keys are even there, how do we get to them?"

There was a pause for a moment, then Kate smiled. "Jules, do you have the souvenir of the conference you left at everyone's dinner plates?"

Julian nodded and extended his hand. There was a flash of light and the crystal cube appeared in his hand. Taking the item, Kate stood before the Council.

"Gus had limited powers. A three second view of the future, teleportation, and the ability to transform objects into other forms. If you look at this cube, the writing appears on one side." She held it up and the words *Summit 2018* clearly appeared, etched in the crystal. "However, if you rotate it, the refractive surface makes the words disappear." Turning to Julian, she pointed at the painting. "Jules, make the cubes rotate."

All eyes turned to the painting as Julian raised his hand. Slowly the painting came alive and each of the cubes began to slowly turn. A loud gasp reverberated through the crowd as each of the cubes revealed a side of symbols.

Jonathan smiled and walked over to the painting. Lifting his hand, he chanted a long string of Latin words. There was a brilliant flash of light and the symbols transformed from the painting into three keys of gold, held in the palm of his hand.

He turned to Kate. "The Council and the Anderson family owes you a debt of gratitude, Detective Morgan. We thank you for all you have done for the family."

Damian looked over at Leland and his family. "How does it feel, Lucas? To have power so close and not able to grasp it?"

Lucas glared at him then defiantly raised his head. "There is no shame in vaulting ambition. I stand by my words that the Council is past its prime and should step down for a younger generation."

"You should be punished for your disobedience," Marion cried.

Shouts of agreement came from the crowd. Both sides exchanging exclamations of acceptable punishments. Damian raised his hand and the audience quieted. "Lucas and his siblings Larry, Lee, and Laurelle will face a severe punishment, starting with the stripping of all Morgan holdings, businesses, and the family name. Henceforth you shall no longer be a Morgan and all powers and future lives are hereby revoked."

Laurelle let out a scream of indignation and charged toward the Council, only to be grabbed by members of Zion and dragged back to her place in the crowd. "You put us up to this!" she screamed. "How could you betray your own family, your flesh and blood?"

"Yes, yes, Grandmother is to blame," Lucas agreed. "She put us up to this, promising her chair on the council for whoever would bring her the keys."

Kate's mother let out a screech. "How dare you insult your elders? You should be ashamed of yourself. Blaming your grandmother for your bad behavior. Leland, say something. Stop this circus immediately!"

Leland stood quietly, looking at the floor. His expression spoke volumes—a combination of shame and anger.

"Mother," Kate said sharply. "Enough."

"Child," Damian boomed. "Listen to your daughter, for once, and shut up."

Elizabeth stepped back, looking as if she had been slapped in the face. Indignant anger blazed from her eyes, but even she knew better than to defy a Council member's order.

Damian pursed his lips and turned to face his sister. "Lilith, these are serious charges. How do you plead?"

Lily Morgan turned to Damian, her eyes ablaze with arrogance. "You need to ask? Of course, these charges are ridiculous. I am outraged to be the center of these lies."

A chorus of protests erupted from Lucas and his siblings.

Again Damian held up his hand and silence fell over the room. "Ambrose Anderson, step forward."

"Yes, Councilor Damian?"

"You conducted a thorough investigation of Gus's murder scene. Did you find any evidence of the crime scene or an explanation of how he ended up on that flag pole?"

"No sir, there was no video or forensic evidence of the murder anywhere in the hotel or in the tunnels below."

"Yet you have plenty of evidence when he was alive and present in the chateau?"

"Yes, sir. His movements can be accounted for from the time he entered the chateau, the night before the conference, up to thirty minutes before his body was found."

"Interesting. No evidence of his murder, yet he is dead. Multiple family members pointing the finger at Lilith who, coincidentally, decides to retire after thousands of years of reigning and who is one of eight people here who would be capable of committing murder without any evidence at all. Care to change your plea, Lilith?"

"Damian, how dare you? You believe their lies over me?"

"Everyone lies, Lilith. Our family most of all. Hell, it's refreshing when someone doesn't lie. Makes my job a lot easier." He turned to the other members of the Council, pointing a finger at her. "Councilors what do you say?"

"Guilty," Nero replied.

"Guilty," Ronin said.

Lilith's expression turned from haughty to scared as the word repeated itself. Upon hearing the last "guilty" verdict, Damian turned to Lilith. "Counselor Lilith, you have been found guilty of conspiring to upset the balance and steal the keys to the kingdom of heaven. Punishment is hereby pronounced."

"Wait," she cried. "Don't I get a chance to defend myself?"

"No. Judgement is final."

The other members of the Council surrounded her, extending their palms in front of her. Kate slowly backed away as beams of light shot out from their hands. Each beam instilled a different punishment—one lit her on fire, another shot shards of steel that pierced multiple points on her while another one caused her flesh to rot away. Lilith let out a piercing scream that echoed throughout the chamber.

From around them, the screams multiplied, first from the members of both families, followed by an ungodly chorus of torment as a chasm to Hell opened in the floor of the chateau. Lilith's mottled form dropped to the floor, clawing at the carpet as an invisible force pulled her toward the opening. Her screams intensified through the floor until the abyss closed around her and she was gone.

"Blimey," Jake muttered, trying to rub the sight from his eyes. "Is this over yet?"

"Almost, Jake. The Council has one final issue to address before we declare the *2018 Summit* over." Damian and the remaining members raised their arms and started to chant a single word over and over.

"*Coniunctio, coniunctio, coniunctio…*"

Kate felt Grant pull her close, then a wave a vertigo overtook her. Around them, the room changed—the walls replaced by cliffs of rock and the overpowering smell of sulfur. The entire group looked around at the platform they stood on, high above running rivers of molten lava.

"I don't understand, what does *coniunctio* mean?"

For the first time ever Kate saw genuine fear in his eyes. "It's Latin for 'union.'"

She felt her stomach drop as a sick realization set in. They were there to witness The Joining. Her Joining.

CHAPTER 27

No!" she screamed as several guards pulled her from Grant's embrace. "I refuse, I won't participate in The Joining!"

"Let her go," Grant yelled, but it did no good.

With a subtle glance from his grandfather Jonathan, Ambrose and Mark pulled him to the other end of the Anderson group.

"You don't have a choice, Katherine. For too many years you have run from the family. You are a Morgan. Your blood is Morgan and you are to be joined to our maker as all other Morgans have done." Damian glared at her and motioned to the guards. "Bind her."

She screamed until they gagged her with a red scarf. Her hands and feet were bound together with red rope so tightly, they cut into her skin.

"This is barbaric! You can't force her to join against her will!"

Damian glared at Grant as he struggled to shake off Mark's hold. "You and the Anderson clan are being allowed to witness this sacred event as a courtesy. Don't make me regret this decision."

Ambrose hustled him away, giving his body a shake. "This is their way, Grant. It's no different than our sacraments and the traditions we hold as sanctified."

"The difference is we get to choose. We aren't forced to submit."

"Really, Grant? I don't remember your two month old self agreeing to be baptised."

Grant drew his mouth into a tight line. Shaking off Ambrose, he clenched his hands into fists at his side. His silence was enough to appease Damian, who turned to face the crowd.

"Members of the Morgan and Anderson clans, you have been brought here to witness the joining of Katherine Morgan and her maker, our beloved Lucifer. This child of the Morgan clan will follow in his footsteps and work to encourage the harvesting of souls in his name. Since she has indicated her right to refusal, which has been rejected, is there a proxy who will complete the rite?"

"I will be proxy to her."

"So be it, step forward and state your name."

"Elizabeth Morgan, mother of Katherine Morgan and daughter of Lilith Morgan." She approached Kate and caressed her face. "Don't struggle, dear. You'll only make it worse for yourself."

Kate screamed obscenities, unheard due to the cloth that filled her mouth. Her mind filled with fear and every part of her lashed out in protest of this ritual. She felt like she was in a glass box and, by the impartial expressions on people's faces, no one except Grant could see or hear her.

Damian nodded and turned his attention to the audience. "This woman has no spouse. Is there a man to claim her?"

Lucas's head lifted and with a clear voice, he yelled, "I claim her."

"No," Grant replied. "I claim her."

Damian smiled and shook his head. Gesturing to Lucas, he waved his finger disapprovingly. "You are no longer a Morgan." Looking at Grant, he smiled as if somewhat amused. "And you are an Anderson." Damian looked around at the crowd and sighed. "If no one lays claim, then she is free to seek her own mate on her own terms. Let the ceremony begin."

He clapped his hands and the ground beneath them began to shake. The circle of onlookers widened as the ground in the middle of the floor caved, creating a sink hole the size of a swimming pool. There was a pause then a loud rushing sound as hundreds of gallons of liquid filled the ever expanding fissure.

"Wow, bad luck ol' mum," Jake said dejectedly, as he massaged the back of his neck with his hand. The sight of the pool had the opposite effect on Elizabeth Morgan, she clapped her hands with delight.

Grant's eyes grew wider as he realized what was happening. Rage flowed through his veins and, though he said nothing, he felt two sets of hands latch solidly onto him.

"In accordance with the ancient right, we thank The Sculptor for his contribution," Damian said. He nodded to a figure who stood in the shadows, overlooking them on a nearby cliff. "We look upon the blood of six hundred and sixty six sacrifices that will bond this child to her maker in the act of ultimate allegiance."

"Well, now we know why all of those associates went missing," Mark said grimly.

He shifted his glance to Grant, careful to make sure his cousin didn't do anything crazy. From the sounds and smells, he was pretty sure they were as close to hell as they would ever see. It was imperative that they left with the same number of family members as when they arrived.

"Katherine Morgan, do you accept Satan as your maker and agree to act in his name."

Kate shook her head but the motion was useless. Her mother proudly stroked her hair and declared, "She does."

"Do you agree to abide by the rules of the Morgan clan?"

"She does,"

"Do you agree to uphold and abide by the rules and declarations of the Council in the name of maintaining the balance?"

This time, it was her mother who struggled with a response. Kate could see the defiance in her eyes, so soon after her own mother had faced execution for going behind the Council's back. With some measure of anger, her mother finally blurted out, "She does,"

Damian nodded. "Then if there are no other issues, I declare—"

Jake cleared his throat and raised his hand. "I have a debt to settle before we conclude this."

"And what might that be?"

"According to the charter, I can resolve any outstanding complaints before The Joining. It's a personal grievance between myself and my cousin."

Damian stared at him, looking slightly annoyed. Finally, he shrugged his shoulders and gestured toward her. "So be it. Proceed."

Jake walked up to her and winced as hope filled her eyes. He grabbed her from behind and put her head into a choke hold. Announcing loudly to the crowd, he said, "Katherine Morgan, you invaded my privacy by reading my most private thoughts, so I claim this act as a way to right to that wrong."

"What the hell are you doing, Jake?"

"Grant, don't interfere," Ambrose said.

Kate felt the pressure on her neck increase. With the gag in her mouth, she struggled to just breathe. He leaned into her, whispering in her ear. "Our powers don't work here. I can't get you out of this, luv, but I can make it easier for you. Trust me, Kate. Focus on the person you love the most. It worked for me."

She nodded and focused on Grant as spots began to appear before her eyes. She heard nothing but the pounding of blood in her ears. Jake gripped her harder, cutting off her air until he felt her body slump forward into unconsciousness. Looking around, he stood up and dusted off his hands. "My debt has been paid."

"What the hell did you do?" Grant yelled.

He broke free of his guards and lunged at Jake, sending an upper cut into his jaw. As a small platoon of Anderson men dragged Grant back, Jake held up his hands in a show of forgiveness. "It's okay, mate, I deserved that."

Elizabeth rushed to Kate's side, her face crimson with anger. Standing up, she pointed a finger at Jake. "What did you do? She's supposed to be conscious. You've robbed her of the experience!"

"Enough, Elizabeth," Damian declared. "The rules only state that she not be dead and she isn't. No harm has been done, and Jake's debt has been paid."

"Son of a bitch," Grant growled as he struggled to free himself.

Ambrose motioned to the men. They hustled Grant farther into the crowd and away from the ceremony. "That's enough," Ambrose hissed. "Jake did you and Kate a favor."

"How so?"

Ambrose grabbed him by his lapels. "She's a fighter and will fight to the end. At least when she goes in, it will be quick and painless for her. There was no chance to save her, and Jake knew that. Do you really want to spend the next five minutes watching her drown in that blood?"

Grant faltered as grief hit him dead on. "But she's on her third life."

"And if the ceremony goes according to plan, she will be resurrected by Lucifer as part of his pact to the Morgan family."

Grant watched as her mother pushed her unconscious body into the pool of blood and grimaced as she floated for a minute then disappeared into the depths. His heart shattered as a single burst of air bubbled up, temporarily disturbing the glassy surface. "But that means—"

"That means that the Kate we knew is gone."

CHAPTER 28

Kate sat on the bus, staring out at the countryside, deep in thought. Restlessly, she shifted in her seat, drumming her fingers against the arm rest, then lightly on her outer thigh. She was always restless these days, as if she had taken the coffee obsession one step too far, except she didn't drink coffee and tea never quite cut it for her.

Her thoughts drifted back to her last therapy session. It was a day just like this, cold and rainy.

"So Katherine, welcome back. How was your vacation?"

She had sat in the chair, drumming her fingers and wondering why she was there. "Fine. Relaxing, why?"

The doctor raised her eyebrows at the tone in her voice. Avoiding Kate's question, she posed another. "What did you do?"

Kate paused for a minute, then frowned. She tried to remember details but nothing came to her. A flash of some random guy and scotch, but a splitting headache quickly pushed the memory away. "Not much, just kicked around the city, running errands." Pausing again for a moment, she realized the question irritated her. "Why do you want to know? Why do you care?"

There was silence again as the doctor looked down at her note pad and scribbled something. "Because I care about my patients and you seem different than before."

Kate shrugged her shoulders. "Clearly, you're mistaken.

It's been two weeks since I saw you and I know I haven't changed, so I guess you don't know me as well as you think."

More uncomfortable silence had Kate looking at her watch. The therapist sagely nodded again and Kate rolled her eyes. The woman's calm exterior covered the less-than-courteous thoughts coming from her. She really thought Kate to be impatient and rude.

"Okay. How about your career? I understand you're finding it hard to concentrate at work. You also have a short temper, lately? I understand there was an incident, so why don't you tell me about that?"

Kate smiled. Clearly the doctor had spoken with the department psychologist, given the plethora of notes swimming through her mind. "Look, Doc, why don't we cut to the chase? I don't like you. You don't like me, and the only reason I'm here is because I hate the shrink at work even more."

The woman was stunned by the forwardness of her words. "I—uh—what do you propose we do about that?"

"Good question. How about, you're fired?"

"I—okay, so you're agreeing to see the psychologist from the NYPD?"

Kate shook her head. Pulling out her cell phone, she called her captain. "Yeah, it's Morgan here. I'm sitting with Dr. Trask and she and I agree the best therapy is no therapy at all." She watched as the woman waved her hands, trying to get her to hang up the phone. "Uh, huh. Okay. Actually, I have a solution for that too. I quit."

Now, three weeks later, the restlessness was relentless. Even as calming as the countryside was, she wanted to get off the bus and walk, run or do anything but sit there. Silently, she cursed herself for not hiring a driver but this had been a spur of the moment decision, just like the rest of her trip.

"Have you been to Britain before, dear?"

Kate glanced over at the old man sitting across the aisle.

His wife was nose deep in a tourist guide, nattering excitedly to another senior citizen who was trying to show her pictures on her tablet.

"No. First time out of the United States."

"It's a mystical place, you know."

"Yeah? can it change this dismal weather?"

"Anything is possible, my dear." Leaning across the aisle he extended his hand. "Charlie Anderson."

Before she knew it, she was shaking his hand. "Kate Morgan." He smiled and she felt a warm surge and, with it, a calming of her agitation. She leaned back in her chair and relaxed, feeling for the first time in weeks like she was at peace. "So, Mr. Anderson, how is this place mystical?"

"Well, the most popular tales revolve around a worshiping ground for the Druids or the magical creation of Merlin himself, but I think it has healing properties."

"Really?" Amusement filled her voice. "Well, then I guess it's a good way to spend the day, despite the weather."

"And what brings you here? You seem to be travelling alone."

She exhaled a long breath of air. "I am. New York was feeling a bit claustrophobic. I needed to get away." She looked out of the window and saw the stone circle approaching through the rain-splattered window. She wasn't sure why, but the old man was so warm and open it was impossible not to confide in him. Sadness filled her eyes. "Truth is, I'm feeling a bit lost lately."

"And you think what you're looking for is here?"

"I don't know. Perhaps. Seemed like a good place to start." She smiled at him and started to gather her jacket and bag.

"Well, Miss Morgan," he said with a wink, "I'm sure you're going to find what you're looking for."

Kate stepped off the bus and surveyed the countryside. There was a visitor's center and cafe down the road and, near a winding path, the ring of stones. Most of the people on her tour gathered around the guide who rattled off departure times. Kate nodded her goodbyes to the old man, then started toward Stonehenge.

Every step she took was accompanied by a strange sense of déjà vu. With the exception of the winding observation path, guarded by a low wire fence and signs warning to approach no farther, the setting seemed strangely familiar. She searched her memory, trying to recall if she had ever been there before, but the more she sought, the less she found.

Somewhere in the back of her mind, she reasoned that pulling the umbrella out of her backpack was probably a good idea but she couldn't stop to take the time. In minutes, the rain plastered her hair and chilled her to the bone. She felt the restlessness returning, like an itch incapable of relief no matter how hard she scratched.

Behind her, a voice called out to her, warning her to stop her approach to the stones. She knew she should stop, act properly, and turn away. She felt torn, as if different commanding voices were telling her what to do. She chose to ignore them all and examine the monument in front of her.

"What am I doing here?" she asked, touching the stone. In the pouring rain, it felt no different than any other stone. Cold and rough in some places, smooth in others.

She didn't know what to expect from the circle as she walked through the stones, following the well-worn paths between the rock, never lifting her hand as she passed from stone to stone.

Nothing happened as she wandered between them, not that she really expected anything to change. She felt cold, wet, and foolish, not sure of what she was doing there.

"Hello, Kate."

She looked around one of the stones and stared into the face of a handsome man. The haunted look in his eyes was familiar to her. She had seen the look many times before in the faces of victims who had lost loved ones. It took a second, but she placed him. He looked so haggard she almost didn't recognize him.

"Special Agent Anderson?"

His expression changed and hope filled his eyes. "You know me?"

"I almost didn't recognize you, but yeah. Junior Malone. I don't know if you remember about a month or two ago? We were trying to apprehend the same man."

He looked down, anguish filling his heart. The stories were true. She didn't know who he really was. She didn't remember.

He held out his hand, his voice faltering slightly. "Of course, Detective Kate Morgan, from the NYPD. It's good to see you again."

She shook his hand then pulled away, focusing again on the stones. "So what are you doing in England? Bit of a long way from home."

"Thought I would take a vacation with my girlfriend and decided to come here for fun."

Kate looked around. In the pouring rain, they were the only ones to trudge across the wet grass and actually touch the stones. "I guess she's not much for wet weather, huh?"

"Speaking of which…I'm a bit soaked. What do you say about getting out of the rain?"

She smiled and shook her head. "Still a bossy SOB, huh? At ease, Agent, I'm not the enemy here."

He wiped the water from his eyes and smiled, remembering his exact words from their first encounter. Shoving his hands into his pockets, he shrugged his shoulders. "All right, Detective, you look like you're on a mission. Can I help you find something?"

"Not detective anymore. I'm done with that life. Anyway, you're going to think I'm crazy."

"Try me."

She finished scanning the rock then moved on to one of the largest pieces—one with a capstone stretched across the top. "I'm looking for something. I don't know what, but I'll know it when I see it."

"Maybe it's not something you can see. Maybe it's something you have to feel."

She let out a snort, turning away from the large stone. After a minute, she returned and stood facing it again. He might be right, so what did she have to lose? Taking a deep breath, she closed her eyes and stood with her hands touching the rock. In her mind's eye, she saw the stone clearly. Not covered with rain and smooth, but a thicker, rougher, and taller stone. As she stared at the surface, she felt the vibration of something hitting the rock, then a white light obscured her vision. Kate opened her eyes and looked at the base of the structure. Dropping to her knees, she began to dig, shifting dirt and handfuls of grass out of the way.

Grant stared at her, covered in mud, hair plastered to her head. "What are you doing?"

"It's here. The stones have sunk with time but it's here." She looked up at him, annoyance crossing her face. "Don't just stand there. Make yourself useful and help me."

He dropped to his knees and shrugged his jacket off his shoulders, digging alongside her, pushing the mud out of the way. After a couple of minutes of digging, she grabbed his arm, shoving it out of the way.

She sat back on her knees and looked at him. "There. See? I'm not crazy."

He glanced down at the symbol of a mountain top next to the letters MMXVIII, wiped his hands on his jeans, and stared at the symbol. "Son of a bitch, it was real."

She looked at him with surprise. "You know what this means?"

He nodded and looked away, pain filling his eyes again. "Yes, and so do you."

"Me?" She bristled at the remark. "How would I know what this means?"

"Because you know, Kate," he said, grabbing her hand. "And you don't remember, but you know."

She jerked away, shaking her head with disbelief. "You're crazy."

"No, Kate. I love you and you love me."

"I don't even know you."

"Yes, you do. You've just forgotten because something happened to you."

Kate snatched her hand away, angrily, throwing her back against the stone. "Why does everyone keep saying that? My ex-therapist, ex-boss, and now you. I haven't changed, I'm still the same."

"No, you aren't, Kate. For starters you can't remember me, can you?"

"Of course, I can. I told you that when we met."

"What about the second time? When we met at the Summit and spent the week together?" She hesitated, unsure of what to say and he took it as a good sign. "Something in you knows what I'm saying is true. I put that symbol there, and you watched me do it."

"You put it there? When? Why?"

"A long time ago. That Summit mark doesn't just represent the place where we met, it's a symbol of the challenges we went through to stay together. Kate, this is just another obstacle, but we can conquer it, I know we can."

She shrank away from him, shaking her head with disbelief. "I don't know you. I barely remember you from a random chance encounter, and you expect me to believe we're a couple?"

"I don't expect anything from you, Kate. I know how crazy this sounds, so I'm just asking you to give me a chance. Spend some time with me. Let me prove my worth to you."

She shook her head, covering her face with her hands. Every word he said grated on her nerves, reigniting a pounding headache that no amount of medicine could erase. Anger filled her again and the restlessness increased to an unbearable level. Taking a deep breath, she pointed at him. "Go away, Agent."

"Kate—"

"No. I don't want to know you. Hell, I don't even want

to talk to you. I don't care if we were once involved, all I care about is the here and now and I just want to be left alone."

She could see her words cut deeply into him, but she didn't care. Despite the cold, her skin felt like it was on fire, and all she craved was to lash out at something. Do something to ease the anxiety that threatened to consume her.

"That isn't you talking."

"Really, then who is it? Is it this place? Do you think I'm possessed? Because you're looking at me like I'm crazy." She charged back to the monument and pointed at the symbol. "Do you think it's this symbol? Because now that I've seen it, I'm good. I've killed the morbid curiosity and am ready to move on with my life. If fact, let me bury it again for some other poor sap to find."

She bent down, shoving mud and grass back into the hole. Turning to grab a random rock to cover the etching for good, she slipped and fell onto her knees, her hand slamming against the Summit symbol.

Her actions ignited a maelstrom. All around them, thunder and lightning tore open the sky. A brilliant white light ignited the rock face and, like fire, spread to the other stones. One by one, each of the rocks lit up until the circle of light joined, connected, and swept her into its path. Kate looked at the ball of light that was her hand. She let out a loud scream as the light crept up her limbs and overpowered her, absorbing her into the ring of light.

Images filled her mind. People and things she had forgotten—every memory ever encountered, good and bad, replayed in an instant as if someone had plugged her into a thought-enhancing machine. She saw walls breaking down around her. Every spell, every effect from a supernatural power shattered and the truth of what happened to her was revealed. The time spent tracking Rocco Morgan in Texas, her experiences with Grant at the Summit, and the temporary power she had received from the Council. She let out another scream as she relived The Joining, the feeling of helplessness as the dark devoured her. Every life she lived, every joyful high and heart-wrenching blow struck her at once, and she sobbed uncontrollably. Tears streamed down her face as years of guilt washed over her, cleansing her of her restlessness like water consuming fire.

"Kate," Grant yelled.

He ran over to her and caught her as she fell, blinking furiously when the light consumed him as well. She cried hysterically as he pulled her into his arms. Cradling her, he soothed her pain by speaking words of love to her over and over again.

As quick as the light began, it was gone and they lay amid the stones. He rocked her, protecting her with his arms as she cried.

Slowly the rain stopped, and glorious beams broke through the clouds, filling the meadow with streams of warmth and light. Long moments passed as she sobbed and clung to him. It was only after her breathing had calmed that he released his protective embrace.

"Kate, say something," he said anxiously. "Talk to me."

She drew back from him then reached up and caressed the side of his face. Tears filled her eyes as she brushed a strand of wet hair from his eyes. "Hey, stranger. Long time, no see."

"Oh, thank God," he gasped, pulling her to his chest and kissing the top of her head.

"I'm back, Grant," she murmured, clutching his hand with her own. "I remember everything. The Summit, the Council, Lucas, and Jake."

"Me too, honey," he replied. "Everything from Texas too."

Kate looked up into his eyes and smiled at the man who had fought for her and refused to give up, despite impossible odds. The one who trusted in her and believed when even she gave up on herself. "I love you, Grant Anderson."

He grinned back, a beautiful radiance filling his handsome face. "I love you too, Kate Morgan. I don't know how but you came back to me. You survived The Joining, and you came back to me." Before she could reply he leaned down and kissed her softly.

"It's the stones. He was right. It really is a healing place."

"Who was right?" he murmured, covering her face with tiny kisses.

"Charlie Anderson. He's a senior citizen I met on the bus."

Grant paused for a moment and looked curiously into her face. "Charlie Anderson?"

She smiled and nodded. "He's a relative of yours. I didn't know it at the time but I could feel he was one of your Andersons when I shook his hand."

He kissed her forehead and mulled over her words. "We had a Charlie in the family. He was a member of the Council, but he died."

"You're sure of that?"

He let out a laugh, shaking his head. "Nope. Remind me to bring it up at the next Summit in fifty years." He rose to his feet and pulled her into his arms. "Until then, let's just live happily ever after."

About the Author

Born in Winnipeg, Canada, Christine Wall is an author, screenwriter, and actress in her current hometown of Toronto, Canada. Her love of storytelling has led her to Hollywood with her success in screenplay contests and a decent ranking in the Nicholl Fellowships(Oscars) 2011.

When she's not writing, Wall is acting, singing and pursuing her love of Crossfit. Her first novel, The Fog (2012), delves into the worlds of science fiction and romance and is currently enjoying success on Amazon and Barnes and Noble.com.

Growing up, watching Saturday matinees filled with science fiction, adventure, and fantasy, led Wall to create compelling universes for a younger generation to explore. With her debut YA novel, Showdown at Evil High (Black Opal Books 2013) she combines the world of angels and demons with the daily challenges of the modern teenager.

Wall can be found on her website www.christinewall.com, Facebook and on Twitter @chrstnwll.

www.ingramcontent.com/pod-product-compliance
Lightning Source LLC
Chambersburg PA
CBHW071308200626
46813CB00015B/611